LAST
CHANCE

ALSO BY T. G. AYER

Young Adult Paranormal

THE VALKYRIE SERIES

Dead Radiance

Dead Radiance Audio

Dead Embers

Dead Embers Audio

Dead Chaos

Dead Chaos Audio

Dead Wrath

Dead Silence

Joshua - Dead Radiance

Joshua II - Dead Embers

Joshua III - Dead Chaos

Joshua IV - Dead Wrath

Joshua V - Dead Silence

THE HAND OF KALI SERIES

Fire & Shadow

Blood & Gold

Time & Fate

Fury & Virtue

Spirit & Soul

THE DARKWORLD ORIGINS

Pyros (Logan)

Ailuros (Kailin)

~

THE DARK SIGHT SERIES

Dark Sight

Cursed Sight

Vissarion

Shadow Sight

Dark Prophecy

Cursed Prophecy

Shadow Prophecy

~

THE APSARA CHRONICLES

Immortal Bound

Gods Ascendent

Dominion Falling

Vengeance Born

Last Legion

~

A SEASON OF ASH AND BONE

Heartfyre

~

Adult Sci-Fi

HANDS ASSASSIN

Death Dealer

Death Mark

Death Strike

Hand's Assassins Series

∾

NEW ADULT CONTEMPORARY THRILLER W/A TONI VALLAN

Beautiful Collision

Beautiful Conviction

∾

PSYCHOLOGICAL HORROR W/A TONI VALLAN

Dark Shadows

Splinter

Last Chance

A SkinWalker Novel #3

Cover art by Eduardo Priego

Editor: Cassie Kelley McCown

ISBN-13: 978-0995112544

LAST CHANCE

USA TODAY BESTSELLING AUTHOR

T.G. AYER

CHAPTER 1

A Walker funeral isn't that different from the funerals of any other species. Flowers, coffins, mourners. Tears, grief. Regret.

The subtle difference lies in the species itself, and maybe in particular religious preference. Most Walkers regard the goddess Ailuros, cat god of the Greek pantheon, as their deity of choice. Worship isn't in any way similar to most other EarthWorld religions.

Ailuros just is.

She is a constant, like the air in your lungs or the rain falling from a moody sky. The goddess is nature personified. She gives no gifts, answers no bargains. She is merely the god of all things.

Ailuros has no temples, not in the modern world. Not after the tsunami that was the annihilation of 'witches'. Call a Walker or a Mage a witch and it was a laughably simple feat to eradicate entire clans. Places of worship were and always will be an open invitation to the religious zealots.

Now, the temple must exist inside your soul. Or else you were truly lost.

I often wondered how different life would be if humans knew we existed. What would they think if their son or daughter brought home a werewolf or a Fae for dinner? Cross-species reproduction? I shook my head, the movement jerky and short as I swallowed a bitter laugh. I walked, past faces some familiar, many not, to the front row of white aluminum foldout chairs. My father's lawn, and the weather had cooperated in my sister's honor. The ground was firm, the grass a bright, cheery green. The sun streamed down, not so warm that we'd have to shed our coats, but with enough heat that an afternoon outside was a pleasant experience.

Seems Mother Nature had remembered to pull out all the stops for Greer's farewell.

I'd already said my goodbye to my sister. I sighed, my thoughts taking me back a few days. We'd had our last conversation in a way I'd never expected. How many people get to talk to the dead?

I recalled Greer's last words.

"So many times I pushed you away and yet you still came to help me. I didn't deserve you. I don't deserve you... Thank you, Kai."

Words I never expected to hear, not from a sister who had always remained just that bit out of reach, just that bit colder than necessary.

I recalled the expression on her face, the sincerity in her eyes, and even the love as she spoke. So unexpected. Those words. Tears blurred my vision as I sat blindly on the nearest seat. I wished we'd had more time, I wished we'd been able to be close. But fate didn't want it that way. I sighed and felt the lead weight in my stomach settle deeper into place.

I should be happy that Greer and I had made our peace but the harsher, more awful truth hung over me, a dark, accusing cloud threatening to loose a storm of emotions. I'd failed my mother. I'd failed to save her daughter. What mother could forgive me? I didn't deserve forgiveness. I'd failed her.

Failed them both.

Murmuring from the back of the seated crowd drew my thoughts away from the cesspit of my self-pity. I shifted in my seat and glanced behind me. My father Corin, brother Iain and four other men I didn't recognize, walked steadily along the center aisle bearing the weight of Greer's coffin between them.

Made of molded concrete, shaped to fit the curves of Greer's figure, the coffin was finished with exquisitely fine detail. The sculptor had paid close attention to Greer's aquiline features, replicating them so closely that I would have sworn that Greer herself lay there. The rest of her body was sculpted wearing a peplos, an ancient toga-like garment draped elegantly around her body in the style of the Greek goddesses. Within the carved casket, Greer was dressed in a similar fashion.

Her body had been gently bathed, perfumed oils rubbed into her skin. Her long ash-blonde hair, was washed, brushed and draped over her shoulders and allowed to fall off her body at the waist. Her hands had been positioned at the center of her chest, her fingers entwined around the feet of a stone statue of Ailuros, the statue stood straight up, its feminine curves enhanced by the fall of the fabric of her simple peplos. With the head of a panther the statue hearkened back to the days before Ailuros had evolved into the external manifestation of a cat, the days when the goddess bore the head of a lioness. Today, each Walker tribe saw Ailuros with a head that signified their own species.

Only the cats, of course. Wolf Walkers bowed to the feet of Anubis.

With a start, I recognized Byron Teague, the local wolf alpha, and Justin Lake, alpha of the cougars, behind my brother and father. Again, I was reminded that attendance at the funeral would be more a show of support of those grieving her death rather than an actual payment of respect to Greer herself. The lynx and jaguar alphas brought up the rear of the pallbearers. I turned and faced the stone bier at the front; a simple table constructed from white marble, and surrounded with vases of white roses.

From somewhere around me a lone violin sang sweet sad notes. A song I didn't recognize but which brought tears to my eyes anyway. I swallowed the lump in my throat and blinked away the moisture. I'd just regained my composure when a tap on my shoulder pulled my attention from the pallbearers who were setting the casket onto the bier. Behind me sat Lily, Logan, Saleem and Tara. Logan's hand felt warm and comforting on my shoulder and I held tightly onto it. I drew strength just from the touch of the man.

Tara leaned forward, her dark hair glinting in the sun. "Mother couldn't make it but she does send her apologies and her condolences," she whispered in my ear before giving me a small encouraging smile.

I nodded. "Thanks," was all I could think to say. I was overwhelmed by their support. Even more so when I caught a glimpse of Storm and Chief Murdoch sitting in the back row. Proof that I managed to gather my own little band of friends over the last few years. The one person I didn't see was Clancy. Clancy McBride, my best friend, my supervisor at the rehab center, taken from me by the same Walker who, in the end, had killed my sister too.

The chair beside me squawked and I twisted around as Grams sat down. I took her hands and she squeezed them back. We were both dressed in white, me in a skirt suit, and Grams in pants and a matching jacket. Walkers shunned the nothingness of black. We saw death as another step in our journey, not a marking of the end, the beginning of nothing.

Grams and I had long supported each other in our grief, and then guilt clawed at me, ripping open old wounds. When my uncle Niko had died we'd had no body to bury. They'd had a small memorial service but with everything that had happened, and everything Niko had done I couldn't bring myself to attend.

Grams and everyone else had understood. I'd been weak from the Wraith-sword poison, grieving for Clancy, terrified for Mom and Anjelo and Greer, all innocents sucked into Niko's crazy schemes.

I tried to banish those thoughts, bring my attention back onto the ceremony. With the casket in place, the pallbearers dispersed and my father and brother came to sit beside us.

The light glinted off the carved face of the coffin as a woman glided slowly toward a lectern. The white podium stood beside the bier, covered in white fabric and decorated with a swag of white roses and baby's breath. Etina was our equivalent to a pastor or a priest. The priestesses of Ailuros presided over deaths and births and marriages within the Walker communities. Etina, her red hair held away from her face by a band of matching braids, came to a graceful stop behind the flowers and turned to smile at the gathering.

I listened with half an ear as she spoke a little about Greer, an extolling of virtues that steered clear from her leaving home without so much as a goodbye, from her involvement with Pariah Walkers Niko and Brand, and from any references to how she finally met her end. I swallowed a sob. Everywhere I looked I saw the image of my mother's face, superimposed on everyone, saw the look of disappointment in her eyes everywhere I turned. A look I would need to face soon. My heart thudded as Etina motioned for my father to come forward to speak.

I didn't hear his words, my mind still on my mother and the promises I'd broken. Fingers slipped in against mine and I looked at Iain as he held my hand, squeezing it in silent comfort. I'd refused to speak, not wanting to be a hypocrite. As sisters, we'd never been close. No point in pretending now.

Soon, my father returned to his seat, and Etina resumed her duties. Movement around me brought me back to the present as the small gathering began to rise. The service was over and the coffin would be transferred to a special cart, whose dark gleaming wheels were almost as tall as I was. The cart would draw the coffin and the mourners along the edge of the town and deep into the mountains.

All Walkers have a special place to bury their dead. Living in the world of humans the only safety we had against prying eyes is the ownership of private land. As such, every Walker town would have a special burial ground. Whether they be within mountains or beneath the ground, they were all lead-lined to hide the contents, and the entrances were all so well hidden you'd only know of its existence if you'd been shown it. And as a rule, no human was ever shown the entrance to our Mausoleums.

And now, for the first time, I wondered how that rule applied to Mom.

When the gathering moved to the roadside, only immediate family, elders and the priestess completed the procession. The cart rolled back and forth on spindly wheels, then began to move, drawn by my father and brother. I followed, giving Logan and my friends a weak wave.

"We'll wait for you at the house," Lily whispered as my heels scraped the hard-packed soil of the path.

The procession moved slowly, far too slowly for my liking. To be honest I just wanted it over and done with so I could get back to my normal life. Grams moved silently beside me, sending waves of Jasmine in my direction. When she glanced at me, she threw me a soft smile, her blue eyes darker than the clear azure sky above us. But behind that comforting smile I could see a hint of resignation, with a touch of determination added in for good measure. I sighed and trudged along. If Grams could see it through, then I bloody well could too.

We walked together, following the rugged road deep into the forest of birch and ash whose branches rose high above us, but blessed us with ragged patches of golden light every few yards. I had to admit, no matter how much I wasn't enjoying the walk, the trail through the forest was utterly beautiful. The very nature of it made my panther purr inside me. I pushed her back down and walked on until eventually we moved off the dirt track and into a clearing that seemed to appear out of the forest like magic. We'd reached the base of the mountain at last. My feet gave thanks. *Someone please remind me why in Ailuros' name did I think heels were a good idea?*

Someone up ahead would have pressed his hand against the plate hidden behind a fall of creeping ivy, because suddenly stone ground and scraped, and a large rock shifted aside to reveal the entrance to the burial cave. The threshold was wide enough to accommodate the wheeled carriage, allowing it to pass through comfortably. We followed it inside, and still nobody spoke. The last of the group stepped further into the cool interior and the door grunted and groaned shut.

For the briefest moment, we were plunged into a solid darkness so thick it felt like I was breathing shadows into my lungs. Seconds later, lights began to pop and flicker. Small electric lanterns, strung high up on the stone walls, lit the whole entrance cave up in its stark light.

The Tukats burial grounds were made up of a warren of caves leading off a long central corridor, and organized according to age of family. Each individual room backed onto solid stone, allowing the family to carve deeper into the mountain to expand their space should they expand their families. Many of the older family's had caves within caves allocated to them. It all tended to get a little complicated so I'd only ever concentrated on the Odel tomb. The carriage wheels turned as it traveled to the furthest end of the passage, the thin wheels rolling along the stone floor. As the solemn procession moved into the shadowed depths, I followed, my heart thudding against my ribs.

Ours was the very last of the caves, as befitting of the oldest family in Tukats. The men prepared to remove the coffin from the carriage and the priestess fussed around them, wanting to ensure they didn't damage the fragile carvings. She needn't have bothered. The men, two others including my father and brother, were accustomed enough to funeral preparations as to take the required care with the coffin. Etina was just a fusser.

They slid the coffin off the wooden base of the carriage, then lifted it by the carved metal handles. The pallbearers hefted their burden through the entrance to the Odel burial chamber, finding the empty spot beside my uncle Niko's coffin. Despite the deeds of his troubled lifetime they had accorded him the position in death that had always been allocated to him. His empty coffin lay beside his father, my grandfather, late husband to Grams who stood silently beside me. Everyone within the community had access to the burial caves, many coming and going as they pleased, but I knew Grams hardly ever visited. I'd never understood her reluctance until now.

The walls exuded a deep cold that did nothing to counter the icy fingers of grief. Although I was not mired deeply within the grip of mourning for Greer, I could understand the need to have someone make you feel better. And this cold, underground mausoleum certainly did nothing to help me feel better. If anything, it made me feel a little too close to death than I would have liked. I moved toward Grams, happy to feel the warmth of her arm as she drew me closer.

At that moment, I missed Mom so badly that I felt the stab of longing deep in my gut. It hurt, and hot tears filmed my eyes. I blinked them away just in time as Iain and my father joined Grams and me. The rest of the townspeople who'd accompanied us to the burial grounds moved to position themselves behind us. Etina walked silently to the head of the coffin, a censer swinging from her hand, her skirts rustling. Ribbons of white smoke streaming from the gleaming brass container, curling and spiraling upward until they dissipated above our heads.

The scent of incense softened the icy air, and I felt the tight fist in my gut release its hold on me.

Etina spoke about the eternal quality of the soul and how the ones we lose are never truly gone. I almost believed her.

I recalled the way Greer had retreated into the light, how it had felt so right, as if she was returning home. Or was it perhaps the expression on my sister's face. One I'd never seen before.

Peace.

CHAPTER 2

We were gathered in my father's lounge, the fire crackling merrily away despite the warm sun outside. Once we'd returned, the Odel family had been banished to the lounge to visit with their friends and wind down.

Friends of the family took over the kitchen and food duties, and trays of sandwiches and pastries were brought around by people I barely recognized. Their faces revealed no judgment, maybe a little sympathy, but not even a hint of curiosity about the specifics of Greer's death.

Dad and Ian as well as Logan and Omega had actively ensured the details would be kept under wraps.

That didn't mean the people of Tukats were ignorant of my sister's relationship with Niko and his Pariahs, or that they would be ignorant of Greer's relationship with Brand. People talked and Walkers were just like humans when it came to gossip.

But not one of them would ever ask me directly. I still stood apart from the Walkers I'd been raised among, and even knowing the reason didn't ease the niggle of unhappiness inside my heart. Half-breed. That's what they were all thinking. But if that mattered to me, then I'd have to question my loyalty to Mom, something I simply wasn't capable of.

I shifted in my seat and studied my friends. A Fae, a Djinn, a Fire Mage, and a lynx Walker. What an interesting circle of friends I'd joined to my heart. It wasn't often that Corin Odel's house contained this many non-Walkers, and I knew this time tomorrow, the Tukats' gossip mill would be having a field day.

I felt the heat of the fire on my right, my cheek now uncomfortably hot. My fingers fiddled with crumbs and the oily tissue that remained on the empty plate on my lap.

Lily and Tara were talking in low voices beside me, and I caught snatches of their conversation. Something about a jamming safety lock and poison bullets that got repeatedly stuck in the chamber.

Salem and Logan sat on the couch opposite me, seemingly in deep conversation. But even while he interacted with the Djinn, Logan never stopped watching me with those deliciously dark eyes.

He caught my gaze and gave me a small smile, and I understood his reluctance to come too close to me. The Tukats community wasn't without their own prejudices, and I knew despite the well-meaning words and polite social behavior, my friends would have been given the whole outsider treatment.

And Logan wouldn't do anything to make it worse for me. I was gripped by the urge to grab him and kiss him senseless right in front of all the prying eyes and judgmental gazes.

But I maintained control of my urges and got to my feet. "You guys want some fresh air?"

They rose in unison, and I hid a smile. They were as eager as I was to get out of the room, now suffocating with heat and curiosity.

Heads turned, drawn to our sudden movement. Dad looked up from a conversation with Iain. They both stood beside the fire, the golden light dancing on their fair hair.

Our little family was now balanced between the dark-haired and the light. I blinked, pulling myself up short. What a horrible thing to think about right now. All the stress of Greer's death and the funeral must be turning my brain to mush.

I stuck a thumb in the direction of the patio doors and they both nodded. They knew where I would take my little party.

I headed to the glass doors, unlatching one and walking out into the sunshine. The afternoon was cooler now despite the warmth of the sun.

Nobody spoke as I hurried out onto the lawn. A little gazebo sat at least a hundred yards from the house. Painted white, it was octagonal in shape, with four thresholds and four windows.

A pillar marked each point of the eight sides and was now overgrown with a creeping white rose. Little white buds peeked out from the sea of green leaves and branches.

Once inside, we all burst out laughing. The space wasn't big enough to fit five adults all standing.

I sighed and sank onto the nearest window seat. "This used to be my most favorite place in all the world."

"I can see why," said Lily as she took one of the seats opposite me. The strong warmth beside me made me want to smile.

Logan sat next to me, his long legs stretched out in front of him. There was barely enough space on the seat to fit two people, but we seemed to manage well enough.

Lily stared around at the creeping roses and the flaking paint. "Did your dad build this for you?"

I shook my head and almost bumped my forehead on Logan's chin. "No. This place was built for Greer. When she was six, she wanted a tree house. Dad, of course, was reluctant, but Mom had liked the idea. Eventually, they came to a compromise. A gazebo would do just as well, where it was nice and safe on the ground. But Greer was the only one who wasn't satisfied. She was never the compromise sort, and once it had been built, she barely gave it a glance. It eventually became the place I would go to have a quiet moment. Somewhere I could hide away with a book."

The day Mom left, I'd been reading in the gazebo, a daisy-chain crown draped on my head. I'd heard a door slam and glanced up to see Mom getting into her car. Dad was standing on the porch, his hands hanging at his sides as if he had no idea what to do with them.

The look on his face had chilled my blood, and when I looked back at Mom, I'd known something was wrong. Her eyes gleamed with tears and she'd swiped at them roughly before peering down at the keyhole to start the engine.

Once she'd gunned the engine, she released the brake and drove off without a backward glance. The wheels had skidded, spitting gravel, and I remembered the empty clacking sound of the stones as they were thrown around in the wake of the disappearing vehicle.

Later, I remembered wondering if that had really been the sound of the stones. Because I was sure it was the sound of my heart shattering.

"So how are you holding up?" asked Logan softly.

I glanced at him, met his eyes, and smiled. I wanted to run my hands along his cheek, to hold him and thank him for being so kind and attentive. "I'm fine. Really, I am."

I fell into silence, my thoughts returning to Greer. *It wasn't as if we were ever as close as sisters should be.* Logan shifted and I looked up. From the looks of all the faces around me, I knew what had happened. "I said that aloud, didn't I?"

Saleem's eyes twinkled, and both Lily and Tara nodded. Tara had an odd look in her eyes, as if she were worried about me but was trying not to get too suffocating with her concern.

I raised my eyes at Tara in question, and her features relaxed a little. "Kai, you do know you don't have to have a close relationship with a family member to mourn them." I nodded. "Because that's what I think you're doing. You're stopping yourself from mourning her because you think you have no right. Because you weren't close or because you were so different from each other or because you never clicked."

I sighed and leaned against Logan. "I know, but somehow I seem to keep doing it to myself. Even when I feel like crying, I just feel like a fraud. Why do I deserve to cry for a sister who I never really cared for?"

"But was that really all that true?" asked Logan as he gave me a squeeze. I craned my neck to look at his face. "You said in the end it seemed almost as if she cared. And maybe she always had, just never really knew how to show it. Just because you didn't have the perfect-world relationship doesn't mean you weren't sisters. She was your family. And now she's gone and it's okay to mourn her. Nobody will judge you for it."

I stiffened a little, but Logan didn't move away. I didn't want him to either. He was right. They were all right. I'd been doing this to myself all along. Making myself feel like I had no right to mourn her loss. Missing her or reminiscing about good times would be a lie. But mourning her wasn't. "Why does everything that goes on in my head have to be so darned complicated?"

"Because your name is Kailin Odel." Saleem spoke, his face gleaming with a smile. For the briefest moment, I thought I saw tattoos along his eyes and forehead, dark markings creeping along his neck and throat and disappearing into the neckline of his shirt. I blinked and they were gone. And I would have thought it was all just my imagination had it not been for the look he gave me. A knowing look.

I blinked. Was he using a glamor to hide his markings?

Not that it was any of my business what he showed to the world and what he didn't. But I still had unfinished business with the gorgeous Djinn.

We'd never discussed his strange need to collect Blue Stones while we were in the Graylands. I made a mental note to speak to him about that. But for now, I needed to just relax.

CHAPTER 3

When Logan and the gang left, they were followed closely by the rest of the visitors. I found the house quiet.

Too quiet. I wandered back inside, heading upstairs to my old room, and ended up on the window seat, inhaling the mustiness of old curtains and carpets. Seemed Dad hadn't brought himself to redecorate.

Sometimes I wondered what it did to him to live in this big old house, missing more than half his family. There were times when I could totally understand the icy cage he'd locked his emotions in all these years.

I leaned my forehead against the window and sighed, staring out at the garden, where the trees grew dark and gloomy now in the blush of evening.

"It's not all that bad, is it?" a voice broke into my reverie. I jerked my gaze to the intruder so fast my neck snapped and my heart gave an uncomfortable thud.

Justin Lake stood in the doorway, a lazy smile on his face. He was leaning against the threshold, his arms folded, the thin cotton of his shirt stretched tight over bulging muscles. He watched me, golden eyes observant, not missing a thing.

Then he blinked as if some thought had caught him short. "Not that I'm making light of Greer's death." His expression was apologetic, and I knew he meant it. With Justin, you trusted what you saw.

I tilted my head toward him and nodded, unsure if I should get up and take him back downstairs or remain seated. Justin always had the ability to fill a room with his presence. And here alone in my bedroom, he made me decidedly uncomfortable.

I gave him a weak smile and an equally half-hearted shrug. "It's okay. I know you weren't."

"She was pretty troubled." His statement filled the room, and I wanted to do something like knock on wood or throw salt over my shoulder because I wasn't convinced that talking ill of the dead wasn't bad luck.

"She had her moments." I laughed, seeing images of Greer sneering in the Graylands when she controlled the Deadland demons, bleeding after Brand had sliced her up, apologizing before disappearing into the light. "She certainly didn't do things by half."

Justin chuckled, then strode into the room. He had an air of dangerous power about him, like a threatening cat waiting to pounce, waiting to kill. He headed for the bed and sat on the corner of my mattress as if it were the most natural thing in the world. As if he weren't alone with another woman in her bedroom.

The cougar hunched and placed his elbows on his knees, leaning over. He stared at the carpet for a while, linking his fingers, sitting there deep in thought as if he owned the place. It grated on my nerves a bit, more probably because I wanted him out of my room, away from me. Being alone with Justin was asking for trouble.

Only when I was about to ask him what he wanted did he lift

his head to speak, as if anticipating the question. "I'd like to discuss something with you." His voice rolled over me like honey, thick and delicious. I blinked against the alpha effect and concentrated harder, watching him, the way the muscles in his shoulders bunched, the way his jaw tightened, granite hard.

And I wondered if I was going to like what he had to say.

He cleared his throat, then held my gaze. "I'm not sure how to say this."

"Take a deep breath and let me have it," I said, giving him an encouraging smile, all while something pinged inside—the warning he was probably right and I should rein myself in if the urge came over me to toss him out on his sexy ass.

He obeyed and said, "I'm concerned… I hope you're not going to be making a decision you'll regret."

Immediately I bristled, staring at him. My own shoulders tightened as I held his gaze. "What's that supposed to mean?" Who was Justin to wonder about my decisions? I would have asked him, but I'd noticed how difficult it had been for him to speak in the first place, and now I really wanted to know what he'd intended to say.

He cleared his throat. The fingers twisted, then loosened. "Okay, I know this is going to piss you off, but I don't have any way of avoiding it." He fell silent for a moment. "This Logan Westin you're seeing…" I said nothing, just waited as my blood began to simmer. "Do you really think it's wise?" he asked, concern darkening his eyes.

I fisted my hands and made a concerted effort to keep my fury in check. "Is it any of your business?" I pushed the words past the tight anger in my throat.

Justin lifted his head, meeting my eyes dead on with his brilliant golden gaze. "It is when it concerns an alpha."

"Did Iain send you?" I folded my arms, my body moving from relaxed to aware. Justin was sending off waves of power, confidence, and control. None of which made me in any way agreeable to him or his line of conversation.

"What?" Justin's brow furrowed and he looked momentarily confused. Then he shook his head, a little annoyance leaking into his gaze. "No, Iain has nothing to do with this conversation."

I believed him, but I waited a moment while I gathered my thoughts. "Justin, what is it you want?" All I wanted was to have this conversation over and done with, but it didn't seem my desires were up for consideration.

"I just wanted to tell you I think you're making a mistake. And I think you can do a whole lot better than Westin."

There, he'd said it. I'd suspected that was where he'd been heading, yet all the while, a part of me had hoped he wouldn't. My eyes narrowed and anger flared in my veins. "Really?" I asked, getting to my feet. My hands vibrated with anger.

Justin rose from the mattress and held out his hands, although supplication was the last thing I would think he was capable of. His attempt to placate me fell flat, just like his little attempt to stick his nose in my business. "Look, don't get all hot-headed about it. All I'm doing is saying my piece," he said, giving me a short shrug, as if he thought I wouldn't figure out something bigger was going on here. He wouldn't have opened his mouth, especially when he knew I'd bite his head off, if he didn't have a good enough reason. And mere concern didn't cut it.

My spine tightened as I said, "Well, now that you've said it, you can leave." I folded my arms and gritted my teeth. I waited a few moments for him to vacate the room, but not once did I expect him to. And true to my gut, all he did was stand there watching me with those alluring honey eyes. I lifted my chin. "Fine. If you won't, I will."

I stalked to the door, my back ramrod straight as I tried to contain my anger. The audacity. "Just because you're an alpha doesn't give you the right to interfere in my life," I said over my shoulder as I moved past him. I would have said more, but a warm hand grabbed hold of my elbow, setting my skin tingling. I'd always been half in love with Justin, but now was the worst time for that attraction to rear its ugly head.

He spun me around to face him. I opened my mouth to tell him where to get off, but I didn't get the chance to get a word out. He curled his arm around me, placing a hot palm at the base of my waist, and pulled me against him. My body remained stiff and I meant to struggle for a way out of his grip, but he was strong, not to mention the thought of struggling had disappeared entirely from my mind.

We stood there for a moment, heated skin sizzling against each other from chest to hips. I was sure it was my anger, but I knew it was probably something a little more passionate for him. Justin had always felt things to their fullest. His eyes blazed, but I didn't get a chance to look at them too long. His head descended and he kissed me. Caught off guard, I wasn't sure how to react.

Certainly not by kissing him back.

His lips sent sparks of heat racing up and down my spine, and my panther purred. The moment I felt myself liking it too much was the moment I shoved him away.

I took precious seconds to catch my breath and then I glared at him, my eyes narrow and all panther. "I get it. You want Logan out of my life because you want me for yourself."

He shrugged. "I can't deny that."

"The question is, why? Is this some alpha power play? Marry the daughter of an alpha and gain power over another clan?"

He shook his head, his eyes going dark. "No, Kai. You know that's not the case."

"I don't know anything," I said through gritted teeth. "You proposition me out of the blue. What do you expect me to think?"

"I didn't proposition you."

"Justin, this kind of dominance went out with the dark ages. You can't just force yourself on me."

"It didn't feel like I was forcing you. I kissed. You kissed back." His attitude was nonchalant, and he had a point.

I blushed, unable to deny that charge. "That's irrelevant. And don't go getting any ideas. I'm in a relationship with Logan. And I'm not interested in you that way. You've known that for a long time." I glared at him and shook my head, hardly believing his audacity.

"Why? Because of Sonia?" He met my eyes and held them, intent on seeing my reaction to his question as if he'd also be able to see into my soul.

I shook my head. But I had to admit the ghost of his sister did stand between us. His sister, my brother's wife. Killed by Logan. I blinked, fear flitting through my stomach. Justin would go berserk if he ever found that out. I thrust the thought away and concentrated on the cougar in front of me.

"Then what's standing between us?" he asked as if he genuinely wanted to know.

"Apart from the fact my heart is elsewhere you mean? You're an alpha, and the last thing I need is to get involved in that political game again. That's the very reason I left, and you know what? I'm very, very happy with my life right now. I have my own responsibilities to think about, and I'm happy if it just stays that way."

"So you won't even consider it?" His nerve never failed to amaze me.

"What's to consider?" I asked, lifting my chin. I didn't want to look into his eyes.

With a hand beneath my chin, he lifted my face and I was forced to look directly into his golden eyes. Then he leaned forward and kissed me again. This time he deepened the kiss, and I kissed him back just as passionately. When I found myself leaning into him, icy reality washed over me and I jerked away, shocked at my wanton response.

What in Ailuros's name is wrong with me?

I stared at Justin for a long moment, my heart thudding against my ribs. Then I shook my head and walked straight out of the room without looking back.

I'm not sure what the hell he expected from me. I knew he was manipulating my attraction to him, but for what purpose? Was it purely emotional or did he have an ulterior motive? A heavy iciness settled in my gut. And all the while I kept asking myself why I'd responded to that kiss.

But I didn't really feel as if I'd betrayed Logan in any way. Justin and I went way back. I'd been in love with him since my teens. Only falling out of love with him when I realized the true reality of being an alpha. Not that the reality had caused any of the attraction to disappear. From the heat of that kiss, we were both still pretty much into each other. But that wasn't a reason to pursue anything with Justin Lake.

My heart belonged to Logan.

CHAPTER 4

My feet took me to the kitchen, which was bright and empty. I pulled up a stool, sat at the counter, and stared at the gleaming red-and-chrome galley. I'd always loved our kitchen, the way the sun would stream inside and stay in the room for the better part of the day. We had a huge range and a center island big enough for a professional chef.

Elbows on the counter, I rested my chin on my hand and surveyed the silent space. Heaviness weighed me down, despite accepting what my friends had to say. I knew what it was. Now that the funeral was over, I could get on with my next mission. We'd held Greer's ceremony and burial within days of her death only because Dad and Iain knew I'd need to get myself to Wrythiin as soon as possible.

Mom and Anjelo waited. And as far as I was concerned, they'd done enough of that.

I looked up to the sound of footsteps entering the kitchen. Grams reached out for my hand, and when I took it, she gave it a little squeeze. Dad followed close behind her. From their expressions, I could tell they'd had some sort of disagreement. They covered it well. The old Odel strength when facing the outside world.

But not well enough so I'd be unable to see. "What's wrong?"

They looked at each other, a brief glance filled with worry. Then Grams turned to me. "It's just an old disagreement, dear. Nothing to be worried about?" She gave me a lukewarm smile. Then her gaze flitted away.

"Is it about Mom?" I asked as she hovered, unsure what to do with herself.

"What makes you say that?" she asked, her eyes still evasive. She rounded the marble counter for want of something to do, but our friends had done such a masterful job at cleaning up that not a speck of dust was left behind for her to attend to.

I snorted. "Because it's obviously going to be on everyone's mind. Greer is buried and now I leave for Wrythiin."

"When?" Just that one word from Dad.

"As soon as I can get my things together. I just need to make sure I have the right ammo, and I'm good to go."

He was shaking his head. "Grams wants to go with you."

My mouth dropped open, but when I looked over at Grams, she was shaking her head. She clicked her tongue and said, "What your father is trying to say is he doesn't think it's safe for you to go alone." She glared at him before she continued. "He thinks Iain should go with you."

I scoffed. "Even if Iain wanted to come with me, he doesn't have a portal key," I said, raising an eyebrow.

Dad shrugged. "We do work for Sentinel. A portal key is a small matter."

"At what cost?" I asked, the memory of the blood promise filling my thoughts. It would dog me until the day she asked for payment.

"Cost? What do you mean?" asked Dad, his forehead scrunched.

"If she extracts a blood promise, what then?"

His lips curled as he gave his head a slight shake. "If that's what she wants, it's a small price to pay." Then he frowned. "Is that what it cost you?"

No point in evading the question. I nodded and didn't miss the disapproval in Grams' eyes. "I did what I had to do," I said, a little too defensively.

"You still have your mother's key to the Wraith world?"

I nodded, then got to my feet. "I should get a move on. I need to stop at Tara's and then get some sleep. I'm going to leave in the morning."

Dad's forehead creased and he opened his mouth as if he wanted to say something but wasn't sure how to. Then he sighed and his shoulders slumped. "Of course you know I don't want you to go."

I smiled softly, feeling a little sorry for him. "I know. But I'm still going." I knew he would be struggling with it. As Mom's husband, he would want to be the one to save her, but his hands were tied. So many restrictions and rules.

"Always your mother's daughter, aren't you?" he said, and I grinned.

"Look, if Iain wants to come, I won't stop him. Mom's his mother too." I offered the option and really meant it.

Dad glanced over at Grams in a triumphant way that made me smile. Then he looked back at me. "I'll let him know."

I nodded. "Don't forget I'm leaving in the morning."

"I'll be sure to let him know."

I frowned, a thought just jumping into my head, one filled with saddening suspicion. "Does Sentinel want to have something to do with this mission?"

Dad's jaw tightened. "They don't approve, of course, but no, they don't want to get involved. The Wraith kingdom is in enough turmoil without Sentinel meddling in their affairs. Just be careful, though. Get in and get back home as fast as you can."

"That's the plan."

Dad rose and drew me into a hug. A strange action coming from a man who'd shown me such coldness for most of my life. And at that moment, I knew I no longer held it against him.

I sighed as he let go. "I have to get going before it gets too late." I snuck a glance out the window at the deep blue of the night as it snuffed out the light. I considered running home, but heels and a skirt weren't conducive to speeding through the forest and brush all the way back to the city. I gave my feet a wry glance and peeked up at Grams. Hopefully she was going my way, considering we both lived in the same apartment.

"You need a ride?" she asked, her blue eyes twinkling.

"Since these shoes weren't made for runnin', I certainly accept." I grinned as she got to her feet and rounded the counter. She patted her son on his arm, giving him a look that failed to hide her concern. He'd lost his daughter. Good enough reason for him to fall apart. But the man seemed to be hanging in there.

My gut twisted. I'd been so focused on my own feelings I'd lost sight of the fact that my father had just lost his child. I couldn't imagine a more horrible thing. Grams hesitated in front of him as if she wanted to give him a hug, but he held himself a little too stiffly. Enough for her to know he wasn't ready for more comfort. It made me more certain that Mom needed to get her ass home. And soon.

When Grams moved away, I followed her out of the kitchen, leaving my father alone, surrounded by strangely shadowed chrome and red that looked more like dried blood. I paused in the doorway and glanced back at him. The tilt of his head, the weary bow of his shoulders, even the elegant splash of gray at his temples all made me more aware that he wasn't getting any younger.

I'll bring her home soon. I promise.

Following Grams out the door, I frowned as I saw her shadowed form disappear into the garage. I followed her inside and almost jumped when the automatic door grumbled loudly. A quick glance around and I couldn't hide my smile. Grams stood beside a gleaming Ducati, the motorcycle seeming far too mean for the likes of my grandmother. She grabbed her hair in her hands and knotted it at the back of her head.

Then she picked up two helmets, holding one out to me with a cheeky smile. "I'm not exactly dressed for a bike ride, but I think I need to feel the wind on my face."

I snorted. "How will you do that when the helmet is jammed on your head?" I'd always disliked helmets, and whenever I rode, I'd find some reason to conveniently forget to put it on.

She shook her head at me and tutted. "Kai, you're a Walker, not an immortal. Smashing your head into the ground will kill you, just like it would any human."

I stiffened.

"I take it you haven't gotten over that yet?" Grams' lips twisted wryly.

"Oh, you mean the fact that after eighteen years of existence, I find out I'm a mongrel? Yeah, I've gotten over that." My voice was cold despite the fact that I wasn't so angry anymore.

"Kai," Grams said, reproach dulling the usual sparkling bright blue of her eyes.

"I'm sorry, but that's the way I feel. It's got nothing to do with Mom. It's not like I hate her for being human. For Ailuros's sake, I'm kinda falling for a human myself, so I can't be judging. The thing is I lived almost my whole life and I never knew the truth, so you can't expect me to switch off my feelings just like that." I came to an abrupt stop and took a deep, shuddering breath, wishing the shadows in the dark garage would swallow me up. "Sorry, Grams. You didn't deserve that." I sighed.

Grams, hit my arm with a pair of elegant black leather gloves. "Don't apologize for feeling emotions, Kai. Sometimes you're too much like your father." My gaze snapped to her face, my forehead wrinkled. "He's always kept his emotions bottled up inside. The deeper he feels, the harder it is for him to reveal his feelings. It's not healthy."

I nodded. I'd felt the ice of his emotional detachment after Mom left us. I knew I should learn from his actions and deal better with my feelings. Tossing the shiny black helmet from one hand to the other, I said, "I know. It's just hard."

"How hard is it, dear?" Grams tilted her head up at me. "Have you thought about your own children? What if sometime in the future you marry Logan, or a man of another species? What would you think of your own little mongrels then?"

I stared at Grams. Trust her to force me to think about something that hadn't even occurred to me. Marriage. The last thing that had ever been on my mind. Even with my relationship with Logan. Although, if I had to be perfectly honest, I wasn't the sort of girl to waste time on a guy who I didn't consider long-term material. I'd grown up with the belief that Walkers and humans could not have children, but finding out about my mother had certainly put that fable to dust. Here I was half human, half Walker, fully capable of watering down the gene pool further. I wasn't sure how my family would feel about that.

"But wouldn't that be frowned upon? I'm already only half Walker. Wouldn't I obliterate the Odel genes if I had children with a non-Walker?"

Grams frowned, then looked up at the dusty ceiling. She thought for a few moments, then said, "I don't think the Walker bloodline is at all dilutable. Look how strong you are. You're still an alpha even though you're half Walker. Sometimes I wonder if the Walker gene simply just takes over. I've never seen a human-Walker pairing that produced non-Walker children."

I frowned. "Then what about Greer?"

"Greer was Pariah. Just like Niko. And your uncle was full-blooded Walker. Unless I'd had an incubus visitation without my knowledge." She winked.

"Grams!" I scolded but couldn't help laughing. "Okay, I see

your point. Half Walker but full strength. And still alpha." I sighed and grabbed my hair in one hand, twisting it into an ugly bun before jamming the helmet on my head. Grams did the same and threw a long, lean leg over the motorcycle.

I eyed Ivy Odel as she moved with lithe grace. Grams was pretty sexy for an older woman. Sometimes I had to force such thoughts out of my mind. Poor Gramps would be turning in his coffin if he knew how hot she still was. As she thumbed the starter switch and the engine revved, I grabbed her around the waist and tried to stop thinking of everything but the ride.

CHAPTER 5

Sighed as I unlocked our apartment door and fell inside with relief. Grams kicked the door shut behind me and headed to her room. The day had sucked out all my energy, leaving behind an empty hole in my chest. Not to mention my run-in of the personal kind with Justin. I just couldn't figure him out. He'd never behaved like that before, so interested, so passionate, so forward. Not that I would have considered his proposal if he had. Justin was pretty much off-limits by my own stipulation.

I sank onto my bed and was about to remove my shoes when I remembered I'd intended to see my favorite weapons expert as soon as possible.

I sighed and got back to my feet. At Grams' door, I paused and knocked lightly before opening it.

I frowned at her as she hovered over her travel bag. She always carried a change of clothes in her rucksack along with her weapons. "Another job already?" I asked, frowning.

"Not much I can do about having work to do." She shrugged as she folded a pair of black jeans.

"They could give you a personal break, especially now," I said, raising my eyebrows in annoyance. Sentinel seemed to control her life.

She just smiled at me. "Like you're giving yourself a break?" She was watching me, her head tilted, her hands stilled.

I shook my head as if the mere action negated her argument. "You know I'm going for Mom and Anjelo. I can't stand the thought that they'll have to be there one more night. I'd go now if I could. I would have gone after Greer died if you had let me." I didn't care that my words came out tinged with accusation. They'd forced me to wait until after the funeral. Even when I'd tried to convince them I may be able to bring Mom back to say goodbye to her daughter.

But nobody had listened, and I'd begun to wonder if there was something they hadn't wanted me to know. Some big secret they were keeping from me. Now I could see all they wanted was for me to take care of myself.

Grams' eyes hardened and she returned to folding a black turtleneck. "Kai, jumping from plane to plane can have a huge impact on the health of your body. You went from Wrythiin to Earth, filled with obsidian blade poison, then you went to the Graylands still weakened by the poison. Then you came home and went back again, all while still healing. The last thing we needed was for you to die from too much cross-veil travel."

I didn't say anything because she had a point. Having finally fully recovered, I knew now how much the poison had affected me. And no matter what I tried to tell myself, it was more important for me to be healthy because that meant I'd be more capable of completing my mission.

I sighed, then paused. I had another thing to ask before she disappeared on me. "So... Any news from Sentinel on the prophecy?"

Grams' face darkened and she shoved the top into her bag. There was a moment of silence in which I let her fold and stack while I waited, leaning against the threshold. Growing impatient,

I opened my mouth to urge her to answer, when she said, "There is something, although nobody is sure what to make of it."

Ominous. "What is it?" I asked, burning with curiosity.

Grams looked up and her eyes were dark and filled with worry. She cleared her throat, her fingers trailing the edge of the bag's zipper. "The scholars studying the manuscripts have come across a translation problem. They think they were wrong about the specifics of what or who the Ni'amh is."

"Wrong how?" I asked, my heart thudding. All along, the idea of being this special being, the potential savior of the world, had intimidated me. And now Grams was saying they were wrong? Suddenly, I wasn't sure how I felt about possibly being free of the responsibility. I cleared my throat. "They've found I'm not the Ni'amh?" I asked her far too eagerly.

Grams grinned, although the smile failed to hit its usual brightness. She shook her head, her blonde waves brushing her cheeks. "Sorry, my dear. You're not off the hook that easily. The scholars believe there was some confusion in the wording. They now believe the Ni'amh is not a singular description."

"What? So they think there's more than one Ni'amh?" To say I was disappointed was an understatement. I'd welcomed the thought of being off the hook from the whole saving the world business.

"They aren't sure yet, but they do suspect the Ni'amh refers to a *group* of women. They are delving deeper into the semantics and also looking back at what they've already translated, since a change in the meaning now could have an impact on older translations."

I nodded, my stomach lying heavy in my gut. "So there's more than one of us?" When she nodded, I said, "Well, I suppose that's better than carrying the burden all on my own."

Grams zipped up her bag, then walked toward me, placing her hands on my upper arms. "Even if you're sharing it, it's still a huge responsibility, so don't kid yourself."

A shaft of ice scraped down my back. I had enough to think about without this hanging over my head. Not that I was about to disappoint Grams by whining. I nodded, then gave her a quick hug. "I know. And I guess I will carry that responsibility until I know what I'm supposed to do with it." For a moment, the skin at her eyes tightened. But I wasn't going to apologize for that. Up to now, nobody had been able to give me better information on what exactly it was I was supposed to do to fulfill that responsibility. Not even the Titan Jess. I sighed. "I'm sorry. I shouldn't have said that. It's not your fault."

But Grams was shaking her head. "No. You have every right to be frustrated. It's not easy when all you have is a hazy idea of what you're meant to do." Grams sighed. "How about we all deal with this one day at a time? Okay?"

I nodded, feeling slightly better. "Okay. Now I'd better get going. Tara has some orders ready for me."

Grams smiled and waved me off, and I hurried out of the apartment. Once outside, I gave the street a quick check. When I was certain I was alone, I took off at Walker speed and got to Tara's in less than two minutes.

CHAPTER 6

The light was on inside, and I pushed open the door, listening for the tinkling of the bell above me. The door shut behind me and my eyes adjusted to the dim storefront. It seemed Tara was already wrapping it up for the day. I headed for the inner door that led to Tara and Gracie's apartment, my heels tapping the worn wood floor. The counters were bare and so were the glass cases that usually held their display of various weaponry.

Odd.

I frowned and stopped at the threshold. I looked over my shoulder at the shelves that held a variety of weapons from around the world. Tara marketed herself as a stockist of antique and exclusive weapons from the past. As such, her shelves overflowed with armaments from Persian daggers to ancient tribal machetes made from animal jawbones. But today, even the sight of those overflowing shelves did nothing to ease the feeling that something was wrong.

I turned to enter the apartment as the sound of voices filtered to me. I hesitated, but being already halfway into Tara's dining room, it was too late to leave. Inside, the table was piled high into two distinct stacks of weapons and ammunition. Two women were deep in conversation, their attention focused on one pile of munitions. Tara glanced up as I paused, clearly aware that I'd been there from the moment I'd entered. As a Fae, Tara had strange and impressive powers, ones I wouldn't want to mess with.

"Hey. Look what the cat dragged in," she said with a laugh. I laughed too, figuring she was at a loss as to what to say. That told me one thing: Tara was on edge; something was distracting her.

I walked to the table and the other woman glanced up, pushing her long black hair away from her face, her gray eyes sparkling. The smile she gave me was well returned. "Hi, Mel," I said, grinning at the tracker. I'd liked her from the first time we'd met when she'd helped me track Greer.

I held out a hand to shake hers, but it only felt weird. I was saved any awkwardness when she leaned forward and gave me a quick hug. "Kai. How are you?"

"I take it you two are acquainted?" said Tara with a smile as she began dropping ammo into a line of waiting boxes.

Mel nodded, giving me a soft smile. "Yes. I worked with Kai not long ago," Mel said to Tara, then turned her gaze on me. "I'm really sorry about your sister, Kai. If there's anything I can do to help, please don't hesitate to ask."

I nodded. "Thanks. Sometimes I think it was Greer's time and sometimes I just think it's all a cruel joke."

Mel looked at me, a sad expression in her eyes. "Yeah. I know the feeling." Then she sighed and turned her attention back to Tara, who had placed the boxes of ammo into a rucksack. Mel helped her pack a few pistols and a rifle into the bag and then grabbed hold of it. "I'll get going and let you two catch up. Thanks so much, Tara, and don't stay gone too long, okay?"

The Fae smiled. "I'll try. No promises." She gave Mel a small wave as the tracker swung the bag onto her shoulder and headed for the doorway.

"Take care, Kai. And don't forget; let me know if you need any help. I'll be there in a flash." We all laughed as Mel disappeared into the front of the store, and I recalled Logan had mentioned the tracker was also a Teleporter and quite a powerful one at that.

I turned my attention back to Tara. "So what was she talking about? Are you going somewhere?" I knew my reaction was a little harsher than I'd intended, but after Greer's death, I was still a little sensitive. Guess I really had abandonment issues. Tara leaving without telling me would hurt more than I was willing to admit.

"I'm sorry, Kai. You were going through so much with the funeral I didn't want to dump it all on you."

"I could have dealt with it, you know. I am a big girl." I swallowed the hurt, careful not to let her see it.

"I know, but I didn't want you to. It's not such a big deal anyway. I have to go home. The Fae Court has demanded my presence. I think they've gotten fed up with having an absent queen."

"But I thought Gracie was back in the Faelands already." My brow furrowed with confusion and my gut was telling me something was wrong.

"Well, there's been a development. Mother returned thinking she could perform her duties, but the court council believed she was past the age to rule. They've insisted the next in line to the throne claim it now or lose it forever."

The revelation hit me like a wave of arctic water. "What? But can they force you to do this?"

She looked solemn as she responded. "Yes, they can. You know what councils are like. They can change their minds in the blink of an eye. Or take a decade to make one decision." Tara sighed, and I knew how she felt. The idea of the council had always felt unnecessary, but I'd understood the reasons they were installed in the first place. The danger of having one's peoples at the mercy of a single despotic ruler was a danger most species preferred to avoid. Hence the installation of councils. Our own Walker Council often gave my father a difficult time, and usually when the Supreme High Council called, it sent all paranormals into a panic.

"So when do you leave?" I asked, trying to behave like I wasn't about to lose it.

"Probably as soon as you leave." Tara softened her words with a small smile. "Sorry. It is sudden. I knew you'd come so I didn't ring to tell you."

"I would have come sooner if you told me," I offered, although I knew that would have been easier said than done with everything that had been going on.

"And how would I have been able to spend time with you while delivering orders and redirecting the rest?" asked Tara with one hand on her hip, reminding me of her mother.

I stared, too distracted by Tara's plans to be offended by her not being able to spend time with me. "You're canceling orders?"

"Of course I am. I have no choice. People like you come to me to get a job done. If I'm not around to fulfill orders, then I have to redirect them. As much as it pains me to pass work on, this is the only way I could keep my loyal customers satisfied while I'm gone. In case I return, I want them to be happy with me."

"In case you return?" I asked, beginning to feel like a parrot. When I saw the shadows in her expression, my stomach sank. "So you think there's a chance…?"

Tara nodded, her amber eyes downcast. "I need to be ready for every possibility. I hope I can come back, but I can't make any promises." Tara waved me into the kitchen as she spoke, and I followed her in silence, still absorbing the enormity of her revelation.

I sat and swallowed the lump in my throat. While I simmered in my thoughts, Tara busied herself making coffee and slicing cheesecake. Just watching her activity made me want to cry. What a wuss I was.

Glass tapped against Formica as Tara set down mugs and plates. She sighed as she pulled her chair forward. "I'm so sorry to do this to you now."

I shook my head. "No. Please don't feel bad. Our lives are just as important as our friendships." I searched her face as I asked, "Do you need me to come with you? Or help you in any way?"

A smile curved softly at the edges of Tara's mouth. "No. And thank you for offering." She sipped her coffee and stabbed a fork into the pale cream of the cheesecake. "As much as I would love company, unfortunately I need to deal with this shit myself."

I chuckled as I reached for my mug. "Yeah. We all have our own shit to deal with."

The next few minutes were spent just talking about nothing and everything. To be truthful, I wanted to prolong our time together, but I knew we were both pressed for time. Tara had to leave, and I had to prepare for my trip to Wrythiin.

"So how do I contact you if I need to?" I asked, a little afraid of the answer.

And when she shook her head, I had a sinking feeling this was a goodbye that could likely be final.

And one that I did not like in the least.

CHAPTER 7

J left Tara's with my weapons and ammunition. And with a heavy heart. I hoped she'd be back soon because I was so damn tired of losing people.

I made a concerted effort to shrug off the negativity that sought to weigh me down and moved into Walker mode to race all the way home. The wind in my hair did a little to relieve my sadness. But only until I got home.

Again, I entered the apartment through the front door, something that was becoming far more common these days. I hardly ever used the old fire escape anymore. Maybe it was the fact that last time I'd used it to enter my apartment, I'd been caught off guard and then abducted.

Not something I wanted to ever repeat.

I'd barely made it inside before Grams came hurrying to me, placing an arm on my elbow and turning me around to face the door again.

"What? What's going on?" I squawked, twisting my head to send Grams a questioning glare.

"The Walker Council has requested our presence at Lake's property. And we leave now. Get rid of your bags and let's go."

"Okay," I said as I slipped the bag of weapons off my shoulder and dropped it just inside the front door. Then I allowed Grams to pull me outside and lock up. As we hurried down the stairs, I asked, "So what's the big hurry?"

Grams' jaw tightened and she gave her head a short shake. "All I got from the council was a summons. Every Odel who is alpha would have received one."

"I didn't," I said without checking my phone. Now I wondered what I'd see if I did. Grams raised eyebrow seemed to wonder the same thing.

We rushed down the stairs to the old boiler room beneath the apartment building. Gram went straight to her bike, grabbing the helmets and throwing one at me. In one smooth move, she shoved the helmet on her head and swung a leg onto the bike. I mimicked her actions and we were soon out on the road, heading toward the cougar colony.

My stomach tilted as my mind returned to memories of kisses that shouldn't have felt so good. I shook them off. They were the leftover emotions of first love. Hardly anything to worry about.

I felt a little off balance. This whole evening wasn't going at all as planned. First finding out I might have company in the status of Ni'amh, which wasn't too bad, then finding out my best friend was flying off to Faeland and may not return for a long while, which pretty much sucked. And now a summons to the Walker Council that had all the signs of being bad, bad news for everyone.

As it turned out, it wasn't bad news for all alphas. Just a few of us.

Grams skidded to a stop in front of Justin's wraparound porch, uncaring that she littered the steps with stones from the drive. We got off and hurried up the stairs, tossing our helmets onto the chair beside the doorway. Justin's house had the style of a dude ranch, all wood and glass with a huge wrap around veranda. To be honest, I kinda loved his house.

We swept inside without knocking and headed straight to the meeting room that sat beside Justin's study. All alphas ensured they had the facilities to accommodate a Walker Council meeting. Even my father's house had a similar setup: a large meeting room with a table long enough to seat the twelve councilmen as well as sufficient seating along the walls of the room to accommodate all the alphas of the American colonies.

I sighed as we approached the double doors to the meeting room. "Be happy this meeting wasn't in L.A. or New York for that matter," said Grams in response.

"Yeah," I replied with a wry smile. "Let's hope we can get this wrapped up as soon as possible."

Grams cracked the door open and we slipped inside. A few heads turned, but most of the people within the room paid us little attention. A discussion was in progress, a heated one, hands shaking and heads moving. The alphas sat back, seated with their family members. As a pack, the alphas could tear every member of the council to pieces, but to do that for whatever reason would spell anarchy. The rise and fall of negative energies in the room told me this wasn't a good place for the alphas right now.

At the far end of the room, Justin looked up, meeting my eyes with an encouraging nod. He sat alone, his sister Sonia having been his only living relative. For Justin, his line ended with him, unless he married and produced a few little cougar alphas. I nodded back and walked along one edge of the room, heading straight for the two seats beside my father and Iain. Grams and I sat quietly, giving Dad inquiring glances.

Grams leaned over my lap and whispered to Dad, "What's going on? I was heading out on a job." She wasn't holding back her annoyance.

But Dad just shrugged. "They've been deep in discussion for the last half hour. Looks like they themselves have a problem with whatever this announcement is." His voice rippled with annoyance, probably at being in the dark. I knew how he felt.

"So you both have no idea?" I asked him, noticing Iain face us from where he sat on the other side of Dad.

Both Iain and Dad shook their heads. Iain leaned forward. "All we know is it's some sort of new codex to the alpha laws."

I frowned. "Can they do something like this so suddenly?"

"No. Whatever rule they intend to pass will take time to take effect. So everyone has time to air their disagreements."

I nodded and sat back. Having been to a few of these meetings before, I was used to the politics, but it wasn't often the entire alpha families were called to attendance. Around me, I recognized the faces of alphas, cougar, lynx, panther, and more. Alphas and all members of their families that had reached the Change.

We sat and waited a while longer before a hush fell over the members seated at the table. A gavel smashed against a block somewhere at the head of the table and the room fell into silence. "Attention, please. I call this meeting to order." It was purely as a matter of routine that he spoke. Everyone was already waiting with bated breath, having been seated here too long already. I could smell the tension in the air clearly enough even without the aid of my panther senses.

"We've called this meeting with the intention of adding an addendum to the Codex of Rules. We are aware this new rule will not sit very well with many alphas, and we are instilling a three-year timeframe in which each alpha family can table their disagreement and/or propose an amendment to the new ruling."

The speaker certainly had little personality, and I almost stopped paying attention to him as he droned on.

Almost.

"Now we come to the new ruling. I hand you over to the Walker Council Leader Joseph Marsden to speak to you on this." He waved his hand at Marsden, who got to his feet to address the gathering, his hands folded behind his back. The man was ancient and seemed to have been ancient for decades.

Years ago, I'd wondered when he'd keel over and die. As I

watched him look down at his notes, his bald head shining in the soft light of Justin's chandelier, I felt a spike of unease. I'd never liked this idea of a non-alpha Council ruling over all the alphas. To me, it defeated the purpose of having alpha families, but I knew too that it was politics that had brought about the Walker Council. In recent years, their power had increased, new rulings included in the codex that placed more constraints on the alphas.

I'd heard Dad and Iain argue over it, often threatening to leave and form an independent clan not affiliated to the Walker council. But that in itself had seemed treasonous at the time. Not so much now when I faced their power directly.

Finally, Marsden cleared his throat and the low murmur of voices hovering in the room faded to silence. "We have been in discussion these past months and have come to an agreement that the new ruling we are considering is applicable and appropriate given the situation. I apologize to you for having to wait today. Although most of the council are in agreement, there are some that have expressed their concern and have registered their disapproval. As will be your right, you are free to do so as well in the coming years."

He stopped speaking and took a moment to survey the gathered alphas, his gaze panning the room. I studied his eyes, once blue but now gray with age, his skin where it sagged beneath his eyes and under his neck, giving the impression of a bewildered turkey. Then he spoke and what he looked like was the last thing on my mind.

"Our concern is the dilution of the Walker bloodline, more specific the dilution of the alpha bloodline."

My heart stilled in my chest and I didn't dare look at Dad. I knew what they meant, and it was bullshit. Why should the council even care? Everyone knew the Walker gene was always dominant.

Although nobody spoke, there was now new tension in the air that hadn't been there before. Despite the rising pressure,

Marsden continued unperturbed. "The new ruling is: alphas who have more than fifty percent non-Walker blood will no longer have a legal claim to alpha-hood."

"And who are you to say that?" asked one of the outlying jaguar alphas. "Being an alpha is a natural trait; it is either there or not. Many of the families you see here have a number of descendants that don't qualify as alpha with your new ruling. I'm not sure what it is you are trying to do here." The jaguar alpha who spoke had a pure, untainted bloodline, so I admired him for standing up and posing the question.

It was clear enough to everyone present that a ruling like this could imply there was more that the Walker Council was keeping up their sleeves. It brought suspicion on their intentions, and in this case, I thought it was probably a good thing. If alphas with watered-down bloodlines had to go, then what about alphas who are Pariah or alphas who are crippled? Pariahs never took the roles of leaders in their clans, but they did still retain their alpha status. On the other hand, alphas who were crippled, maimed or born disfigured still became alpha if it was their blood right.

This new ruling could be expanded to change that. And that was where the danger lay.

Marsden waited patiently as the noise subsided. "I understand your concern, but this is a serious issue that you must take the time to consider. We know the Walker gene is stronger. We know that a pairing with a human or another species still produces offspring with a strong alpha gene. But what we are concerned with is the next generation. How many second-generation alphas do we have seated here that have only one grandparent that is Walker. They are technically only twenty-five percent Walker, and what right do mixed-bloods have to control a colony, to oversee other full-blooded Walkers, to control their lives?"

His words were designed to incite the prejudices of the alphas, but it didn't seem to be an all-out success. A few heads were nodding, but many more were shaking in disagreement.

As I surveyed the room, my eyes met Justin's. The sadness in his expression made my heart ache. Not that it mattered, but I wondered how he felt about a union with me now. Would he think it was such a good idea anymore?

Marsden cleared his throat. "The ruling includes the following: all second-generation mixed alphas who are part of a Walker/non-Walker union will automatically be disqualified from alpha rights."

His words chilled me to the bone. The new ruling meant, should I continue my relationship with Logan and we settle down, then I lose my right to alpha-hood.

CHAPTER 8

*J*didn't like it.

Not that it had ever meant much to me considering I'd always rebelled against my alpha responsibilities, but when your rights were being removed, then everyone had the right to be concerned.

"I'm afraid I don't see what right you have to instill this ruling," said the jaguar alpha who'd spoken earlier. I struggled to remember his name. Deacon. Matthew Deacon. "It doesn't make sense. Sometimes alpha genes are extremely dominant in third-generation offspring. Sometimes they are stronger and more alpha than most."

What he was saying was true. I knew of alphas who were third-gen mixed-breed that produced a feline counterpart that was stronger and more powerful than many of the full-bloods.

"That does not mean they have a right to rule." A voice cut through the hum of disagreement. Francine Waters. An icy voice to match the icy blonde.

"We haven't had a problem with it for centuries. Well, forever if you want to be specific. Why now? Why are you making a minor issue into something bigger?" Deacon asked, still not backing down.

"It's not a minor issue," Waters snapped. "It's a matter of the dilution of the bloodline."

"Bloodlines are diluted no matter if you are alpha or not," said Deacon, his tone kind, his eyes far from it. It was clear to anyone watching that he didn't particularly like Ms. Waters.

"Be that as it may, we believe the right to rule must preclude those who will dilute the bloodline."

"We aren't royalty to be bothered with bloodline purity. What exactly is this all about?" an irritated voice piped up.

"So what? Are we going to go back to the dark ages where our mates are chosen for us? Will the Walker Council now act as marriage advisors to the ruling families, then?" another voice shouted.

Marsden held out his hands, waving down the rising voices. "You will have plenty of time to record your disagreement to the ruling. Please take your time to think about this from all angles."

"So are you saying if we don't agree with this ruling of yours, you will not ratify it?" Marsden glanced at the speaker, a lynx alpha from Colorado. The expression on the council leader's face was stony. The lynx alpha laughed. "I see. We have time to voice our disagreement, to table our dissatisfaction. But in the end, you will still ratify the ruling anyway."

The room erupted into cries of disagreement.

"That isn't fair…"

"We should have a say…"

"This goes against our rights…."

"The council is taking their responsibilities too far…"

The secretary banged his gavel again, but nobody seemed to care. I was numb, trying to process the whole thing. Beside me, Dad and Iain had remained strangely quiet. I wanted to know what they thought, but a tiny part of me wondered if they agreed. Maybe they also had issues with my relationship with Logan. Iain had certainly disliked him to begin with, but I'd been under the impression it was because of the whole Sentinel-Omega rivalry.

Around us voices rose and fell. Most of the alphas respected my father and would stand with him in this case. It wasn't as if I'd ever done anything for the colony that would make them want to sacrifice anything for me. So I wasn't expecting them to stand up for me personally. I just hoped there were enough first and second-generation mixed-bloods within the alpha families that would ensure the alphas didn't allow the ruling to go through.

I leaned over to my father. "So what if the majority of the alphas disagree with this ruling?"

"It certainly seems like it doesn't matter who disagrees."

"But can they really do that?" When he didn't say anything, I asked, "So what if they decide the Walker Council now chooses the alpha leaders, that dominant Walker blood no longer has a say?"

"As ridiculous as that sounds, it looks pretty much like they could do that too if they wanted," said Iain, a cold, hard anger in his voice.

"Then I think the Walker Council has gotten way too powerful if they can stand all the alphas down when and if they want to."

"We agree, but little can be done about it. We're left with lobbying the current council members to ensure the vote doesn't go through." Dad shook his head as if he couldn't fathom what was happening.

"So one nay will stall the ruling from being ratified?" I asked, curious about the process but fuming at the reality of it all.

Dad nodded, but his eyes were hooded with worry. "But I'm not sure now if they can be stopped."

"How the hell did it get to this?" A voice at Dad's back made him swivel around in his seat. A jaguar alpha elder from the north spoke with Dad and Iain in low tones for a few moments.

When he left, I asked, "What was that about"?"

"Just someone as unhappy with this whole situation as we are. Seems the alphas are pulling together on this. It's not a matter of the bloodline issue any longer. It's more to do with the fact that the power of the High Council has reached a danger point. The alphas no longer have a strong vote in major decisions. It used to be that we were consulted, that our opinions were taken into strong consideration. But it seems the balance has shifted. Something has changed that we aren't aware of."

"Did you even see this coming?"

"I'm afraid we did see this coming." A voice spoke behind me, and I twisted around to face Justin. "It's been a point of concern for a number of years, but this ruling is worse than we ever expected. Something has to be done."

I said nothing, but Dad looked at Justin, his gaze dark with concern. "Are we meeting?" was all he asked.

Justin nodded. "I'll let you know the details as soon as I hear."

"Will they want us on board, considering?" Seems the alpha bloodline issue had struck a chord with Dad too.

"Of course, Corin. Don't even think that the alphas will sideline you on this." His tone was sharp, as if it annoyed him that Dad had even asked the question.

Dad just nodded and Justin left his seat and walked further down the line to stop and talk with another alpha family. I scanned the people in the room and for a moment, I was relieved to see that few eyes were on me or any of the other half-bloods with relationship issues.

Until my gaze fell on Michael Waring. He was staring straight at me, caring little if I noticed his attention. The look he gave me didn't disguise his dislike. The Warings were one family I'd never want to contend with. If you wanted to see entitlement in action, you only had to look at the Waring alphas. They were cougars from Washington and seemed to think their location meant they got to tell everyone else what to do. Most alpha families paid them little attention, and the reality was they had more enemies than friends.

Now Michael, whose father was the reigning alpha of his clan, stared at me with a potent hatred in his eyes. Michael, whose advances I'd deflected just before I'd fled to Chicago. It didn't make sense though. Why hold a grudge against a half-breed with the new ruling now coming into effect? But a niggling thought still remained. I was one of the most powerful alphas in the US. If we had to step back into the Dark Ages and fight amongst the alphas for the right to rule, I'd pretty much wipe the floor with Michael's ass. Was that it, then? He hated me for rejecting him?

I sighed, wanting to rub my forehead to ease the ache behind my eyes. But that would be a show of weakness, and alphas were not weak.

I just wanted this to be over so I could go get Mom.

The gavel knocked again and the room subsided into silence. During the discussion, the council members had remained at the table, had not mixed with the alphas at all. Smart move since so many of the alphas were so unhappy.

"Now that we have the ruling on record, we can adjourn the meeting. You will all receive copies for the addition via email within the next day. And of course, we welcome any discussion regarding the new ruling. Meeting adjourned."

The moment the gavel hit the block a final time, the room erupted into discussion. The council members filed out in a hurry, and it was easy to see why. They weren't the most popular people around. A large number of alpha families gathered around us, and a few of them patted me on the back or the shoulder, murmuring words of support and encouragement.

We stayed until the first alphas began to leave, an Odel family rule of old. We were officially the highest-ranking family, and even in Justin's home, Dad acted as the host. Not that Justin minded, either. He'd been an honorary member of our family since we'd joined his in marriage.

As soon as Grams and I got back to the apartment, she rushed into her room and grabbed her bag. She glanced over her shoulder as she headed for the door. "I really have to go. I'm not sure if I'll get back before you return, so be careful, Kai. I mean it. Don't go taking any unnecessary chances."

"Yes, Grams." I agreed, knowing as I spoke that I merely said the words to satisfy her. Whatever happened when I went to Wrythiin, it would happen as needed. I had no plans to avoid anything the Wraiths may have in store for me.

The apartment was silent after she left, just the soft tick-tock of the hall clock to break the deathly pall. I was bone tired and needed some sleep, but the insistent vibration of my mobile told me I had at least one message waiting to be attended to.

A glance at the list of texts confirmed a message from Lily and one from Logan. It was well into the early hours of the morning when we'd returned from Justin's, but I responded to both messages, hoping both senders were asleep and would receive them in the morning, thus relieving me from any further disturbances.

No such luck.

The phone buzzed and I was forced to answer. "Hey, Lily. Why are you still awake?" I asked, keeping my voice light.

"Where the hell have you been?" came the strident question.

"Sorry, it's been a freaking long day."

"I was worried," Lily replied, an accusing note to her words.

"I'm sorry. I got home late, then saw Tara, then had to head off to a Walker Council meeting that still makes my stomach turn."

"Walker Council?" Lily asked. "What do they want?"

I sighed and sank into the couch. "Nothing much. They just want to make sure half-breed alphas who don't partner with another full-blooded Walker lose their alpha-hood."

"What? But, Kai, what about Logan?"

"Hey. It's not as bad as it sounds. It looks like the alpha families won't be taking the council's shenanigans lying down."

"So someone is going to do something about it, then?" she asked hopefully. She seemed as upset about this as I was.

"I certainly hope so. And by the way, Lily, this has nothing to do with Logan, okay?"

"What do you mean? If what they say stands, then you won't be allowed to be with him." Her voice was strident and almost panicky, as if the thought that anything happening to Logan and me would devastate her.

"Lily," I said, keeping my voice low and even. "I'm young and so is Logan. We both have a lot of life left before us. This isn't the time in either of our lives to be making long-term life choices."

"But…"

"But nothing, Lily." I fell silent for a moment, and it seemed she had nothing to add. I hoped she wasn't pouting. "Look. I have to get some rest. I'm falling asleep on my feet."

"When do you leave?"

"As soon as I wake up."

"Well, I'm coming with you, so don't leave without me."

"Look, Lily—"

"Don't *look Lily* me. I'm not letting you leave me behind this time, okay. Anjelo is in Wrythiin too. I have stakes in this too, you know, so you can't cut me out. You don't have the right." No matter how I looked at it, I couldn't negate her words.

I sighed in silence. Lily had me cornered with her argument. Besides, how could I refuse her the right to save the boy she loved? "Okay. I'll text you when I get up."

"Thanks, Kai. I promise I won't let you down. I'll be useful too."

"I know you will. Now let me sleep and we'll talk in a few hours. You get some rest, too. No telling how long it will be before we rest again."

CHAPTER 9

My sleep broke a few hours later, and I knew that was all the rest I was going to get. I wriggled in the bed, my eyes squeezed shut, reluctant to open them. Already my heart was thudding in anticipation of the mission.

I stiffened as warm lips traced a heated trail down my neck. Logan's hair brushed softly against my cheek, and I smiled, inhaling the musky, piquant scent of him. It had been a different kind of hell during the funeral, unable to touch him or let him touch me. I'd have said to hell with propriety and manners, but Logan was all about the rules.

Now, though, it seemed he was prepared to break a few rules with me. The strap of my racer back tee slipped off my shoulder, and he kissed my collarbone, sinking his teeth into the sensitive skin, sending shivers of desire along my body, all the way to the pit of my stomach.

I cleared my throat and tilted my head down to look at him. "Just what is it you think you are doing?" Although I tried to be cool, even bossy, my voice came out husky and filled with desire.

"What does it look like?" he asked as he raised his head to look at me, his black eyes filled with fire. My collarbone felt bereft of his warmth, and the look in his eyes destroyed any facade of resistance I might have raised.

"What it looks like is breaking and entering," I said, my breath coming in short, sharp bursts.

He moved closer, skin sizzling against skin. "Oh no, I entered the property on good authority that the owner was in need of saving."

"Oh really? Saving from what?" I raised an eyebrow, but it went unseen as Logan returned to burn kisses along my neck, all the way back to my collarbone, and then further. I wasn't about to complain.

"Saving from need," he whispered, his voice hoarse. "You see, need is all-consuming, and she has to be saved or else it will mean the death of her." The other strap of my tee slid off my shoulder, the fabric skimming sensitive skin, heightening the ripples of desire that engulfed me.

"You sure this need isn't really an Incubus?"

Logan snorted and his breath puffed against my ribs. He'd certainly made progress. I was now down to just one article of clothing.

Logan groaned and pulled me closer, sliding his body up mine, sending sparks of lightning across my skin, firing my senses. The feel of his lithe, muscled body against the length of mine did unmentionable things to my insides. His mouth descended on mine, his tongue driving me to seek more of him.

And at that moment, time stood still. I wasn't thinking about heading off into unknown danger. All I could think of was the man who held me so tenderly in his arms.

For now, the moment was all ours.

I WOKE with a start and blinked drowsily. Something had pulled me from a deep, dreamless sleep. I accessed my panther sight, the dark slowly melting away until I saw Logan struggling in the bed beside me. I'd been so fast asleep I'd forgotten he was even there. And I didn't have time to feel bad either. He thrashed about, tossing his head this way and that. The muscles in his neck were strained, tight with whatever stress his dream created in his mind. He mumbled something, but many of the words were smudged. I managed to make out a few words, and it sounded like he'd said, "Where is she?" and "What happened to her?"

A light sheen of sweat bathed Logan's body, and he was so hot to touch that I hissed when I put my hand on him to still his frantic thrashing. I ignored the burn and gripped his muscled shoulder, shaking him hard. Who knew what he'd do, but I was prepared.

He slid out of his nightmare slowly, blinking at me as I bent over him. He dragged a hand over his slick face and groaned, dropping his head back against the pillow.

"You okay?" I asked as I hovered.

He gazed at me, his eyes dark and troubled. Then they cleared as he gave me smile. "I'm fine. Just a bad dream." He was trying to reassure me, and I didn't want to push him.

Selfishly, I was aware I didn't have the time to spend convincing him to confide in me. I just had to hope we had enough between us that he could eventually be comfortable enough to bare his soul.

I WALKED out of the shower to the enticing aroma of fresh coffee. Dressing quickly, I headed for the kitchen to see Lily sitting at the marble counter, sipping at her mug and blowing carefully on the steaming surface. Logan stood on the other side of the counter, a mug in his hand. He'd dressed and looked pretty decent considering we'd gotten about two hours of shut-eye. Handing me a mug, he smiled as I approached, and I slipped into the seat beside Lily.

She looked at me, then quickly glanced at Logan and then back at me. I hid a smile. Lily was a little uncomfortable being alone with us.

"You're early. Wanted to make sure I don't leave without you?" I asked with a teasing smile.

Her eyes narrowed, unamused. "Something like that," she snapped, clearly grumpy because of the hour of the day.

"You tell Storm where you're headed?"

Lily nodded. I was being motherly, but I didn't have a choice. I had to be sure she'd checked off everything that was necessary.

"Did he have any objections?"

She snorted. "Of course he did. He seems to think he's my father or something." She rolled her eyes, then returned to blowing on her coffee.

"Lily, he is your guardian, you know. It's what you agreed to. And it shows that he cares."

"I know." She sighed and set the mug on the counter. "I'm just not used to someone being so overprotective." She rolled her arms, elbows out, as if she were struggling under a blanket weighing her down. I knew how she felt. It was exactly the way I'd felt in Tukats before I decided to hit the road. How could I fault her?

Silence shifted between the three of us until Logan cleared his throat. "You girls need to be extra careful in Wrythiin." He seemed to blurt out the statement as if he hadn't intended to say anything in the first place but had been unable to control himself.

"Any particular reason?" I sipped and wondered what he knew. "Omega know something we should?" Logan's eyelids dropped the tiniest bit of an inch, and in that movement, I knew the answer was yes. "So what does Omega have on the Wrythiin situation?"

"It's not very specific. We've tried to gain information, but it's pretty difficult considering we don't have a Wraith working for Omega, so a deep cover agent isn't a possibility." He paused again, then drained his mug. "Our knowledge of the political and social situation in Wrythiin is solely from back when the Wraiths were originally banished from the Earth. Since their banishment, they've been careful to ensure as little interaction with Omega or Sentinel and even the High Council of Protectors."

"Well, if they weren't allowed to come to our world, how was anyone supposed to keep an eye on them?" Lily asked.

I waited for Logan to respond.

"I wonder about that sometimes too. Surely someone would have ensured that we still kept open a mutual liaison line, but as far as I know, the information coming from Wrythiin is little to none."

"So all we know is based on our limited knowledge of their activity in our world? Does Omega have a standpoint on their current activity?"

"You're referring to their slow and persistent penetration into business and politics?" he asked, a curve to his lips.

I nodded. "I hadn't expected them to be that smart."

"They're Wraiths, not imbeciles."

"Point taken. It's just in my encounters with them, I never got much chance to discuss business or politics." I laughed. "So I'm walking into the middle of a war." The thought was sobering, and based on Logan's expression, he wasn't comfortable or happy about it.

"From what we know, intense conflict, rebellion. There are two resistant factions. One who believes the Wraiths should have access to all the other worlds. They believe they shouldn't be made to suffer for their forefathers' indiscretions."

"I take it the other Rebel faction is led by Widd'en? Or was?"

Logan nodded, a drop from his still-wet hair falling onto his shoulder. A wet patch had spread on each of his shoulders. He'd been so preoccupied he'd forgotten to dry his hair. It worried me now that I worried him so much. "Yeah, with him out of the way, who knows who the next Rebel leader will be? Let's hope his death doesn't mean you have worse on your hands."

I grunted. "Just my luck, right?"

"Well, don't borrow trouble. Who knows what you'll deal with when you do get there?" With that, he set his mug down and stepped around the counter. "I should be going."

I snuck a glance out the window. It was still too early for the sun, but the sky held a tinge of light that teased with the promise of another dawning day.

I slid off the stool and walked him to the door. Out of the corner of my eye, I saw Lily scoot off her seat, scurry to my bedroom, and closed the door. I smiled, knowing she'd want to avoid seeing any farewell kisses. If she'd stayed in her seat, she would have seen that concern was unwarranted. Logan's phone began to buzz and he flicked it open. After a few terse words, he shut the phone and gave me a rueful smile.

He opened his arms and I slid into their comfort. He held me tight for a while, then released me. He kissed me hard on the lips, growling the words, "Be careful," against them. Then he turned and hurried out the door. So. He didn't like long goodbyes.

Neither did I.

CHAPTER 10

*O*ur footsteps sounded off the wood of the pier, echoing around us so loudly I was sure we'd be spotted. Early mornings on the docks weren't usually the quietest time of the day. I glanced around, and thankfully we didn't have an audience. At least not one I could see. I never forgot that Sentinel and Omega were likely to be keeping an eye on me.

I gave my cell-phone one last check and found a message from Iain. *'I won't make it K, bring her home and be careful.'* I hadn't wanted Iain to come with me and now I could not deny that I was relieved he'd changed his mind.

The wind surged against us as I adjusted my overflowing satchel on my shoulder. I was glad I'd dressed in a turtleneck and my warm leather jacket. I had no knowledge of Wrythiin weather, but I decided to dress warmly in case. My black leather pants and sturdy biker boots finished my ensemble. A glance at Lily confirmed she was beginning to opt for a similar style, although in her case, she made do with jeans.

Lily's face was pale in the bland morning light. The waves smacked against the pilings beneath the pier and a light wind swept past, playing with her matching pale hair. She'd been unusually subdued since we'd left the apartment.

"You okay?" I asked, watching her face.

She peered up at me from under her thick lashes, reminding me so much of how young she was. Sixteen may not be all that young for a Walker, but a life on the streets wasn't a good place to find a happy, calm existence. I suppressed a laugh. Lily would be the last person to say she needed happy and calm. She liked the hunt too much. Must be something about being a feline Walker. Something in the blood that drives us along in search of the next adventure.

Lily nodded. "Yeah. I'm good. The sooner we get Anjelo and your mom home, the better I'll feel, though."

"You nervous?" I asked Lily.

She snorted. "I *am* a dimension-jumping virgin, you know."

I laughed softly as I slid my hand into my jacket pocket and withdrew the portal key. It gleamed in the light, the solid weight giving me a strange comfort. A ripple of unease volleyed through me as I recalled the blood promise the high priestess had drawn from me. Sometime soon, that would come back to bite me in the ass. But right now, I refused to think about it.

Now I concentrated on Wrythiin.

I stepped to the edge of the pier and held the key over the water. Lily stopped beside me, silent but sending off waves of nervousness. I understood how she felt, so I let her be.

I threw the key over the water and watched it hover above the heaving black waves. It didn't take long for the light to begin to shine. It streamed upward from the center of the donut-shaped key, so bright that the average human would have had to shade their eyes or risk being temporarily blinded. Not so for Walkers, whose eyes were far stronger.

The column of light filtered through the hole and down into the murky bay, pulsing intermittently as if it had its own heartbeat.

"Ready?" I asked Lily. I watched her face, her stiff shoulders, taut spine. She was a bundle of nerves and that was good. Fearlessness was dangerous.

"Yes," said Lily, nodding as she stared at the hovering key. Then she gave a mock shudder as she glanced down at the pulsing black water.

I laughed softly as another gust of wind buffeted me, throwing my loose locks into my face. I slipped a finger into my pants pocket and retrieved an elastic band, then tied my hair into a low ponytail. Not particularly fashionable, but good for dimension hopping and Wraith hunting.

"Right, then, let's go. On three." I took two steps back and Lily did too. I held out my open palm, and as soon as the lynx Walker placed her hand on it, I gripped hard. Leaning forward, I ran, feeling Lily keep pace beside me.

We both leaped together, flying through the air toward the bright column of light. For a moment, my chest tightened with fear. What if we didn't get close enough? But I needn't have worried. The key itself seemed to have an attractive force around it. It caught us in its path and began to pull on us like a magnet attracting its polar opposite.

We sailed over the water and straight at the portal key. I half closed my eyes as we flew, heading into the center of the key. The first time I'd used a key, I'd been terrified that either I'd never enter the thumb-sized hole, or I'd be squashed forever for the effort. Experience told me I'd be fine, that we would both be fine, but logic screamed in my brain and I felt a dart of fear slash through my gut.

The next thing I knew was darkness. When I squinted against the blackness, I found I was blinded by the light emanating from the column. As suddenly as the light blinded me did it disappear again, leaving us in pitch darkness. My body hurtled through black space, gusts of wind slamming against me and throwing me into a slow spin. I wondered how

Lily was doing and worried she wouldn't be able to handle the ride.

And then I hit the ground and my head slammed into something solid. A sound exploded next to me and reverberated around us. Lily hit the ground with a thud and a small, *"Oomph."*

I sat up and rubbed the bump on the back of my head. The silence was thick, as solid as the darkness around us. I sensed Lily shift beside me. "You okay?" I whispered.

After a moment of silence, as if Lily were giving the question serious thought, she whispered, "Yeah. Wow. That was some ride. Now I know what babies feel like, being shoved through a tiny hole just to see life."

I snorted. Trust Lily to do something as ridiculous as compare traveling through dimensions to the act of birth.

I smiled into the darkness and channeled my panther sight. Heat coursed through my eyes, electric pulses rippling along the surface of my eyelids, surging into my eyeballs. I felt my eyes widen, my pupils stretch wider and adjust their shape from round to the feline almond shape of a cat's eye. The blackness began to fade as it turned to gray and solid darkness transformed slowly into the outline of Lily's body with the ebony rock of the tunnel wall behind her.

I got to my feet, dusting myself off from the black sand covering my clothing as well as my skin. It was the strangest feeling to be immersed in thick shadow, as if swimming in a pool of ink.

Lily struggled to rise beside me. "Be careful. The walls are not smooth and the tunnels are fairly narrow."

"Have you been here before?" came Lily's soft voice.

I nodded, then realized Lily couldn't see me in the solid blackness. "Yes, or at least I'm assuming I landed in the same place I did the last time I arrived in the Wraith dimension."

"How come there's no dark water?" Lily asked.

I frowned and realized Lily had a valid question. Even in the

Graylands, there had been dark water to assist in inter-dimensional travel. But here in Wrythiin, I'd arrived on hard-packed ground. "Maybe the water is close by, maybe on the other side of the wall. Or maybe portal keys don't need dark water in the Wraith world." Lily didn't answer, and I could imagine her frowning as she considered my words. "Right, I think you need to turn on the Walker sight."

"Easy for you to say," came Lily's voice.

"Sorry," I said. "We're in no hurry. Take your time." Being Pariah, even a partial transformation was a task in itself. I knew it would sap some of Lily's strength, but she needed at least a little sight so she wouldn't be a liability to me. The last thing I needed was to have to worry about a blind Lily in this world. She'd come to help, so I hoped she wouldn't chicken out just because she was reminded of her Pariah status.

"Okay, let me got my bearings. Where exactly are you?" Lily asked, and I watched her reach out. Then I felt a warm hand on my breast and choked back a laugh.

"Lily, this isn't the time to be fondling me."

Lily snorted, then dissolved into a fit of laughter as she withdrew her hand and placed it on a much safer part of my body. "Sorry, I got my wires crossed there for a moment. I thought you wanted me," Lily said dryly. Then unable to hold the tone, she giggled.

I reached for Lily's hand and lifted it off my shoulder. When I placed the girl's palm on the rock wall, I said, "Here's the wall of the tunnel. Now concentrate on the change. You want to see, so open your eyes."

"Okay," said Lily, a nervous lilt to her voice. A few moments passed and Lily sniffed. "I don't think I can do this."

"You can. Otherwise, you'll make me regret bringing you. You wanted to be here to help me, right, not to be a distraction? I don't have time to spend concentrating on you instead of the mission." I spoke sharply and hoped I wouldn't hurt her feelings too much, but I had to be blunt. I wasn't planning on sugar coating anything. She needed to channel her sight so she could also be an asset. Otherwise, I should really just leave her right there to wait for me to find Anjelo and Mom.

The soft susurration of Lily's breathing was the only thing to mar the solid silence that fell upon the tunnel. Until Lily yelped and the high-pitched sound echoed around us.

"Gosh, Lily, a little louder please. I don't think they heard you in the Graylands. Do you want to alert them to our presence?"

"Sorry. I just felt my eyes transform."

The excitement in her voice was contagious, and I forgot to be annoyed with her. "Good girl. Can you see yet?"

She was breathing fast, excitement and the thrill of lynx sight rushing through her veins. "Yes, yes, I can. The sight isn't the best, but it's not dark any longer."

"Good. Then we can get moving," I said, not waiting for her response as I began to walk forward. The tunnel curved left up ahead, and I moved quicker, determined to get this job done fast.

"Kai?" Lily asked as she hurried to keep up with me.

"Yes, Lily?" I responded without looking back.

"Thank you." Her voice filtered to me, soft and hesitant.

"What for?" I frowned but kept walking, eyes open and alert.

"For being so patient with me. And for bringing me along." Her voice revealed she'd known all along how close I'd been to saying she couldn't come.

I shrugged, but the movement was obliterated by the weight of the weapon-laden satchel on my shoulder. "Don't worry about it. Just don't make me regret bringing you, or I will have to send your ass back home immediately." I smiled to myself. Sometimes it was hard pretending to be an adult.

My feet hit the stone floor as we moved down the tunnel, sending low thumping sounds echoing around us. I cringed, but there was nothing to do but plod on.

"Will you really do that?" Lily asked hesitantly, and I considered her question.

Then I nodded without looking back. "Yes. If you become a burden or jeopardize the mission in any way, I will take you straight back home."

Lily grunted and I could just see her pout. "Geez. You're such a slave driver."

I snorted. "I don't expect any more of you than I do of myself."

"I guess you're right," Lily conceded before falling into silence. She hurried to keep up with my long alpha strides, but I didn't slow down. Lily would think I was being easy on her, and the last thing I wanted was for her to become complacent.

Not in Wrythiin, when all our lives were at stake.

As we took the corner, the sound of oncoming footsteps slammed into me. For a moment, I was fixed to the spot, unsure of what to do. Then I fell into a fighting stance. Lily heard the footsteps too and stopped just at my shoulder. I could taste the tension coming off her body in waves.

A hooded figure stalked toward us, head down, footsteps in a fast, purposeful rhythm.

CHAPTER 11

Just when I thought the Wraith hadn't seen us, he looked up. His face was within folds of shadow, hidden by the large hood of a Wraith cloak. I watched as he slowed to a stop, one black-gloved hand flipping aside the folds of his dark mantle. The black sword at his hip glinted in the meager light. Even in panther sight, the obsidian blade flickered ominously, making my stomach roil in response.

My hand followed suit and my fingers curled around the hilt of my own appropriated obsidian sword. But it was stupid. The whole hand-on-sword-hilt move was meant to be threatening, but it held no substance. Not when these narrow tunnels made a true swordfight near impossible.

The Wraith stood stiff, shoulders straight as he waited for my next move.

Moments passed in which we both seemed to be waiting for the other. I felt he had the advantage, as he was able to see my face while all I could make out was black shadow under the hood. It seemed we both decided at the same time, launching into a run.

Lily's voice echoed behind me, her cry of, "No!" reminding me I wasn't in this alone. In the moment of studying my enemy, I'd forgotten I had her to back me up. Now I just hoped if this fight went south, she'd be strong enough to help me.

I moved fast, panther blood pumping through my veins, energy burning through my muscles as they thrust me forward, closer to the enemy that bore down on me. The tunnel was silent and all I could hear was the thumping of my heart, the rush of my breath as I ran. We closed in on each other, only a part of my awareness registering the slimness of my enemy's legs, the feminine shape to the thigh, the elegant arch of her neck.

This Wraith was a girl.

But I paid little attention to that knowledge, just ran headlong into her. I hit her in the middle of the chest, fingers curled in a tight punch. The power rippled through her, the force of the blow reversing her forward momentum so swiftly I heard a crack as her neck snapped forward then back.

I slowed as she stumbled backward, arms wind-milling as she attempted to regain her footing. She was lithe and light on her feet, though. She skidded to a stop, the hood of her cloak finally falling off her head to reveal her features. I'd always considered Wraiths ugly, but the girl's femininity seemed to give her Wraith features a certain elegance. Wide, almond-shaped eyes, an expansive forehead, a long aquiline nose in a face at least a third longer than a human's. Silky white hair framed her face, falling all the way to her shoulders. A Wraith's cheekbones were much higher, their cheeks more sunken than a human's, making their faces look gaunt and corpse-like, but in this girl, the elongation simply contributed to the serene elegance of her features.

Anger flashed in the dark pupils of her obsidian eyes and she clenched her jaws, muscles bunching in her neck. She bent forward and ran at me, and I could see her intention clearly. She intended to hit me shoulder to abdomen and use her weight to drop me onto my back, but I had other plans.

I reached deep for my panther, accessing my ability to move with speed and agility. I ran as she did, straight for her, until she was about five feet away. I ran faster, reaching an optimum speed. Even as she reached me, I kept running, using the wall to keep moving. A foot low on the tunnel wall, I pushed against the rock, propelling myself higher and over the Wraith girl until I landed behind her. I spun around just in time to see her skid to a stop and stare at me, stunned.

Lily crept up slowly behind her, her gun trained on the Wraith, but the creature remained unaware. Her attention was focused on me, and that's the way I wanted it to stay.

"What are you?" she asked, her voice vibrating. She squinted and reminded me it was still densely dark in the tunnels. Thank goodness for my feline sight. But I wasn't stupid enough to assume she was blind in the darkness either. I knew nothing about Wraith physiology, but I had to wonder if they were born with the ability to see better in the dark than the average human, considering they lived all their lives in these burrows.

I moved closer and she stilled, watching me with her strange black eyes, her whole body tense, waiting.

Then Lily stepped closer, her foot scraping the stone floor ever so softly. But not softly enough. The sound must have been enough to draw the Wraith's attention, and she spun around, forgetting I had my full attention on her.

She moved smoothly. I watched her shoulders lean forward, her back tense, telling me she was about run straight for Lily. And I couldn't let that happen. I grabbed her before she launched herself into a dead run, wrapping an arm around her neck, pressing my forearm hard against her throat. I held onto my wrist with the other arm, keeping her in a tight headlock, and although she struggled violently, she remained imprisoned.

The more she struggled, the more pressure I placed on the lock. But something else was happening. I wasn't sure if it was me being so close to a Wraith, but my hands began to glow. The skin on my fingers gleamed gold. I could hear the high-pitched sobs of the Wraith as she struggled for breath. The more she struggled, the brighter the glow became.

Fascinated by the glow, I paid little attention to the Wraith girl and her ever-lessening struggles. Paid no attention to the advancing thunder of boots coming straight at us.

A shout sounded, and it took me precious seconds to recognize what he said. "Kai, don't." The words were repeated, echoing around the tunnel and in my brain.

"Anjelo?" I asked, peering beyond Lily, who spun on her heel, her spine stiff.

"Kai, please don't hurt her. Let her go." Anjelo held out a hand toward me, his eyes begging me to stop, and I did. The Wraith dropped hard to the floor as I took a step around her and headed straight for Anjelo. I reached him seconds after Lily grabbed him and squashed him into a death grip of a hug. He laughed and squirmed, returning the embrace, his face revealing embarrassment as well as joy.

Odd.

Lily released him and glanced at me, her eyes and cheeks wet with tears. She stepped aside as Anjelo hugged me. There was a new strength and confidence in my old sidekick's muscled arms.

"Anjelo, how are you?" I studied his face, but a movement beyond him distracted me. A pair of Wraith guards stood stiffly behind him. "Who are they? Are they holding you? Is that why you haven't come home?"

Anjelo shook his head and placed a hand on my arm. "Kai, it's okay. I'll explain everything." Then he walked around me and headed to the girl Wraith. Lily's eyes flashed, and I knew a little of how she felt. I turned to watch Anjelo as he hurried to the fallen Wraith. She sat there, hand to her neck, leaning against the stone wall. Anjelo reached her side and hunched down, the wide swathe of his cape billowing around him. He knelt beside her, spoke words we couldn't hear, then held out a hand. After helping her up, he waited while she steadied herself. She seemed well enough as she began to walk toward us with Anjelo at her side.

I didn't miss the small fact that Anjelo walked a few inches behind her. A little bit of deference that made me tamp down any concern that Anjelo's heart may have moved owners.

The Wraith girl was in charge it seemed.

Anjelo whispered something in her ear, and she gave him a swift nod. Then she stopped in front of me.

"Few people would be allowed to survive after doing that to me. Consider yourself fortunate that Anjelo has spoken for you." Her eyes sparked angrily, and I understood her position. She'd had her ass kicked and she didn't like it. I wouldn't like it either.

"Thank you, I guess." I had to respond and couldn't think of anything else to say.

Anjelo cleared his throat. Clearly he hadn't lost the ability to tell when my anger levels were rising. "Kai, this is Illyria, leader of the Rebel army. Illyria, this is my alpha, Kailin Odel."

I held out a hand, and the Wraith girl stared at it for a moment as if watching for any sign of a golden glow. Then she glanced up at me and grasped my hand, her grip strong but not macho.

"Good to meet you. Sorry about the whole near-death thing," I said, although I wasn't entirely sure I was sorry. She was a Wraith, and I found the fact the Anjelo deferred to her a little disconcerting.

She laughed softly. "I'm not that easily killed."

"You are when Kai gets all glowy hands on you. No Wraith has ever survived her golden touch," said Lily, her voice holding a faint tightness as her gaze went from Illyria to Anjelo. I wanted to tell her there was no need to be jealous. Not that I could see anyway. Sure, Anjelo seemed attentive to the great leader. But that could mean any number of things.

Illyria stared at me for a moment, her eyes studying my face a little too long for my comfort. Not that I felt threatened. "How long have you had this power, Kailin?" asked the Wraith leader.

Although I really thought it was none of her business, I answered, "Just over a year now."

She turned and glanced at Anjelo over her shoulder. "Is she the daughter of Celeste?" she asked, something in her tone implying she knew my mother personally.

Anjelo nodded. "And if she's here now, it means she's looking for Celeste."

A hint of shadow passed over Illyria's face, and a shiver ran down my spine as I wondered what that expression meant. "Why, what's wrong? Has something happened to my mother?"

Anjelo and Illyria exchanged worried looks. Then Anjelo said, "We've been keeping track of Celeste's movements. As far as we know, she's being held captive by Widd'en's followers. They blame her and you for his death."

I frowned. "So how did you get away from them?" I still found it odd to see Anjelo unharmed, unaffected by his stay in Wrythiin. Especially the fact that he seemed comfortable here.

"Illyria's army attacked Widd'en's compound. In the confusion, I was saved, but Widd'en's men managed to get away with your mother. We have a mole within the army. But the information we get from them trickles in a little at a time. The problem is we only get the information after the fact."

"Have you considered the possibility that perhaps the mole is manipulating you?" I asked, raising an eyebrow.

Illyria gave me an admiring glance. "Yes, we have considered that, but unfortunately we have little choice. We have to ensure your mother is safe. She's a very valuable part of this rebellion."

I shook my head, frowning at the girl's words. "What does my mother have to do with your rebellion?"

"Your mother has spent many years among us. She's one of the very few non-Wraiths who understands what we're going through. We can never repay her for the amount of help she's given us over the years. And now we have you, her daughter, to thank for killing one of the most notorious Wraiths in Wrythiin." She smiled at me, but before she removed her gaze, something flickered in her eyes. Something I couldn't quite put my finger on.

I brushed away the thoughts and said, "I only did what I had to. My sole purpose in entering the Wraith world was to retrieve my mother and Anjelo." I kept my tone measured and clear of emotion. At this point, I wasn't entirely sure what I felt, but looking at Anjelo now was beginning to annoy me. "Why did you not come home as soon as you were freed? You must have known we'd be worried about you all this time." I glared at him, not giving him a chance to avoid the question.

He had the grace to flush, but his features remained composed. "I knew I should return, but I owed Illyria and her army for saving me. I couldn't just let her down and leave."

"But it was okay for you to let us wait back home, month after month, not knowing if you were alive or dead?" asked Lily, her tone devoid of emotion. I had to admire the girl. I'd have been vibrating with fury at that point, and my voice would have shown it.

Anjelo turned his gaze to Lily, touching her arm as he spoke. "I didn't only stay for the Rebels. I stayed because of Celeste. As long as Widd'en's army had her captive, I couldn't leave. I had to find a way to free her, and Illyria and the Rebels have been helping me."

"Twice now we have attacked their strongholds, and twice we have almost saved her. The one thing we do know is she is alive and healthy. During the last raid, she looked well, and I am hoping she remains so. One cannot trust Widd'en's men. Without their leader, they are lawless, unruly, and at times vicious. Who knows what they are up to right now?" Illyria's voice was musical, the lilt a bit unsuited to her odd looks. But it seemed to work.

Out of the corner of my eye, I watched Anjelo sidle up to Lily and take hold of her hand. Lily tensed for a moment, her arm going stiff. Then she looked at him and relaxed. Good. There was no trouble in paradise that couldn't be repaired.

I nodded at Illyria. "Thank you for keeping Anjelo safe, but right now I think the best thing is for me to take him and Lily back home. I will return immediately to search for my mother."

"Kai," both Lily and Anjelo protested together.

CHAPTER 12

"No way," said Lily.

"Hell, no," said Anjelo.

They both spoke together, their anger almost tangible, enough for my panther to raise her head and give them a tentative sniff.

Illyria remained silent as she watched the conversation progress with a small smile. I stiffened. I was sure her own army didn't rebel against her instructions the way these two half-wits were. I glared at them. "I can't have you two hanging around just so you can get hurt." Couldn't they see that, in the end, I was responsible for them?

"I'm not a baby," Lily whined as she folded her arms angrily against her chest. Fury had darkened her honey eyes to a warm gold.

Anjelo cleared his throat. "Kai, I've been in Wrythiin long enough to know my way around and to know how to defend myself and fight back. I haven't been sitting on my hands these last few weeks." There was a confidence in his voice I hadn't heard before. Even so, I wanted to cut him off and say that was all irrelevant because I was here now. But something in his expression made me realize that doing so in front of Illyria and the two wraith guards would demean him in a way that would be irreparable. I let him speak. "Illyria's guards have been teaching me hand-to-hand combat," he added as if that would impress me. It did.

"I'm impressed," I said allowing a grin to curve my lips. As much as I worried about Anjelo I really couldn't demand that he return home. "Looks like I really shouldn't have been worrying about you all these weeks."

Anjelo's teeth flashed a smile, then he ran his hands through his hair. A bloom of pink tinged his cheeks and I thought it was so cute how he was embarrassed to be complimented. I wondered what sort of treatment he'd been getting down here. Sure he'd said the rebel leader's guards were training him but he could still be a captive without looking like one. I needed to tread lightly and I hoped Lily wouldn't put her foot in it too quickly.

I glanced at the lynx but she was still staring at Anjelo with that adoring look in her eye. She wasn't holding back how she felt and I could tell it was making Anjelo uncomfortable which in itself was odd since he'd always doted on her. I studied Illyria for a moment but she seemed unaffected by Lily's mooning. Either she didn't give a damn or she was way confident. That was if, and only if, there was something going on between the two of them.

Now that we got the fight to stay part out of the way, I knew we had to get on with it. "Okay, Anjelo. Is there somewhere we can go to talk? You and I need to figure a few things out."

Anjelo glanced at Illyria, waiting for her response, and all the while I watched. She gave him a curt nod, her eyes still masking her emotion. "You can use the small war room." Then she flicked her fingers at the guard behind her. When he scurried over she said, "Have quarters prepaid for the ladies please and make sure they are comfortable."

I inclined my head at Illyria and despite my reservations I felt myself slowly warming up to her. Of course, I had to remind myself that a show of hospitality was merely that. It could even just be a ploy to entrap us. Then I wanted to laugh. What in Ailuros' name would they be wanting with me. "Thank you, Illyria."

"No thanks required." She smiled as she moved to leave. Then, as if on an afterthought, she turned to look over her shoulder at me. "After you speak with Anjelo I would like to talk to you about your golden hands." The smile she gave me must have been meant to be neutral but it did nothing to hide the glimmer of fear in her eyes.

My stomach hardened. "Of course, Illyria it would be my pleasure." She seemed happy with my response and I watched the stiff hold of her shoulders as she moved down the tunnel. She was afraid of me. That was all I needed; for a woman in a powerful position to see me as a threat when my sole purpose here was to find my mother. Then I gave a mental shrug. All I had to do was convince her that I was no threat to them, maybe try to win her over to my side.

Well, that was the plan anyway.

After Illyria left, leaving behind one of her guards, I turned to Anjelo. In time to see him watch the rebel leader's back as she disappeared into the shadows. There was a strange look in his eye, a look that caused me to frown and glare at him. He must have felt my stare because he glanced over at me and asked, "What's wrong?"

Lily moved away to retrieve our bags from where they'd fallen a few yards away. I watched her go for a moment then pinned Anjelo with a cold glare. "I saw you looking at Illyria. What's going on between the two of you?" There was a long pause in which Anjelo remained silent, while his jaw tightened. "Don't tell me you've fallen for her? What about Lily?"

Anjelo did a double take, then stared at me, amusement sparkling in his eyes. "What? Are you insane?"

I lifted my chin, now more than a little embarrassed for my

assumption. "You can hardly blame me considering your eyes have barely left her in all the time we've been here."

He shook his head, the short buzz cut now gone to be replaced by shaggy blond curls. "It's not what you think." He stopped short as Lily hurried back, then grabbed me by the elbow. "Let's talk when we get to the war room."

The guard watched from a few paces away, his wraith features inscrutable. I sighed. "I guess I'm going to have to find an excuse so you and I can talk privately?" His shoulders rose and fell in time with his sheepish smile. "She's not going to like it."

"Tell me about it," Anjelo said dryly as he fell in beside Lily. He took the bags from her and threw them over his shoulder. Lily smiled and slipped her hand into the crook of his elbow and they walked off leaving me to trail behind them as if I was the side-kick. I swallowed my laughter. Whatever Anjelo's current issue was, I was glad that I'd finally found him to be safe and healthy. And it certainly pleased me to see the sheen of joy on Lily's face. Whatever was wrong with Anjelo could wait until I find a way to get Lily out of the way.

Now to figure out what that way was.

WITH THE EVER-SILENT guard in tow, Anjelo led us quickly through dark tunnels whose walls gleamed with moisture, and we soon reached a set of double doors made from unbroken pieces of a wood so dark it gleamed like black pearls. The hinges were as thick as my arm and made from twisted black metal. Anjelo pushed on the door and it swung open soundlessly. We entered a gigantic hall filled with trestle tables and long wooden benches. The stone roof hung low, just high enough for the tallest Wraith to avoid bumping his head. The entire hall was carved out of solid stone, no mean feat.

I looked around and saw no hearths, no fire, and I wondered

how the Rebel army kept warm. Then I snorted. They were Wraiths; they didn't need warmth because no blood ran through their bodies. I'd killed enough of them to know.

"Follow me. The war room is through here." Anjelo waved a hand at another doorway set into the left wall. His boots tapped on the stone beneath his heels as he strode with raw strength and confidence into the next room.

I think I like this new Anjelo.

"What is this place?" asked Lily as Anjelo dropped our bags on the seat of a very slim wooden chair. Again, furniture designed for Wraiths, chairs for thin, wiry creatures. A shiver ran up my spine at the reminder that I was standing in the middle of a Wraith Rebel compound. But it shouldn't have been so surprising considering we'd had Wraith company all this time. The guard now stood just inside the doorway, still silent.

"Outside is the meeting hall where Illyria speaks to the army, and this is the war room where she plans her strategies for each mission." Anjelo untied the leather strips at his neck and swung the heavy black cloak off his shoulders. He threw it onto the nearest chair, completely unaware that both Lily and I were staring.

Lily glanced over at me and raised her eyebrows. I raised my own in response, then mouthed, *He's hot,* at her. She didn't seem offended by my observation, just returned her gaze to ogle Anjelo. He wore a close-fitting leather vest that left his taut, bulging biceps bare. Strange snakelike buckles ran down the front of the jacket, holding the thick leather of the front edges together, but just barely. Beneath the garment, his skin was bare, his pecs full and muscular. I didn't dare look at Lily. Ailuros knew what she was thinking right this minute considering she hadn't seen Anjelo in weeks.

My attention fell on Anjelo's forearms, which were covered by leather braces imprinted with symbols I'd never seen before. Another reminder of the Wraiths that surrounded us.

I cleared my throat as Anjelo sank into a chair opposite me. Lily sat too and remained oddly silent. I was pretty sure she had her own problems to deal with. Perfect timing.

"Lily?"

"Er... yeah?" she answered, her voice sounding far too throaty for my liking.

"Why don't you take our bags and get this nice guard to take you to our rooms?"

That made Lily turn her full attention on me, although she still had a glazed look in her amber eyes. She hesitated, her mouth opening as if she wanted to protest, but then she stopped and glanced back at Anjelo. Pink bloomed in her cheeks and her gaze settled on me again. I'd probably never know what went through her mind, but she seemed to decide she'd be of no use to any of us panting at the sight of her boyfriend while we talked. She was right.

"Um... I'll just... I'll just go, then. I've got to check the weapons," she muttered as she turned to leave. Anjelo stared after her, frowning as she neared the doorway and spoke to the guard.

"Was it something I said?" His inquiring expression was somewhere between bemused and confused.

"More like something you did," I said with a dry laugh.

"Eh?"

I laughed out loud at that. "Anjelo. Have you looked in a mirror lately?"

"What do you mean?" He touched his shaved jaw and then ran a hand through his curls.

"I don't mean shaving and brushing your hair. Have you looked at yourself lately?" I asked as I moved slowly toward him, rounding the table, deliberately letting my gaze run along his muscle-bound arms, his trim waist. When I got behind him and was about to get a full eyeful of shapely ass, he spun around, spluttering.

"What in Ailuros's name are you doing?" he hissed, glaring at me, his eyes wide in disbelief at my blatant perusal of his body. He looked about ready to grab the cloak and wrap it around himself. And when he did give the cloak a longing look, I burst out laughing. So hard it brought tears to my eyes.

"I'm sorry, Anjelo. I couldn't help it."

"What couldn't you help? Staring at my body like I'm a piece of meat?" he asked as if my admiration had been an offense.

It brought me up, his words. Because guys didn't usually take it well when they're on the receiving end of the meat study. "I'm sorry." The thought sobered me a little. "It's just the way you took off the cloak… and Lily… She stared so hard…. and…" I couldn't help but burst out laughing again. Anjelo just folded his arms, classic protective stance, and watched me.

I just laughed some more.

njelo waited patiently while I laughed and wiped at the tears flowing from my eyes. From the tightness of his shoulder muscles, I knew my mirth wasn't impressing him, but I couldn't help it. My laughter had to run its course or I knew I'd keep laughing until I was doubled over with a bellyful of pain.

Anjelo sighed and took a seat as my laughter subsided to a few hiccups and then slowly to nothing.

At last I was able to breathe evenly, and I glanced up at him and gave him an apologetic shrug. "I'm sorry, Anjelo. It really was funny."

"Pity I couldn't see the joke." He raised an eyebrow distastefully.

"It wasn't really a joke and I certainly wasn't making fun of you."

"Then what exactly was it that made you almost die laughing?" He leaned forward and I could see the tiniest twitch of his lips. He was already seeing the funny side, so I knew I hadn't mortally offended him.

"Well, for one thing, you got hot." He scowled at me, his face going dark. He folded his arms again, only the actions caused his well-shaped biceps to tighten. I pointed at them. "And for another, Lily's reaction was priceless."

"She noticed?" He suddenly looked interested. That was a very good thing.

I nodded. "Um… If you could call staring at you on the verge of drooling *noticed*, then yes." I laughed, feeling the giggles rising again. I took a deep breath and said, "Right, I think we need to get down to business before I start laughing again."

Anjelo snorted, then leaned his elbows onto the table.

I took the chair beside him and shifted it to face him. "So tell me what happened after Greer and I went through the portal. I know I killed Widd'en, but what happened to my mom?"

He was silent for a moment. Then he took a deep breath and said, "Remember, I was imprisoned somewhere away from the main hall, but I got the information pretty soon. They threw your mom in the cell next to me after you killed Widd'en, and then they left." Anjelo's face whitened as he recalled the horror of it all. "I don't think I need to tell you they were royally pissed off. Without Widd'en running things, his army is a little bit of a mess. And of course, they worshiped him so they weren't very pleasant to your mother considering her child had killed their master."

"Did they hurt her?" He nodded. "Torture?

"No. They aren't smart enough to even think of torturing her. They just shoved her around a little, starved her. But she was okay while I was in the cell beside her. I shared all my food with her."

Tears filmed my eyes and my gut hurt. "Thank you, Anjelo."

"No need to thank me. I would have done it for anyone, but seeing as she was your mother, she was special to me. I couldn't stand seeing her suffer. I worry every day about her. How she is, if they're treating her well." He looked at his hands, his features dark and shadowed with worry.

I swallowed the lump in my throat and needed to change the topic. Talking about Mom wouldn't change the fact that she wasn't here for me to save her. I cleared my throat to loosen the tightness. Then I remembered I'd hit Anjelo pretty hard when Widd'en had taken possession of his body. "Did I hurt you?" I asked.

"When?" asked Anjelo, brow creasing in confusion.

"When Widd'en took over your body in the lab. Don't you remember?"

"All I recall from Niko's lab is you and Lily in those glassed-in cells. Then I remember him pumping me with something that made me transform. It was fucking painful." Anjelo started at his use of profanity, then glanced up guiltily. But I ignored it, didn't react at all. And he continued. "Then I remembered almost biting Niko, although I don't recall why I would have done that."

I shivered as the memories drifted back. "He provoked you. Used the defibrillator on you to try and control your transformation."

"Geez. Good thing Widd'en didn't put me in the same cell as him. I'm sure I would have ripped him to pieces because of what little I did remember. But he disappeared not long after he arrived. Him and Greer. Somehow the both of them ended up locked up beside me."

"Yeah, that would be my fault. Mom and I arrived, and Widd'en's guards caught us. When I saw him, I demanded to know what happened to you and Greer. Niko's body was brought to the hall and thrown next to the pool. Then Widd'en just kicked him into the flaming water. I guess he wanted shock value, and he succeeded."

"So Niko's dead?" When I nodded, he continued. "I'm sorry, Kai, but I can't say he didn't deserve it."

"I thought the very same until I learned a little bit of information not too long ago about Pariahs."

Anjelo's gaze snapped to my face. "What about Pariahs?" His tone was edged with awareness.

"According to Grams, there is research to indicate the chemical imbalances that cause a Walker to be Pariah could also have psychological effects. That and the use of the Synthe or any related drug turns the brain to mush."

"God, Kai, that must suck. Niko and your sister?" I nodded but couldn't force a word past my tight throat muscles. "Did Greer make it through the portal safely? Did you find her?"

I looked at him and was about to ask him how he knew she'd gone through the portal, but I realized he'd said Mom had been in the cell beside him. I shook my head. "I guess I did, but it's complicated."

"That's bullshit, Kai. I'm not asking for chapter and verse. Just tell me what happened."

I raised an eyebrow at his outburst, but I continued. "Widd'en moved the key at the last second, and when Greer jumped, she went straight to the Graylands. When we scryed for her, we found her, but it wasn't so easy to just go fetch her home. Let's just say I made it to the Graylands, rid the world of a few dozen creepy demons, and brought Greer home in one piece."

"So she's okay?" He leaned forward.

When I shook my head, his face fell. "No. Greer's dead."

"What?" He whispered the question, and I knew instinctively that he wasn't grieving for Greer herself, but for Mom's loss. Anjelo had known Greer when we were kids, had been on the receiving end of her taunts and bullying. He was the last person I'd expect to shed a tear for my sister. "What happened?"

"Brand happened."

"Brand? Hiro's boss—that drug dealer dude?" Anjelo's brow furrowed as he stared at me, his expression a study in confusion.

I realized he'd left before I'd discovered Brand, aka Sully the club owner, was the mastermind drug lord supplying Synthe to the Walker clubbers. "Brand and Sully are one and the same. He owned the club, but he was also distributing Synthe. He got Lily onto the drug in the first place." I hated to remind him of that, but it was something we needed to talk about. "He was also

Pariah, hence the association with Niko. But if that's not bad enough, here's the kicker —Brand and Greer were an item."

"You're kidding me, right?" Anjelo was so shocked I'd have forced him to sit if he wasn't already.

I shook my head. "I wish I was. Every time I think about it, I wish I could turn back time and make sure Greer never got mixed up with him. He got Greer on Synthe too."

"So what happened to Greer when you brought her back from the Graylands?"

"The DeathTalker was convinced Greer was having mental difficulties, and that was true. She seemed to have lost it a bit while she was there. But when she got home, she played us all. Pretended to be on the mend and wanting to do everything right. But the next thing we know, she's run off with Brand. Long story short, I fought Brand, Greer got in the way, and Brand accidentally slashed her throat open."

"Shit." Anjelo rested his head in his hands, then ran his fingers through his hair. "Man. That totally sucks. Your mom was always talking about the two of you and how she couldn't wait to see you again."

I sighed. "To be honest, I'm not sure I want to see my mom."

"Why the hell not?"

"Because I didn't save Greer. I brought home her daughter only for her to die in my arms. Some sister I am."

"Kai, you're priceless." Anjelo snorted and shook his head at me.

"What did I do now?" I asked, confused by his criticism.

"You saved Greer. You did what you could. The last thing your mother would do is hold you responsible for Greer's decisions and actions. Greer was a big girl, in case you didn't notice. And not that Celeste didn't know exactly what she was dealing with when it came to her daughters."

I watched Anjelo as he spoke. I'd missed him all these weeks, and hearing him say those words was exactly what I'd needed. I sighed. "Right, back to Widd'en?"

"Okay, right," Anjelo said as he stared off into space, filtering through the memories. "Celeste was in the cell next to me for a few days. Then something happened. Lots of activity, as if the whole army were moving out. In the middle of all their moving, Illyria's army attacked. They flooded the tunnels and almost overran Widd'en's troops. But it wasn't enough. Widd'en's men managed to grab your mother, but they were interrupted as they headed to my cell. That's how I was saved. Only because they left me behind." Anjelo laughed in a self-deprecating way that I didn't like very much.

"So Illyria and her team have been tracking Widd'en's army?"

Anjelo nodded. "The last known sighting was on the grounds of an abandoned castle out west. We raided the place, but again, we were too late." His frustration was clear as he fisted both hands.

I frowned. "How often has that happened?"

"Too often for it to be a coincidence. We're always getting there a little too late or not quite on time. There are times we arrive and the place is deserted. And others when we end up catching stragglers because the army had only just relocated themselves."

"Any idea where they are right now?" I asked.

"Not yet. We're still waiting on the intel."

I sighed, suddenly exhausted after the rehash of everything I'd been through in the last few weeks.

Anjelo's eyes widened in concern. "Are you all right? Do you need to rest?"

"No. It's just that I realized how much we've all been through in the last couple months. It's a wonder we've all survived at all."

"I think we've all avoided the clutches of death on the odd occasion," he said dryly.

"You can say that again." I laughed. Then I grew serious as I remembered what I wanted to ask Anjelo. "Now tell me what the story is with your Rebel leader. Do you two have something going on?"

"No." Anjelo seemed affronted by the question as he raised his hands, waving off my words. "No, it's nothing like that."

"Then tell me what it is, because soon, I won't be the only one to notice you watch her all the time."

"Look, you have to understand something. Illyria is a female Wraith—"

"Got that part." I nodded and sat back.

Anjelo glared at me, then continued. "Females here aren't exactly trusted within any army. The king's army in Wrythiin refuses to allow women in their ranks, so it's hard enough having her as part of the Rebel army, let alone at the helm." He paused as I nodded, understanding the mechanics of the oppression of female rights. "But with Illyria, sometimes I'm not so sure. She's strong and smart and powerful, but sometimes for her it's never enough."

"And you're wondering how far she would go to prove herself as a capable leader?" I asked.

"Yeah, something like that." Anjelo nodded, then stared at the table. "So I keep a closer eye on her than I probably should."

"Well, we don't have to concern ourselves with them too much longer. Once we have Mom, we can go back home." I watched his expression in case I saw something that would make me suspect he had no intention of returning home with us. But all he did was nod and look eager enough at the sound of home. "Now, I have one more request."

"Which is?"

I got to my feet and said, "Take me to your leader."

CHAPTER 14

Not much later, Anjelo walked me to a small room a few doors down from the hall we'd occupied. He knocked and entered without waiting for an answer. I waited in the passage.

"Illyria, Kai has a moment to speak to you if you have time?" he asked, so polite and so precise. It looked like they stood on ceremony here in the Wraith dimension.

A chair scraped and Illyria spoke. "Please ask her to enter. She is most welcome here."

At that, I entered the room without waiting for Anjelo to summon me. The Rebel leader smiled and waved at one of the three empty chairs in front of her work desk.

I chose one and Anjelo turned and left the room without waiting to see if I needed him. Although I was slightly annoyed, I tried to put it out of my mind. I turned my attention to my hostess. In this room, now well-lit by dozens of candles squished down in melted wax and placed over every available surface, I was given the full effect of the Rebel leader's looks. And I had to admit that even for a Wraith female, she looked pretty good.

"What would you like to talk about?" I asked more as a way to get her started. She'd already indicated the subject of this discussion, but I didn't want to wait for things to get awkward.

"Anjelo tells me you are a SkinWalker just like him?"

I nodded, not sure how this was relevant.

"And in addition, you are his alpha?"

I laughed. "Only by Anjelo's own choice. I am part of the ruling alpha family of my clan, but it is my father who is the alpha leader. Anjelo and I relocated to Chicago some time ago, and he has looked up to me in many ways. He decided I was his alpha, and I didn't have the heart to divest him of the idea."

I was beginning to wonder where this conversation was headed when Illyria leaned forward, an intense expression filling her eyes. "Now tell me about this ability you have. This golden glow that helps you kill Wraiths."

I lifted my chin an inch, a little unsettled at her penetrating gaze and her eagerness for information about the glow. Even I still didn't understand its intricacies. "I inherited it from my mother actually. We have the ability to kill demons, a power beyond a normal demon hunter's skills."

"And you use this skill to kill Wraiths? And demons?" There was an edge to her voice that could only be interpreted as judgmental.

I nodded. "Of course, I do. We seem to be having a run of Wraiths infiltrating our city and since I have the ability to kill them with ease, it's turned to me to get the job done."

She studied me for a moment, then leaned back against her chair. "These Wraiths, these infiltrators. What are they doing that would necessitate you dispatching them in such a... permanent manner?" I could see she was choosing her words carefully, but the answer to her question was important to her.

"It used to be a simple case of possession, just taking over a human and draining their life force from them." As I spoke, I noticed the strange tightening of the skin around her eyes. The dislike that emanated from her made me wonder if the Wraiths I was talking about were known to her, but I continued. "In recent months, it has escalated to something more strategic, much more planned."

"How so?" she asked, picking up a pen and pulling a sheet of paper toward her. She dug in a drawer in front of her and pulled out a little bottle of black ink, which was when I realized that although the pen looked like standard modern issue, it didn't come with a pre-filled tube of ink. Seemed some technology was ignored here in the Wraith world.

I cleared my throat. "I used to find just random people being possessed. Just normal family men, nobody significant. But slowly, recently, there have been possessions of senators, mob bosses, drug dealers, pimps, and people in various positions of power. It makes me wonder what else is going on that I don't know about."

"And your investigative organizations do not have a theory as to why?"

I shook my head, wondering again what this interrogation was all about. "They are as blind to the inner workings of these Wraiths as I am. Believe me, none of them talk when they see me." Illyria nodded at that and didn't seem to take my comment as offensive. "So what's your take? What do you think are the reasons these Wraiths are using this new strategy? And who are they anyway?"

The underlying question was if these Wraiths belonged to Illyria's Rebel army, but again, she didn't seem offended by my suggestion. "From our own investigations, I am confident to assume that the Wraiths coming through the Veil to your world are members of Widd'en's Elite. They have a tactical advantage over the rest of the army because of their strength and training."

Her words chilled me. Strength and training? Then how had I managed to kill them with such apparent ease?

Surely these trained killers would have stood up to my junior vigilante skills? I forced my attention back on Illyria as she spoke again.

"Which brings me to your abilities. Widd'en's men are similar to what your world refers to as SEALs or Special Forces? Yes?" When I nodded, she asked, "Then how is it that a lone Walker, still young, with little battle training is able to wipe out a significant portion of Widd'en's team?"

Although I had to admit I was a little impressed by her summary of my exploits, I kept my expression neutral and shrugged. "I told you. I inherited the power. At first I had no idea how to use it apart from the fact that I could see their trails."

"Trails?" She leaned forward again, picking up on what would seem an odd reference to her. "What trails are these?"

"Wraiths leave trails, signatures of their own biological substances. I think it may be perspiration or some sort of substance that comes off their skin, but whatever they touch, they leave behind a residue. And I can see that residue. Whether it's on people or walls or furniture. I see it and follow it. At first, I just followed the trails and watched what I saw."

"So you were totally green when you started this… tracking?" she asked, and again, I felt like I was being interrogated. I cast her a sharp glance, but all I saw was honest curiosity. And that pen that kept scratching away every so often.

I nodded. "Yes. I had no training and no knowledge of how to advance. I just worked with what I had."

"What made you think you had to kill these Wraiths?" she asked, her pen ready.

"Apart from the fact that they were abusing people, you mean?" She gave me a tight smile and I could see a sense of pride there that wouldn't allow her to apologize for the question. I let it go. "To be honest, in the beginning, all it was about was saving the humans the Wraiths left in the wake of their destruction. They would possess an individual, take over their lives, and while they bided their time, live on their life force and abuse the person's family members. Things began to change when I noticed oddities."

"Oddities?"

"Like the Wraith would possess a parent, but the child is paranormal. Or the possessed man is a mayor or a senator or an important businessman. Soon there were no longer random possessions. They all seemed planned somehow."

"Strategic." Illyria was nodding. "I know what you mean, Kailin. We have solid intel that Widd'en had formed a plan to infiltrate government and business organizations and the underworld within your realm. Their plan had always been to act as sleeper agents, take possession, and wait it out until the right moment. Until they met you, that is. We had been getting information for a while now on the assassin that seems to be targeting Widd'en's men. They were of the opinion that this assassin was one of mine, sent to decimate their forces in your world. Sadly, they overestimated my knowledge and my reach. Although, I will not relieve them of that suspicion as yet."

I nodded. "How very strategic of you," I said with a grin. I was beginning to like this woman. She was strong and smart, but she did have a ruthless streak that made her trustworthiness a little questionable. In any event, I didn't plan to stick around to get mixed up in her machinations. "So is that all you wanted to know?" I asked leaning forward as if I were about to rise. I was done with the interview, if that was what it was, and I really wanted to get on with finding Mom.

"As a matter of fact, there is one more thing." I sat back, schooling my features and hoping my irritation was well hidden. "I want to know a little more about your golden glow. I'll be perfectly honest from the start. My intention is to find out what causes this emanation from your body and how we can replicate that to aid us in our fight against Widd'en's army."

I cleared my throat and this time didn't bother to hide my shock. "You want to experiment on me to create a weapon against your enemies?" I was tempted to glance frantically around me, looking out for members of Illyria's army ready to grab me and drag me off to the nearest lab. But I controlled the urge and remained still.

Illyria was sitting forward again, waving her hand in front of her, a look of apology on her face. "No, no. I'm sorry if I gave you that impression. You are right in one sense. We want to find a way to make this fight easier, but we would never harm you in the process. In a way, you have been on our side all along. Enemy of my enemy, right?" She nodded with a slight smile.

I shook my head, "Don't you have weapons?"

"Yes. But our weapons are old and outdated. Both sides were using similar weapons until recently. We have wondered how it was that such a small band of Wraiths could be so successful in the defense of their company, but we found out recently that a few Earth world weapons have been brought to Wrythiin and modified with our ammunition. These weapons are faster, shoot more ammunition, and seem far more deadly than our Rebel army's."

I held up a hand. "Okay, so this does make sense. Widd'en's men are in the Earth world to find more efficient weapons." Then I paused and thought of Tara. "What about your ammo?"

She frowned. "Standard royal army issue, reproduced by our men of course. Black stone ball ammunition like we've been using for centuries."

I cleared my throat. "Well, maybe you should start with advancing the type of ammunition."

"In what way?" she asked. She seemed curious, but her brow was twisted in confusion too.

"Has it not occurred to you to put some attention to your ammunition? It's what will make you stronger in the long run. Weapons and ammunition, that's where I would start."

She had a faraway look in her eye, as if she was turning the idea over and over in her head. Then she snapped her gaze to me.

"Do you have any suggestions in terms of ammo? I'm afraid I'm more skilled in hand-to-hand combat." Then she looked at my face, a little startled, and laughed. "Well, when I am fighting anyone else but you, that is."

I laughed, coloring a little. "You can't be blamed if I have an advantage."

"That is one hell of an advantage, Kailin." She laughed again, and I admired her more for her ability to laugh at herself even when the topic should be deeply embarrassing.

It guided me to make a decision I normally wouldn't have done so quickly. "I can help you. If I gave you one bullet, would you be able to reproduce it?"

"It depends on the type of material required," she answered. "We are at the mercy of what Wrythiin offers."

I thought of my bullets, specifically designed for me by Tara, with poison obtained from mysterious places. I sighed. "Unless you have the ability to reproduce a specific poison, I'm not sure how to help you. You will have to figure out what your weaknesses are as a species and use that to your advantage."

Illyria frowned, tapping the pen on the paper. She hadn't written anything on her sheet in a while now.

"Is there a substance in Wrythiin that is deadly to any Wraith? A mushroom or a viper's poison maybe?"

She pushed her seat back, and I winced at the sharp screech of wood on stone. Illyria seemed unaffected by the noise. She rose and paced. "There are a handful of deadly plants that I know of and a viper and something like a scorpion. Also a cuttlefish that is quite deadly."

"Right, get them all into your labs. I can give you my bullet so you can study the housing and the method used by my weapons person. I'm not sure how else I can help you beyond that."

She clapped her hands together softly. "No. No. You have been an amazing help." Then she came toward me. "Thank you,

Kailin. I apologize for being a little curt with you earlier. It isn't every day I get my butt kicked."

I laughed. "Not at all. I know how it feels. But it's refreshing to be reminded of one's own mortality."

"Right. We are waiting for the next batch of Intel to come in. I am sure with that information, we will have a location on your mother. You are welcome to sit in on any of our meetings, and if you wish, you may contribute your thoughts on strategy."

"Thank you, Illyria. I appreciate that."

"Not at all. We need all the help we can get." She grinned as she headed for the door. I followed and found Anjelo waiting outside.

"Anjelo. Make sure your friends are fed and allowed to rest. And come and get me as soon as you have the next batch of intel."

Anjelo nodded. "Will you be in the training hall?"

When Illyria nodded, I asked, "Would you mind if I trained with you?" The idea of loosening all those tight muscles was very appealing right now.

Illyria laughed. "Of course. Why didn't I think of that? Let us spar and you can teach me a few of your special moves."

We left Anjelo staring after us, and when I looked over my shoulder, he had one eyebrow raised as if to say, *Really?*

CHAPTER 15

I followed Illyria down the tunnel to a room about twenty yards along. It had a wide entrance and no door. Inside, the stone-walled practice room was alternately lined with banners and weapons. Along the back wall, I could see large shelves that held hundreds of different weapons. Some of the axes and spears looked similar to what we used in the Earth world. In fact, it seemed the Wraiths had borrowed some weaponry design from human technology. Not surprising considering in the old days they were regulars in our world.

As Illyria swept into the room and threw off her cloak, I prompted, "So you never said exactly what side you're on." I kept my voice deceptively light but concentrated on her answer.

"Side?" she asked as she hung her cloak on a hook beside the entrance. Was she hedging for time to fashion a suitable response? Or was she just distracted?

"Yeah, what's your take on the banishment of Wraiths from the Earth world?"

She tilted her head as if a different angle would help her come up with an answer I would like. Stalling. Definitely. Then she walked to the middle of the stone floor, then turned to look at me. "I don't agree with the banishment, but I'm not about to go and overrule a law. The only way we can bring about change is through our actions. The right kind of actions. What Widd'en's men are doing is wrong. It will only make the council stand stronger against us."

Good answer. I wasn't buying it though. I planned to keep my eye on the Wraith leader. "Is that the reason you're set on destroying his army?"

She nodded. "Yes. They need to be stopped before they destroy any hope we have of putting our petition to the council to allow us to regain our access." Then she began to roll up the sleeves of her white silk shirt. She too wore the same fitted leather waistcoat as Anjelo, but she had chosen to wear a blouse beneath it. It was a good look, the soft leather blending well with the silk, offset by her long white hair.

"But why do you feel such a strong need to be granted access? You have lived for centuries without us. Surely you've managed to survive well enough so far?"

Illyria was already in a fighting stance, her knees soft and bent. At my question, she stood and looked straight at me. "It is not something we are proud of, but Wraiths are a naturally parasitic race. We need the human life force to have a healthy life. This..." She waved both her hands at her body. "This is not what we truly are. We are meant to be stronger, healthier, meant to have offspring that live longer than a month after birthing. We are meant to have long lives too, but the lack of the human life force weakens us, increases our mortality. It has damaged our race in ways you cannot understand."

I nodded. "I actually do understand. You need humans to be healthy, and the council banished your people so you're suffering as a species. I understand that, but what assurance can you possibly give the council that will allow them to even consider your petition? They would need to see what measures you have in place to ensure the whole thing doesn't happen again."

She considered my words, her head tilting to one side. "We do have measures in place. We have laws against killing humans." Then she sighed. "But I know those laws weren't enough to control the rebellious few who thought they were entitled to all of a human's life."

I didn't intend to pull any punches. Wraiths in our world wasn't a small issue. "I can tell you that you will find it hard to convince humans, and the other species on the council, that they should allow you to feed on people's life forces again."

She was nodding, but not as if the movement was a mark of defeat. "I know it won't be easy, but once people understand we aren't a deadly or a dangerous species, I am sure they will allow us access."

"And what if they don't?" I asked, still holding her gaze. Now she looked away, confused, perplexed. "Have you prepared yourselves for a refusal from the council? Humans have spent centuries free from the Wraiths. In the old days, it was a natural enough thing to accept Wraiths will feed on you and you may never know it, but these days, people are far more attuned to their rights. The general public may not be comfortable about setting loose an entire species of people who are likely to begin feeding on them. Never mind that what you take is so little nobody would feel any different afterward."

"Yes, I understand. It's what you refer to as 'the principle of it,' right? Anjelo has mentioned it in such terms before." She sighed again, but her jaw was tight and her spine stiff. She hadn't liked what I had to say, but tough. She studied the floor for a while, then said, "Thank you for speaking your mind with me, Kailin. Truthfully, it isn't easy to hear those words, but reality is something we do need to be prepared for. Should I put myself in the position of your humans, I would feel the same way."

I cleared my throat. "Humans aren't the only ones being fed on by Widd'en's men." My words brought her head snapping up so fast I was sure I would hear her neck crack.

"What do you mean?" Her question was sharp and her voice high with consternation. "Who else have they been feeding on?"

"Before he died, Widd'en collaborated with a scientist to create a drug that would allow a Wraith to possess a Walker. The possession lasts only for a small amount of time, but while within the Walker's form, the Wraith is immeasurably strong and powerful."

"What?" Her eyes were wide, so wide that not even the tiniest bit of white at the far corners was visible. "Are you sure about this?"

"More sure than I'd like. I've seen the drug in action. Niko used it on Anjelo. Then, not long after the drug was administered, the Wraith possessed Anjelo's body."

She gasped. "Our Anjelo?"

I wanted to smile at the way she referred to him as "our Anjelo," but I concentrated on the conversation. "Yes. He may not have told you because I think he can't remember the possession. I know Niko was looking for stronger Walkers, alphas to test. Widd'en was getting ambitious."

"Until you killed him." She said the words, but I didn't miss the iron in her tone. Odd.

I snorted. "Only because I had my mom's help. He was so very, very strong."

"Stronger than you?" she asked softly, tipping her head to the side, watching me.

"In my human form, I think so. I was slowed down by poison, so that may have counted in his favor. But he was no match for my panther form."

Something seemed to snap her out of her thoughts. "Kailin, I don't like this news. This means Widd'en's army may still have access to these drugs. They may still be accessing Walkers on the streets, using the drug as a lure. Who knows what they may be doing while possessing such strong bodies. I wish I knew what their agenda was." She gripped her hands into tight fists at her sides, and I could see how hard she clenched her jaws. I knew her frustration.

"The last I heard was once the dealer in Chicago was dead, most of the distribution cells closed down. As far as we know, the production of Synthe has ceased, along with distribution so any of Widd'en's men would now be finding it especially difficult to find a willing Walker body to possess."

Illyria looked slightly relieved, but the worry lining her face had not eased. "That is good news. But I am not convinced. That is only Chicago you speak of. What about all the other cities across the Earth world? What if the drug had already been distributed worldwide, giving Wraiths access to Walkers across your globe?"

I nodded, feeling a darkness gather over me. "You're voicing every fear I've had these past months. But all I can possibly do is believe Omega and Sentinel and the High Council are all working together to ensure that isn't the case. I don't think they would have been so calm about it if Chicago were still in danger."

Illyria shook her head and smiled sadly at me. "You are still naive, Kailin." When I bristled at her words, it must have shown on my face. "I apologize for my directness, but you are naive if you think these organizations are being completely honest with you. They each have their own agendas. What makes you think you are getting the right information at all?" I would have been annoyed with her had I not heard the despair in her voice. She was fighting two wars. One against Widd'en's army to ensure they didn't advance with their drug-related possessions and the other to ensure their actions didn't destroy the possibility of all Wraiths rejoining the earth dimension.

Tension had slowly built along the muscles of my back and shoulders, and I felt the bite in my neck too. I shook my hands and said, "Maybe we should put that out of our minds for now. Let's get rid of some of this tension."

Illyria gave me a weak smile and came to stand in front of me.

She got back into position, and I noticed how similar it was to most martial arts stances, soft in the knee, hands at the ready. Then Illyria said, "Show me what you got."

We settled into a slow progression first, testing each other, circling the floor. There was no mat to absorb the impact of bone to stone, so I paid extra attention to tackles. Illyria was good, her movements lightning fast, so speedy she was almost as blurring fast as Widd'en. From what she'd said so far, I realized she lacked Widd'en's experience in both age and involvement within the rebellions.

I managed to get out of almost every hold she got me into, which frustrated her no end. We were both perspiring when she finally said, "How are you able to get out of every grip?"

I shrugged. "Maybe my Walker genes?"

She flipped her hair away from her face and stared at me as if actually considering my words when all I was being was flippant. "Well, there is definitely something giving you a distinct advantage. I have never been bested this way in hand-to-hand combat." She made a disgusted sound. "I'm not sure I even want to bother to spar with weapons."

"Tell me what I can do to help you," I offered, but she just shrugged.

"I don't think there is anything you can do to make me any better. I'm going to chalk it up to a freakish skill on your part. No offense," she said, giving me a careful glance.

"None taken," I said, laughing at the incongruity of it all. "Let's just hope your intelligence comes soon. Or else we may have to have a few more of these sparring sessions."

CHAPTER 16

Illyria let out a loud laugh and was heading to fetch her cloak when a Wraith came to the threshold of the room. At first, I thought he was a guard and Illyria wasn't paying him any attention either.

The Wraith stood in the doorway for a moment, gave me a cursory glance, then set his gaze on Illyria. His face was well hidden beneath the hood of his cloaks and it annoyed me that Wraiths wore these damned garments. I quite liked seeing the face of an opponent. Because that was what he felt like.

An opponent.

I stiffened and watched him watch Illyria. His hand moved to his sword and drew it slowly. I wanted to laugh at his audacity. He knew I was standing there watching him draw his weapon, but it seemed like he'd dismissed the likelihood that I was a possible threat.

Fool.

He held out the sword and the moment his weight moved to his front foot, I yelled, "Illyria, watch out." She glanced up from tying the strings beneath her neck and glared at the Wraith. "Who are you? What do you want?"

"I am Widd'en and I want your life." My eyes widened at the statement, but I knew without a doubt this Wraith was not the one I'd killed. Height and shape confirmed this intruder wasn't the master he claimed to be.

"Show your face," Illyria yelled as she tugged the cloak from her neck and flung it at the wall, where it slithered down the stone into an inelegant heap. I wondered why she cared to see his face, but it was possible this particular Wraith was the mole Anjelo had referred to. The Wraith did as instructed and raised one gray-tinged hand to push back the hood of his cloak. As the light fell onto his face, Illyria drew in a shocked breath. "Ni'kai?" She seemed beyond shock as she uttered the name. Then she masked her hurt features and straightened her back. "Why?"

"Because you are weak. Women should not be allowed to lead, especially not a Wraith army." His voice was low and sounded like he'd swallowed a cupful of gravel.

Illyria didn't seem to care for his opinion. She just sank into her stance, confident of her own prowess. I wasn't too sure considering she stood barehanded while he wielded a four-foot weapon. For a moment, the Wraith called Ni'kai shrank back. Then he stiffened his spine and lunged for Illyria. She backed away, light on her feet, then circled him. He turned with her, and I could see her intention. Eventually she would guide him toward me. All I needed to do was calmly wait until he had his back to me, then pounce.

He lunged again, his blade slicing through the soft silk of her shirt. At my gasp, Illyria said, "Kailin, please meet Ni'kai. Son of the noble house of Wen. Loyal soldier in the Rebel army of Wrythiin, now a traitor to his order."

"Nice to meet you, Nik," I said from beside him with a smile in my voice. He didn't bother to look in my direction, although his neck muscles tightened. But he had no choice except to keep moving away from his commander and closer to me.

He lunged again, and this time Illyria leaped away, leaving me to wonder if she'd allowed him to rip her shirt to give him fake confidence. The next few minutes of failed lunges and strikes made me all the more sure. Although out-weaponed, Illyria was definitely not out-skilled.

She continued to fend off his attacks while guiding him toward me until he was in position. He was already gasping for air, while Illyria had barely broken a sweat. All the while, I'd kept silent, my only words to the attacker that of my initial greeting. My silence had been my advantage because in the battle with Illyria, he had all but forgotten I was still in the room. If he'd thought I wasn't a threat, he was sorely mistaken and would soon be finding out what happens when people, and Wraiths, underestimate me.

I pounced on him, throwing my hands around him, grabbing him in a headlock so firm he would have to break my arms to get out of the grip. Had he been a few inches taller, it would have made things a little harder for me, but thankfully he was almost the same height. The better to keep my hold around his throat. He swatted at my biceps, the movements already feeble. Illyria had done an excellent job in tiring our little traitor.

I held on tight and squeezed harder, the muscles in my biceps and triceps burning with the effort. Despite being tired, he was still incredibly strong, and it was taking longer than necessary to completely overpower him. Belatedly, I realized he was on home turf, that Wraiths were much more powerful in Wrythiin than they were in the Earth world.

I kept squeezing, and only when my hands began to take on a faint yellow glow did I realize I'd channeled the demon-killing power with barely a thought. Imbued with confidence, I squeezed harder, pulling him backward as he hit my hands. He coughed and struggled for air, the choked sounds of his impaired breathing close to my ear.

His feet dragged on the smooth stone as he struggled to get a grip with his heels, but again he failed miserably. He'd made two big mistakes: underestimated his commanding officer and dismissed the Walker in the room. I squeezed harder and the glow brightened. His struggles were losing potency and I could tell he was slowly being overcome by the lack of oxygen. Not for the first time did I thank Ailuros that the Wraith physiology was comfortably similar to humans. It made things easier when trying to kill them.

The sound of his sword clattering to the stone was a welcome relief. He was on his way out at last. I knew I'd been holding back the glow. It would have killed him much faster, but something had stopped me from revealing to Illyria exactly how it worked. And it wasn't because I saw her as a threat or that I feared she would use me because of it. Deep down, I just felt weird about it because she was a Wraith, and my power meant it made it easier to kill Wraiths. The whole concept didn't sit too well with me since I'd met a Wraith I knew and liked.

I glanced down and the metal blade bounced on the ground and came to a stop beside my foot. Even in his almost overcome state, the Wraith was still reaching for his weapon. It was well past time to end this.

I placed added pressure on his neck and ignored the brightening of the glow. One last squeeze and I let go of him, allowing him to fall to the ground, weak and almost unconscious.

My concentration on the Wraith drew my attention away from the blur of shadow that came racing into the room. It headed straight for me, and despite Illyria's shout, the blur didn't slow down. I was hit full force in my side.

My golden glow vanished immediately, but it didn't matter as I was tossed away from Illyria's attacker. He'd managed to regain his strength enough to raise himself to his elbows. Another Wraith now stood over the traitor, and he didn't waste time. Or should I say she.

As the Wraith drew back her sword, I got an eyeful of shapely leather-bound thigh and trim feminine waist. Before I could do anything, she plunged the blade into his abdomen. As she performed the action, the shape of her body blurred, and I shook my head, thinking there was something wrong with my eyes. I blinked away the feeling.

"No," Illyria shouted, her hand held out to stop the Wraith from killing the traitor. But it was too late. The female Wraith stood staring at Illyria as the body of the attacker sank to the floor. Illyria hurried forward and fell to her knees beside the corpse, gasping as she turned him to inspect the wound.

"Did you know him?" I asked, more to break the silence because it was pretty obvious to anyone with eyes in their head that she knew this young Wraith personally.

She nodded, swallowing hard. "He was my cousin. Son of my father's brother. He followed me into the Rebel army. In those days, we both shared the same ideals, the same goals."

"But now he's trying to kill you?" I asked, still annoyed that my kill had been unceremoniously taken from me. Must have been my feline instinct, but I had the deepest urge to end this new Wraith's life just for thwarting my kill.

"If I had only known he'd changed his loyalty," she said as she bent over him.

I glanced again at the newcomer whose hood bunched around her shoulders to reveal her almond-shaped eyes. Again, as I looked straight at her, my eyes felt funny and her shape blurred before me. She watched me, concern in her gaze. Then she sank beside Illyria. "I am truly sorry. I spoke to him in the barracks and he seemed agitated, distracted. Then he left to come here, and I confess I rifled through his belongings and found this." She handed Illyria a note and sat back on her heels. "When I entered the room, it seemed your friend here was unable to kill him. I had to help."

"Kailin was not unable." Illyria defended me. "She was trying to subdue him without harming him so we could get some information out of him."

I stiffened and had to hide my reaction. I'd been trying to make the Wraith very dead. I certainly hadn't been told that the plan was to keep him alive for interrogation. I glanced at Illyria, but her eyes were all for the piece of paper she held in her hand. Maybe she was just trying to save face for me. She cleared her throat and continued. "Had we been given the chance to interrogate him, we would have had information and my uncle would still have his son... alive." Her voice was bitter, but it didn't feel like she was truly reprimanding her rescuer. More like she was upset with the way things played out.

When I looked up at the Wraith, intending to ask her what made her think I couldn't handle him, my vision blurred again. I stared at her harder, but she averted her eyes, the attempt to hide her guilt unsuccessful under my sharp gaze. I would have missed it had I not already had my suspicion piqued.

There was something she wasn't telling us, and I intended to find out. I walked slowly toward her, my hand closing over the hilt of the knife at my hip. I stopped beside her and waited a moment. "What is wrong with you?" I asked, my tone sharp enough to make her flinch. Besides that one failing, she was good. Her features remained implacable, her eyes unreadable.

She turned her head to glare at me, affronted. "Wrong with me? There's nothing wrong with me?" she responded, her voice high-pitched and scratchy.

"I'm afraid I can't agree. Every time I look at you, my eyes go blurry. It's as if you have this film of wavy glass over your body." I stopped speaking and stared at her, my mouth hanging open.

Illyria rose to stare at the Wraith as well, suspicion sharpening her features and eyes narrowed.

And suddenly it hit me. "You're a ShapeChanger, aren't you?" I grabbed her arm and held on tight. I'd heard that Shape-

Changers were able to turn invisible, and the only way to be sure you know where they are is to hold on to them.

And just as I thought, the moment I laid my hand on her wrist, she disappeared.

CHAPTER 17

The ShapeChanger was invisible, but beneath my hand I felt her desperate struggle. She twisted her slim wrist, bending her hand this way and that in a vain attempt to free herself. Unfortunately for her, I had an iron grip and didn't plan on letting her loose.

Footsteps echoed to us from the tunnel outside, and Illyria and I shared a concerned glance. She came to stand beside me, some distance from the door in case this was another influx of Wraiths with murder on their mind. Instead, it turned out to be Illyria's guard and Anjelo with Lily in tow.

They all came to a standstill just inside the doorway, taking in Illyria's torn clothing and my strange-looking struggle that appeared a drunken pantomime.

Illyria motioned for them to wait at the door and they did, although none of them looked too happy about it. Including Lily. She gave me an inquisitive glare, but I couldn't pay attention to her because my struggles with the invisible hand just increased as the ShapeChanger made a frantic, last-ditch effort to get free.

I snorted. "Sorry about that, but you aren't going anywhere. And even if I let you go, you won't make it out of this room. The doorway is blocked. Unless, of course, you also have teleportation abilities."

Anjelo and Lily were looking at me as if I'd finally lost it. From Anjelo's expression, he simply wasn't prepared to take it anymore. "Kai, what the hell is going on here?"

And just like that, the struggling stopped. So suddenly that I had to squeeze the hand in my grip to be sure I still had her. Then a disembodied voice said, "Kai? Kailin Odel?" The question was hesitant, as if the shape-shifter were hoping I would say no, I wasn't this person.

Sorry to disappoint.

"Yes, that's me. Now if you are a suicide bomber, could you kindly get it over with and blow us to bits, or can you take some shape or form so we can have a decent conversation?"

"Yes. Yes, of course." The ShapeChanger slowly became visible, and this time she didn't look anything like a Wraith. Her white-blonde hair shimmered and she glanced at me, her pale-gray eyes apologetic. "I'm terribly sorry, Kailin. Part of my mission was to protect you should you arrive here in Wrythiin. I'm afraid I've failed."

"Who are you?" My voice was sharper than normal only because I'd already suspected for whom she worked. Grams was going to get an earful from me for not giving me at least a little heads-up.

"My name is Cassandra Monteith. I work for Sentinel." She lifted her chin and looked me straight in the eyes. "And I think you already knew that, didn't you?"

"Yeah, I had an idea."

"I do apologize for that."

"No need. Although I think you should be apologizing to Illyria for infiltrating her ranks and impersonating one of her officers." I looked up at the leader of the Rebel army, whose face revealed subdued anger. She had it under control, and I admired her strength.

"Don't waste your breath on apologies. What I want to know is why Sentinel is spying on my army." She glared at Cassandra and folded her arms. I wouldn't have been surprised if she started to tap her feet while waiting on the ShapeChanger's response.

But she didn't have to wait too long. Cassandra answered, "I wasn't here to spy for Sentinel. My mission was to lie low and ensure Anjelo and Celeste Odel remained in good health. Were I to find their lives in danger, I was meant to put a call out for an immediate extraction." Her expression faltered a little. "Of course, once I found out Celeste was not here, I had to notify HQ. I would have been advised to ready myself and the boy for extraction, but an alert came to me that Kailin would be coming soon and my mission was not at an end."

"So your placement within my team was purely to benefit the Walkers?" Illyria looked like she didn't entirely believe her.

"Yes. I do believe they have friends in high places. Sentinel wanted to be certain the Rebel army wasn't a threat to the Walkers being held here."

"Anjelo is not being held here. He can leave whenever he wants," Illyria answered defensively, probably pissed off that she had both a Widd'en and a Sentinel mole in her ranks. She probably didn't need to be reminded of that either. "Because of our treaty with the High Council, I will neither hold you or charge you, but please could you ensure you leave my barracks immediately?" Her voice was clipped and tight, revealing her dissatisfaction.

"Of course. I will request an immediate extraction. And I do apologize for invading your privacy. I was only doing my job." Cassandra's lips twisted in apology, and Illyria sighed.

"I understand. I have nothing against you. Although, you can understand why I feel betrayed." After a pause she said, "As long as you leave as soon as possible."

But I hesitated. "Wait. Maybe we could take advantage of her skills?" Illyria stared at me as if I'd grown another head. "I'm serious. Once we have the intel, we will be making a mission into the Widd'en compound. What better way to do it than with a Shape-Changer who can change her looks as she goes? She could get in and find out where my mother is without raising any alarms."

I knew I had her when she began to nod and looked decidedly impressed with my plan. "I will authorize that as long as you are sure you can trust her."

I looked at Cassandra, my lips twisting as I considered her. "I don't know her so I can't vouch for her, but I know who sent her and I trust that person with my life. So yes, I will trust her."

As WE LEFT the training area and headed down the tunnel, another Wraith came running up to us. He weaved past the front guard and Anjelo and Lily, stopping only when he reached Illyria. She seemed pleased when he handed her a small, folded-up piece of paper, then turned and disappeared down the tunnel again. My heart knocked against my ribs. I hoped it was what I thought it was. The intel that would give us my mother's location.

Illyria had Cassandra taken to the war room where the Sentinel agent was instructed to wait. Despite her assurances that she was going nowhere, she was watched by two of the Rebel guard while Illyria called us into a meeting with Anjelo and her generals. I still found it strange that the hierarchy within the Rebel army was so similar to the armies of the human species. But the Wraiths used to live side by side with humans, much like the Fae until the Wraiths were banished, so it wasn't all that surprising for them to model their army reporting structure on that of the humans.

We all filed into Illyria's office with Lily, who looked pretty impressed that she was being included. I noticed she had my satchel over her shoulder and had brought my crossbow and scimitar, the metal of both weapons peeking out from the top of the flap.

I took a seat in front of the Rebel leader, and Lily stood beside me. Then I wondered if there was some sort of protocol, if maybe only the three generals were allowed to sit. But nobody made a face or chided me, so I figured I was safe.

Illyria opened the message and said, "As you must have suspected, I have in my hand the intel from our mole within Widd'en's army. I am not going to assume this information is untainted. We need to be prepared for anything, including another betrayal. My only hope is the news of Ni'kai's failure to kill me would have died with him. Then we have the element of surprise to our advantage."

Illyria nodded at one of her generals, who now stood un-hooded beside her desk. He turned sharply and went to a shelf behind the desk. The rickety wooden bookcase was filled to the brim with rolls and rolls of maps. He looked through the stack, found what he was searching for, and handed it to Illyria. She opened the small catch that held the roll together and spread the map open on her desk.

Over her head, the general glanced up at me and my heart stopped. The dislike in his eyes was so strong I could almost taste it. Even my panther mewled with concern. What is his deal? I didn't recall having any dealings with him since I'd arrived.

I pulled my gaze away as Illyria began to speak. "Widd'en's army is holed up here." She pointed at a range of craggy moun-tains. "This is called the Black Mountain of Wrygos, and the compound is on the north face of the range. It is a sixty-mile hike to the mountains, over dangerous territory. Between here and Wrygos, the land is bare and frozen, dotted with treacherous patches of thin ice. The ice in certain places is thinner because of underground geysers that spout hot water to the surface. But this is not ordinary water. The Black Lake of Wrythiin contains a liquid similar in construct to oil, sticky and wet. And poisonous.

Drinking this water is a death sentence to anyone not born of Wrythiin.

I raised an eyebrow. Talk about a treacherous journey. I glanced up at Lily, and she immediately sent me a narrow-eyed glare that said, *Like hell are you making me stay behind.*

Illyria looked up, her gaze meeting mine first, then Anjelo's. "If you come, you must be prepared for the journey. This is not a mission for a weakling."

I nodded, leaning forward as if the mere action would assure her. "We will be fine, Illyria." Then I fell silent. I decided the less said, the better. Better not to make light of things in the face of a mission that looked quite likely to take at least one of our lives before it was done. Anjelo looked at me, then glanced up at Lily. She must have given him the same glare, because he almost flinched, then hurriedly looked away. I wanted to laugh but quickly suppressed the desire.

Illyria continued. "Who will be responsible for the Sentinel agent?"

The room was silent for a moment, but I hadn't intended for anyone else to volunteer for babysitting duty. I nodded at the Rebel leader. "I will. You won't have to worry about her, though. If she says she will do the mission, then you can believe her. She did save your life."

"You were saving my life when she barged in and took over," snapped Illyria.

I smiled. "Technicality," I said, and Illyria laughed in response.

"I suppose you are right. She was placed here long enough to have killed us all in our sleep if she wanted to, but all she did was watch. But just to be sure..." She tilted her head in the direction of her general and said, "General W, do a little investigation among the senior officers as to Cassandra's behavior and her actions while she has been with us. And find out how she got here in the first place. I'm curious how Sentinel knew how to get someone inside our compound without alerting a single person. Says a lot about our security."

I shook my head. "All it says is Sentinel is pretty good at their job. Nothing is impenetrable to them. If they want to get in, they find a way and they get in. They have incredible technological advancement at their disposal. You really aren't much of a match for them if they wanted to storm the place and take over."

Illyria laughed. "That's comforting to know."

"Sorry." I shrugged an apology, but she waved it away.

"Either way, we still need to find out how my cousin was turned. And who else they have hiding out in our compound until they find the right moment to strike."

CHAPTER 18

She rose, disbanding the meeting, and everyone scattered. "I would suggest a meal and a good night's sleep. You will need it for the journey." Then she glanced at Lily. "I was wondering if I could enlist the help of your friend?"

I glanced at Lily, whose head shot up, her eyes wide and curious. "Sure," I said, wondering what Illyria was up to.

"Since there are so many of you going on the mission, I thought it would be best to have one of your team remain with me, just in case. There are dangers to having all of one's officers on a mission. Particularly if something goes wrong."

I stared at Illyria, impressed and hurt all at once. I knew exactly what she was asking, and from the stiffness of Anjelo's spine and Lily's clenched hand, I could tell they were both on the same page.

Illyria wanted collateral.

I lifted my head and met Lily's eyes. There was nothing for it. She couldn't demand to come with us without offending Illyria and without raising suspicion. Lily visibly relaxed. Then she smiled and said, "It would be my pleasure. You could show me around and maybe we could gossip a little about Anjelo." I had to hand it to her. Her acting skills were beyond reproach.

Illyria laughed and the tension in her own shoulders eased. "Of course. As long as Anjelo doesn't mind."

"No way. Anjelo has to mind for it to be worth it." At Lily's words, everyone laughed and then got up to leave.

I rose to follow them out, but as I neared the door, Illyria's voice stopped me. "Kailin. I am sorry I had to do that." Her expression, even with her tight Wraith skin, was very apologetic and more than a little sad. "It's hard to place one's trust in every person who crosses one's path."

I shook my head and pursed my lips. "Not to worry. I believe I would have done the very same thing."

Illyria inclined her head in thanks, and then I left her alone to contemplate her conscience.

OUTSIDE, Anjelo and a rather dejected Lily waited in the tunnel. Lily opened her mouth, but I shook my head and she took the cue, falling to silence as Anjelo led us to our rooms.

Once safely inside the small room, Lily turned and faced us. "Do I really have to stay?" The tone of her voice said she knew she had to, but I understood how she felt.

"I'm sorry, Lily. But maybe it's a good thing. Maybe this way you can stick to our Rebel leader like glue, make sure she's not orchestrating some plan to have us killed on the way to the compound."

That seemed to perk her up a bit. Anjelo laughed as he opened his arms for a hug. "That's better."

Lily went to him without a word. "I just found you," she whispered into his shoulder.

"I'm not going away forever, Lily. We go to Wrygos, rescue Celeste, and come straight back."

She shook her head, then let go of him. "I'm sorry, Kai," she said, staring at me with moist eyes.

"What for?" I asked, sinking into the nearest of the beds with a sigh. There were two single beds, what seemed like rope springs and mattresses stuffed with something soft. A strange fur covered the bed, and I wondered what types of animals lived in this world.

Lily cleared her throat. "The mission is to save your mom, and here I am sniffing like a baby because I have to stay behind."

"Oh, Lily, you are certifiable sometimes," I said, and she giggled. "Now can we get something to eat around here?" I looked at Anjelo hopefully.

"What do they eat here anyway? Hope it's not worms or larvae or something."

Anjelo laughed hard. "What makes you think that? Of course they have livestock here, but this is like any normal barracks. Mostly bread and soups supplemented with chunks of meat. And don't worry. Everything is edible and definitely not human."

Lily snorted. "I didn't think they ate humans," she said, clicking her tongue.

Anjelo headed to the door. "Come. If we get there now, we'll be the first ones in. Then we can grab our dinner and bring it to our rooms without anyone asking any questions."

"Brilliant idea. Lead the way." We headed to the dining hall, which turned out to be the same hall we'd first walked through to reach the war room. Now, the far corner of the room contained a few small, sturdy tables bearing platters of hot bread. Beside them sat two gigantic metal pots, the contents of which steamed and bubbled. To say it looked unappealing was putting it mildly.

On the way back, Lily and I stared dolefully at the gray mush, and I knew she was wondering the same thing. *Is this stuff even edible?*

But once were in our room, we were both pleasantly

surprised. Where it lacked in looks, it made up in flavor, and soon the bowls were empty and our hunger appeased.

LATER, we were readying ourselves for bed in the small, cold room. With no fire, we were in for a freezing night, but I suspected the furs would be warm enough. Lily took the far wall, undressing in silence, then diving under the covers.

Fatigue pulled me to sleep, but I shoved myself up onto my elbow. "Lily?"

"Mmh?"

"Are you going to be okay here without us?" I asked, determined to find another way to do this if she even hinted she couldn't do it by herself.

Lily shifted in her bed and the rope springs creaked. "Yup. I'll be fine, Kai. Don't worry about me." She faced me and smiled. "What are sidekicks for?" she asked, giving me a wink.

"You know, I forgot to say I'm going to have to hold interviews when we get back home."

"Interviews?" Lily asked sleepily.

"Yeah, for the position of sidekick. You know... considering Anjelo will be back."

Something came sailing at me, and I heard a soft swoosh as Lily's shirt hit the floor. "Shut up, Kai. You should be sleeping instead of talking crap."

I snorted and snuggled down and was asleep before I even got comfortable.

THE NEXT MORNING arrived with Anjelo shaking us awake. He handed us bowls of something hot and very similar to oatmeal.

Lily grimaced as she ate and so did I. It was like eating the worst bowl of oatmeal ever, like shoveling globs of glue or paste into our mouths. I swallowed it courageously and dressed as fast as I could while Anjelo and Lily said their goodbyes.

With my satchel over my shoulder, I waited by the door as Lily and Anjelo came to me. She leaned toward me and I gave her a hug, then held her away to look her straight in the eye. "Keep your eyes open, okay. You just never know what you'll see. And don't trust anyone. Stick as close to Illyria as you can without making it look suspicious."

Lily nodded, although her eyes had a sad droop. "Sure, I'll just complain I'm lonely. She should believe that." She shrugged, her mouth turning down. "I don't think she likes me very much."

"Don't be silly. Illyria doesn't have the time to like or dislike people. She's too busy trying to fight a war." I gave her one last hug, then set her away and walked to the door. Lily had never been known to be clingy, but I was afraid more for me than her. I had to admit to myself that I was very afraid. If something went wrong, what would happen to Lily?

With Anjelo and Lily behind me, I hurried down the tunnel toward the meeting hall. I glanced back at Anjelo's face, trying to figure out what he was thinking. Then I cleared my throat. "I need to talk to Illyria for a moment before we leave."

"Sure. If you see her, grab her. I'm sure she won't mind." I nodded and followed him as he turned into the entrance to the hall.

We'd just stepped inside when Illyria walked off the podium after having addressed her troops. She headed for us, and I gave her a weak smile. "Thanks for allowing us to go."

"It sounds to me like the most logical option. You need to find your mother, so you will be an asset more than anything else." I nodded, unsure of what else to say. She made it easy for me by saying, "Good luck and take care of yourselves."

She shook my hand and headed off to one of her generals peering at a map spread out on a nearby table. He was eating an apple and had stuck a small dagger into one corner of the parchment to keep it from rolling closed.

I caught sight of Cassandra striding over to Anjelo and Lily. She glanced over in my direction, and I waved at her before beckoning her to join me.

When Cassandra drew abreast of me, she smiled. "Good morning."

"Hope so," I responded wryly. "Could we talk for a moment?" She nodded and led me to the farthest corner of the hall without actually having to leave the room.

"So what do you need to know?"

"It's not... that. I just needed to make arrangements just in case."

"In case of what?" Cassandra asked, seemingly oblivious of my tumultuous worries.

"We have a dangerous mission ahead, and that's not even bringing in the fact that we have to attack a garrison of powerful Wraiths. I just want to make sure I put certain measures in place in case Anjelo and I don't make it out alive."

Cassandra blinked as if the possibility had never occurred to her. Then she cleared her throat. "Okay, what do you need from me?"

"What method do you have of leaving Wrythiin?"

"I was brought here by a Teleporter since I'm not one myself. But I have a way of letting them know there is trouble."

"How does this method work?" I asked. I was more attentive when I heard her mention a Teleporter. I'd gone to so much trouble to obtain a key to Wrythiin; I'd be really pissed if I found out there was an easier way to get here.

"The Teleporter that brought me does a daily quick trip to check on my messages."

"Do you have a specific place?" I asked, and she nodded. "And you can leave messages to let them know you need an extraction or backup? Okay. Is it possible for you to tell Lily where this place is?"

Cassandra fell silent for a moment. Then she sighed. "I see. Should something happen to us, you wish for your friend to have a method of leaving this place safely." I just nodded. There was no need to elaborate. "I think in this particular situation, I would be allowed to provide Lily with the correct information."

"This situation?" I asked.

"Yes. Given that my orders were to ensure your friend and mother were safe, and then you of course. In your absence, the girl is my responsibility, so I will speak with her before we leave." Cassandra glanced around the room and spotted Lily beside Anjelo. She turned and headed over to them, and I followed closely. The moment we arrived, Cassandra said, "Lily my dear, there is some information I need to impart before I head off to the mountains with your friends."

Lily frowned. "What information?"

"Your way out of here in case we don't make it back," said Cassandra, as if it were no big deal.

Lily went white. "What?" she asked, her voice a little too high-pitched for comfort.

Both Anjelo and I shushed her. "Lily, keep it down," I whispered. "Not even Illyria knows about this. We need you to have a way to get out of here if something does happen to us. Now relax and talk to Cassandra." I nodded to the Sentinel agent, and she and Lily took a step away.

When I looked at Anjelo, I found him glaring at me. "What?" I asked.

"Why are you letting them talk without us?" he asked, his eyes still on Lily.

"Because it's safer for Lily to be the only one to have the

information. Besides, I don't think Cassandra would have given the information to anyone who didn't need it. And we don't need it."

Anjelo opened his mouth, then closed it again.

Good call.

As the teams readied themselves to leave, Anjelo disappeared within the throng of bodies, only to return minutes later with three gigantic cloaks.

"These are for you. Essential wear for the journey."

"Is it really necessary?" I asked. We'd already been given our own Wraith cloaks so we wouldn't stand out among the rest of the army. I'd thrown the cloak on a little skeptically. I wasn't entirely sure I wanted to be mistaken for a Wraith, but that certainly was a better option than being recognized as a human. That would likely mean instant incarceration or instant death, and I wasn't sure which one I preferred.

"If you want to make it ten feet out the door, then yes," said Anjelo. I made a face, swung the heavy fur-lined cloak over my shoulders, and fiddled with the ties. Once we were cloaked, Anjelo produced a set of fur-lined gloves for each of us. "The terrain is vicious. We'll be walking through blizzards, so we need to be warm enough. We don't want to freeze to death before we get your mother home."

I nodded, wishing we could just get on with it. "I'm assuming we have a coat and gloves for Mom, in case?" I asked.

Anjelo grinned. "Already taken care of."

An increase in the noise around us announced the beginning of our departure, and we moved into the line of soldiers heading out the door and down the tunnel. Neither Cassandra nor I said much as we followed single file. My only prayer was that this whole arctic expedition wouldn't be a waste of time. I just wanted to get Mom and get the hell out of here.

A blast of frozen air hit me in the face as the tunnel made a sharp left. A set of twelve-foot wooden doors, not unlike the pair that led into the meeting hall, stood thrown wide open, letting in a mix of frigid air and swirling snow.

I shivered against the cold that had already managed to sneak beneath the thick furs. "This is going to be fun," I muttered.

I heard Cassandra laugh beside me as I drew on the gloves and tightened the cloak around my shoulders. Then I followed Anjelo out the doors, stepping into the sludgy snow that already bore the tracks of the soldiers that had gone ahead of us. All I saw before me was Anjelo's back as he hobbled forward, bent over against the driving snow. My vision blurred and I was sure my eyeballs would freeze over very soon. We walked for what seemed like hours, unable to talk, which didn't matter much since our teeth chattered so hard that conversation would have been a little difficult. At last, the group stopped to rest with the strange lukewarm sun straight above us.

As we gathered together, I noticed one of Illyria's generals had accompanied the team on the mission. The same one who'd glared at me so viciously in the meeting. Great. My jaw tightened as he sent me a look that felt colder than the frigid snow that fell around us.

He certainly wasn't hiding the fact that he didn't like us. Although, I assumed he had little choice but to obey his commander. He spoke to a few of the men near him before breaking away and coming over to our little group. Anjelo, Cassandra, and I were huddled close together to keep the wind at our backs. The strategy seemed to be working until the general arrived.

I nodded, keeping my features neutral. "General."

"Odel." He greeted me, then turned to Anjelo. When I'd first met him, I'd pegged him for a sexist, but it didn't fit with him taking orders from a female. But I didn't want to spend time trying to figure out what made General Wren'do tick. I turned my body a little to provide them some sort of privacy to have their male conversation. Cassandra rolled her eyes, clearly well aware of the Wraith's attitude and opinion.

After a few moments, he left and Anjelo turned to us. He was about to talk when I said, "Since you're talking to us, I assume we don't need penises to respond."

"Kai," Anjelo admonished, his eyebrows reaching for his hairline. I wasn't usually that crude in his presence.

I just grunted.

"Okay, I get that he's a sexist asshole, but don't shoot the messenger." Anjelo raised both hands in defense.

Impatient to get on with it, I asked, "So what did he have to say?"

"He warned us to stay with the group, not to lag behind, and to tell him immediately if any of us feel we cannot go forward."

"What? So he can have the last laugh and send the girls packing?" asked Cassandra before I could ask the same question.

"Not you too," said Anjelo, rolling his eyes.

"Remember, I've been here almost as long as you have. I know very well the general's opinion of *weakling* females."

"Surely he doesn't think Kai is a weak female." Anjelo scoffed. "Anyone who saw the way she almost killed Illyria would know better, and Wren'do had a front row seat to that show."

"Be that as it may," Cassandra responded patiently, "the general still retains what is likely years of treating women as second-class citizens. I don't doubt he finds it hard to follow

Illyria's commands, but I do believe he has some sort of connection to her father. There may be other political things afoot."

I snorted. "Don't tell me he wants her as his wife?"

"From what I've heard, that is a distinct possibility, but I don't particularly care who he wants to marry. As long as he doesn't make things more difficult for us. I wouldn't put it past him to test us or to push us to our limits to see if we turn back."

I stared at her, then at Anjelo. "So we'd better get used to suffering."

"Something like that," said Cassandra.

Anjelo was oddly quiet. Someone came around with mugs of what tasted like hot beer, which was pretty disgusting. I closed my nose and swallowed, aware the added warmth from the beer would be an advantage. This trek could soon turn into a game of survival for us.

"Well, team, let's just keep our eyes open. This snow certainly isn't making it any easier," I said, trying to swallow the shiver running through me before it obliterated my words.

"Don't worry. The snow will eventually let up once we reach the Dead Plains." Anjelo seemed rather more upbeat than I would have expected, but I suspected he was pretending so we wouldn't lose faith in the mission.

"What's after the Dead Plains?" I asked, now a little more than curious.

"The Black Lake and then Wrygos," Anjelo said before tipping the dregs of his drink onto the snow beside him. Cassandra and I did the same and handed the wooden mugs to the soldier who came around to take them away.

And then we were off again, walking half bent over against a wind that punched and pounded our bodies relentlessly.

A FEW HOURS passed before I noticed the snow and wind were

both letting up their intensity. My body relaxed a little too, glad to not have to constantly fight the storm. We reached a low rise that led down into a shallow valley. The Dead Plains. And now I knew firsthand why it bore such a name.

The snow stopped just at the ridge and only the soldiers' tracks in the black soil would let an observer know we'd trekked through a snowstorm.

The valley below was black. Hard-packed black soil covered the ground, glistening here and there where tiny pieces of stone gleamed. The valley was littered with dozens of leafless trees that seemed frozen forever in a gust of wind that no longer blew. The branches reached out like bony, burnt fingers, forever frozen, as if reaching out to the setting sun.

"The sun sets in the north, I see?" I asked Anjelo for confirmation, but I knew already it was true. The sun was high on our left and from its path looked likely to set in about six to eight hours. "How long have we walked?"

"In human time, six hours. In Wraith time, three."

"Crap. Has it really been that long?" I asked. Then I stared out over the horizon. "You have to wonder why though."

I must have stopped mid-thought because I heard Anjelo ask, "Why what?"

"Huh? Oh, I wonder why Widd'en's army would choose a compound so far away from the Rebel army. Are they hiding? Is it a trap? Or is there some other reason?"

"We'd better walk and think about it. We're getting left behind," said Anjelo as he picked up the pace.

I glanced back to see only half a dozen soldiers coming up behind us. Then I broke into a jog down the hillside until I reached the bottom safely.

Anjelo checked for me over his shoulder, then said, "From the map, I remember once we cross the valley, we will reach the Black Lakes." From Anjelo's confidence, I knew he'd studied those maps well and I was glad.

I wanted to nod in answer but realized he wouldn't see my reaction as I walked behind him. But all the same, I was thankful for his updates. It made the trip easier knowing we were continually making headway, getting close to freeing Mom.

We fell silent again as we picked our way across the parched black ground. Gigantic cracks ran through the soil, evidence the area was in the grip of a drought. No surprise then that the trees were well past dead. As we drew closer to a stand of trees, I reached out to run a finger over the dark bark. The trunk was rough and felt tree-like, although I found the experience slightly surreal as it looked like nothing I'd ever seen in my life. When I removed my hand, my skin came away black. "This is charcoal," I said, talking mostly to myself as I hurried to catch up with Cassandra and Anjelo.

At the thud of my jogging footsteps, Anjelo turned and opened his mouth to speak. I never heard what he said. The low feral growl that rumbled through the air chilled the blood in my veins. The sound made the hair on my neck rise; worse, it made my feline hackles rise. When Anjelo turned his face, his chin raised to test the air with nostrils already half-transformed, I realized I'd done the very same thing without even thinking about it.

Instinct had taken over.

My ears had lengthened and furred, curved to pick up the smallest sound, and my nose had thickened, nostrils larger and deeper, eyes all panther, one hundred percent sensitivity. I smelled warm fur and hot breath and the spike of urine. My ears picked up the sound of rapid panting, of the wind through tightly packed fur, and of the odd whine that sounded so feral and so dangerous.

Wolves.

My eyes had widened, now larger and with a depth of vision I could only dream of in human form. I didn't need to turn my head to know a pack of black wolves watched us from a nearby hilltop. But I turned anyway. More so I could memorize what they looked like.

It was their eyes that stopped me in my tracks.

Blood-red eyes.

THE EYES, the smell, everything about the proximity of the wolves pulled at my senses. The need to change was all-encompassing and extraordinarily difficult to ignore. My inner cat clawed at me, snarling to be set free, but I did my best to ignore her. I glanced at Anjelo and he met my gaze, his brows furrowed with worry.

"You feel that?" I asked, keeping pace with him. He nodded, his expression somber and a little afraid as his gaze darted back and forth from the caravan of Wraiths in front of us and the shadows that lurked at the ridge alongside us.

The wolves kept pace, moving slowly with us, keeping near as we moved.

Cassandra drew closer as we hurried along the track. "What's wrong? What's happening?" Her eyes raked my face as if she would see something in my expression to answer her question.

"It's the wolves," I said softly, even though it was unlikely any Wraith either in front of us or behind would be able to hear. "There's something about them that's affecting both Anjelo and myself. I feel the pull to change and it's so strong I can barely keep it controlled." Even as I spoke the words, the force of the desire to change shocked me. I had very little control left, as if something had taken over me, making my need to transform the most important thing. I shuddered with the effort to tamp it down.

For a moment, Cassandra looked confused. She looked from me to Anjelo and back again. Her gray eyes darkened. "Change?" she asked, leaning a little closer, as if she suspected she might have misheard and needed confirmation. When I remained silent and just stared at her, her expression cleared, as if she'd realized she faced a Walker, and she nodded. "Oh, yes. I see. Are you going to be okay?"

I looked at her for a moment and decided honesty would be the best move right now. "Actually, I don't know. Just be prepared if either one of us changes. We will need your help afterward." I spoke, keeping an eye on our surroundings, every muscle and nerve ready to spring into action the moment the wolves attacked. Because if there was anything I knew, it was those wolves weren't lurking just for fun. They meant business and right now they were just playing with us, biding their time until the right moment presented itself.

"Help?" Cassandra's voice breached my thoughts.

"Yeah." I laughed, but the sound was humorless and flat as a sudden gust of wind hit us. "We'll both be buck naked so you may need to keep our clothing close by and help us change."

"Oh," she said as her cheeks bloomed with a touch of red. It wasn't surprising, though; most people reacted in a similar fashion when they realized a Walker change meant nudity once that Walker transformed back into human form. Cassandra cleared her throat. "Sure. Clothing. Okay. I can do that." She spoke as if she were trying to convince herself she could do it.

I put my hand on her forearm and gave her a quick encouraging smile. "Don't worry. The first time is always the hardest. And I'm pretty sure I have everything you have."

She snorted. "It's not you I'm worried about."

I laughed, the sound mirthless on the dead air. "Don't worry too much about it. He looks pretty good under all those clothes."

She snorted again. "That's exactly what I am worried about."

We both burst out laughing, and I enjoyed the tiny little island of distraction even though most of my mind remained on the wolves as they followed us along the ridge to our left.

"Anjelo," I called to him, as he'd walked ahead of us, clearly struggling with the call of the change. His fists were bunched, the knuckles of his fingers white. He slowed and met my gaze. "Are you okay?"

He nodded. "I think so." But the look in his eyes told me he wasn't.

"Just be strong. There's absolutely no need to change. They don't seem too much of a threat. The team is too big for them to even consider attacking, so we should be fine. It'll pass." I reassured him, but I myself wasn't so confident.

Even as we followed the line of soldiers across the black plain, the threat of the wolves was too strong to ignore. The scent they gave off was threatening, not a drop of fear or trepidation at all. And that worried me.

Feline or canine without fear meant the confidence to attack.

CHAPTER 20

The attack came so fast I almost didn't notice the blur of bodies as they flew at the line of Wraiths trudging along the black soil.

I changed instinctively, muscles moving, stretching, growing in a blur of pain and electric pulses. My clothing fell to the ground and I shook them off my back with a flick of my spine.

With one part of my brain, I registered Cassandra's shock, the taste of fear pulsing through her, her sweat, pungent and sweet. Another part of me saw a wolf up ahead run straight at a Wraith Rebel, taking him down with one blow, grabbing his neck and sinking sharp yellow teeth deep into his throat.

Black blood spilled, spurting onto black fur, dripping onto black soil.

Macabre.

Everything around me was a picture in black and white.

Except for the red eyes of those terrible wolves.

I also registered the wolves that headed straight for me. They seemed to have a plan, to attack me, but not one-on-one. Perhaps they sensed they had the advantage of numbers, as if they knew I was stronger than I looked. My lips rose, baring my teeth in a feline snarl. I shifted on my paws, adjusting my direction so I stared straight at the three wolves who faced me. They watch me, nostrils flared, teeth bared, muscles tight, and ready to pounce.

An arrow struck the wolf on the left, plunging deep into its side. The blow flung him sideways into his companion, the injured wolf giving one last pain-filled whine before its body spasmed and he fell to the ground.

The other two wolves ignored their brother, keeping their eyes on me. Another arrow came flying at them, landing in the hard black dirt just in front of the wolf straight ahead of me. It should have acted as a deterrent, but it seemed the wolves were driven by something stronger than just instinct, as if they had a deep need to take me down.

The strike of the arrow spurred the wolves to attack. They settled low on their haunches before launching themselves into the air, straight at me.

I, on the other hand, didn't wait. Neither did I run. As soon as the wolves moved, I sprang, meeting the first one head-on, paw to claw. We crashed into each other, landing on the ground and rolling along together, snarling and lashing out at each other.

My nostrils twitched as the wolf's hot breath hit my nose. He huffed as he tried to right himself. I swiped at his face, leaving lines of black as my claws ripped through fur and skin, bringing fresh blood welling to the surface. The wolf yelped when I struck, then growled and pushed away, scrambling to get back upright.

I heard the desperate rush of soldiers behind me but resolved to concentrate on my furry attacker. Beside me, Anjelo snarled, but I couldn't afford to keep an eye on him. Unfortunately, he was on his own until I got this wolf off my back.

He still had his eyes on me, despite his injuries. The skin on half his face hung loose, blood dripping slowly from the open wounds. Yet he still remained focused on me.

Must really hate cats.

I knew he would move before he twitched. The wolf launched himself at me again, a sinister growl leaving his throat as he flew at me. I scrambled to the side and swiped hard at his jugular. For all his lethality, the wolf was no match for a feline who'd trained in fighting for years, both in human and cat form.

My claws struck home, plunged deep into flesh, then pulled free as the wolf's momentum drew him past me and onto the ground. He squealed and grunted as he hit the dirt, and as I turned, I knew I had him. He writhed on the ground, the vein at his throat gushing steaming black liquid. His body spasmed one last time and stilled.

But before the first wolf died, I was already turning to help Anjelo.

And just in time.

This remaining wolf must have been the wiliest of the three. He had Anjelo pinned to the ground. His lips lifted, baring his canines, preparing to rip out Anjelo's throat. I didn't give him the opportunity. I jumped, slamming into the wolf, landing paws to his shoulder. It startled him long enough that when he hit the ground, he didn't immediately rise. Time enough for me to sink my teeth into the throat he left so vulnerable to attack.

He died within seconds.

The moment I pulled my teeth free from the wolf's throat, another arrow landed beside me. This one hit so close to my face that it grazed my cheek. I felt the sting and the heat of the blood as I slipped back into human form. Fury rose within me, but it was hampered by arms that threw my thick fur cloak around my naked body.

I glanced at Cassandra gratefully. She'd moved so fast I didn't think any of the Wraiths had a chance to get much of an eyeful of bare ass. Cassandra drew away to throw Anjelo's cloak around him. The cloak warmed me, but I didn't need it. Adrenaline still surged through my veins, keeping my body temperature fairly high. I surveyed the area around us while I caught my breath. It looked like a massacre. More than half a dozen Wraiths lay dead, mauled, and bloody on the black soil.

Anjelo was on his feet beside me, clutching the cloak around him. "What the bloody hell was that?"

General Wren'do answered Anjelo, having appeared out of nowhere behind him. "That was a pack of wild Black Wolves." Anjelo rolled his eyes as if to say, *Tell me something I don't know.*

"Was there a reason they seemed so intent on killing us? Or is that just their nature?" I asked the general, uncaring that he would likely not bother to look at me when he answered.

Surprisingly, he did meet my gaze, although his expression was icy cold. "They are naturally of a violent nature, but we cannot be sure the odor of a feline did not draw their attention." I bristled. Seemed he was trying to place the blame for the attack at our feet, but I didn't give him the satisfaction of a reaction. The general's face darkened, clearly unhappy that he hadn't gotten a rise out of me. "I think it would be best if you hurry up and get your clothes back on. We need to get moving in case there are more of them lurking around."

I nodded stiffly and turned to Cassandra, who had her arms filled with clothing. She handed them out and I took each piece, dressing discreetly beneath the expansive folds of the heavy fur cloak. Minutes later, she moved on to hand Anjelo his clothing. Even before Anjelo was properly done dressing, the general gave the team the go-ahead to start moving again. I glared at him, furious that he couldn't even give us a decent rest.

But neither Anjelo nor I would ever ask for such a privilege.

ONCE I'D TRANSFORMED, the scrape on my cheek burned. I struggled to remove my glove, then traced the wound with the tip of my finger. And hissed with pain as my icy fingertip touched broken skin. My fingers were wet and sticky and bright red when I examined them.

Anjelo glanced at me over his shoulder, and I swore under my breath. I hadn't wanted to bring attention to the wound, but it was now too late as I watched concern bring him to a halt.

"Keep moving," I growled at him. "I'm not letting anything slow us down."

"You know you can be so stubborn sometimes," he growled, his face a dark cloud.

"I'll be however stubborn I want to be if it means we don't have that overbearing creep of a general reprimand us for lagging behind or slowing everyone down."

"Fine," he grumbled, keeping pace with me. "You got a first aid kit in your handbag?"

"It's not a handbag, you idiot. It's a satchel, for your information, and the answer to your question is yes. You know I don't go anywhere without it. Are you sure you won't faint at the sight of my blood?"

He snorted. "As long as you don't expect me to dig more bullets out of you, I'll be fine." Over the next few minutes, he fiddled inside my satchel for the first aid kit and cleaned and medicated the wound, all while walking alongside me, keeping pace with the team.

When he finished, he gave my cheek a worried glance. "Is that going to be okay?"

I nodded. "It should heal soon enough. Give it a few hours."

"You're gonna have a scar."

I nodded. "Tough bitches should have scars. Gives them character."

He snorted and moved ahead to get in line.

Not two hours later, we reached the edge of the Dead Plains, and I had to admit I was pretty happy to have made it through alive, thrilled too that the wolves had left us alone for the rest of the trek. The plains ended in a low ridge not too different from the one from which the wolves had watched us. The front of the line snaked onward without stopping, and we followed, waiting our turn to see the ridge for ourselves.

The closer we got, the more the reality of what we were looking at hit me. The ridge turned into a low mountain, and for a split second, I thought we'd reached Wrygos. But then I remembered we still had to fight our way through the Black Lake.

I sighed as I followed the track up the side of the ridge. The climb taxed my strength, especially after the whole episode with the wolves. I'd kept an eye on Anjelo over the last few hours, worried his almost-end would be bugging him. He seemed fine, but I'd found Anjelo had always had the practiced ability to hide his feelings.

Every now and then, I turned to surreptitiously examine his face. He bore a few scratches, but nothing as bad as my arrow-inflicted wound. I was still pissed off that the general had allowed his men to aim their arrows so close to me. It made me all the more suspicious of him.

Once we reached the top of the ridge, we had a full view of the valley below us. The Black Lake was nothing more than one gigantic, iced-over lake. The entire floor of the valley was covered with hard, white ice, but even from where I was standing, I could see the spots, small darker areas, where the ice was clearly thinner.

The team didn't pause to take in the view. They walked over the spine of the ridge and continued to make their way down to the valley floor.

Anjelo, Cassandra, and I were following the train of men probably three-quarters of the way down the line. As we descended, our position gave us a little bit of a vantage point. The Wraiths at the head of the line picked their way along the ice carefully. It was clear to me that they knew exactly where they were going. Their route meandered this way and that, a course that nobody could possibly have guessed. We were at the mercy of the Wraith Rebel army.

I glanced back at Anjelo and could see both he and Cassandra were feeling the same hint of trepidation I was. If the commander saw fit, he could ensure we walked right into a trap.

Anjelo caught up with me. As I drew closer, I said, "I think it's best if we stay close to the soldiers right in front of us. The biggest mistake we can make is to allow them to get too far ahead of us. We need to make sure we step where they step, and keep your eye out. You just never know which of these Wraiths is out to ensure we get ourselves killed."

Anjelo nodded. "It's good to see you feel exactly the same way I do."

The team moved slowly. Each Wraith walked behind the other, leaving at least ten feet of space. It made complete sense. Nobody could assume how much weight the ice would carry, so minimizing the amount on any particular point was the best strategy.

Anjelo, Cassandra, and I followed suit, walking where the Wraiths walked, following in their footsteps.

A shout up ahead made my heart trip, but I noticed the line of men in front of us came to a slow halt. The commotion made me more than sure that one of the soldiers had fallen in. There was nothing we could do other than wait in silence. Peering around the bodies in front of us made little difference because the path curved so much that even if we were able to see past the soldiers, the view of what was happening was well hidden from us.

At last, the noise died down, but there was no way of telling whether the Wraith soldier had been saved or swallowed by the black waters.

Behind me, I heard Anjelo say, "Even though I've been on this route before, I can honestly say I would rather be somewhere else right now."

I knew exactly what he meant. All this trekking over wild lands was testing my patience. Part of me wondered whether we were being led on a wild goose chase, yet another part of me insisted I had to follow every lead if I was ever to find my mother.

CHAPTER 21

We were almost halfway across the frozen lake when I heard the distinct sound of cracking. But it wasn't the crack itself that worried me. It was the reverberations that ran through my feet and up the bones of my leg. Instinct told me to run, but common sense said stay where you are.

I stopped in my tracks and turned my head to look over my shoulder at Anjelo. He was strutting toward me, head down, paying little attention to what I was doing. "Anjelo, stop."

It must've been something in the sound of my voice, but Anjelo's head jerked up and he halted instantly. He stared at me, eyes wide, and said, "Please don't tell me…" He didn't bother to finish the sentence, seeing as the expression on my face already confirmed his suspicion. Over his shoulder, I could see Cassandra staring at us, fear filling her eyes. She looked like a frightened rabbit, but she knew, much like we knew, that right here right now there was nowhere to run.

Up ahead, the line continued to snake away, widening the distance between us and the soldiers in front. We had no choice but to get their attention, and as Anjelo shouted for them, I heard another crack. This one was louder and nearer. My heart thudded so hard against my ribs that it hurt.

The column in front of us came to a slow halt. From the shuffling up ahead, I knew Wren'do was coming back to check on the delay. The closer he came, the clearer it was that he was furious. But I couldn't care less for his anger. If I had been one of his men in danger, he certainly would not be reacting this way. His first duty would be to do whatever necessary to save the man. But because it was me, the silly, weak human female, he came strolling in like a thundering storm cloud.

"What is it now?" he growled, his dark eyes flashing, his posture stiff and angry.

As if to answer his question, another crack sounded, reverberating ominously across the ice. I stayed as stiff as I could and tried not to move. The expression on his face told me he had heard the crack as well.

He looked down at the ice at my feet, and I followed his gaze.

Beneath my boots, the ice was thick and white, what should have been comparatively safe to walk on. But around the area of solid ice, the dark shadows indicated the more dangerous, warmer areas.

It was clear I had stepped in the right place, having followed the trail of the men in front of me. The problem was the area around me had been weakened by the soldiers who'd gone through before us. It was only by chance that I was the one to step on it at its weakest moment. When I looked up and met the general's eyes, it was clear too that he could see the fault did not lie with me. There was a softening in his demeanor that should've made me happy. But at this point, I didn't have time to bask in the knowledge that I was faultless. My only need right now was to get out of this mess before I too sank into the dark waters and disappeared forever.

"Whatever you do, do not move," said Wren as he scanned the area around me. He glanced over his shoulder and snapped, "Get me the equipment." To the team behind me, he said, "Find another route out to the left and keep moving. I don't want anyone else sitting there weighing down this area and causing more stress on the ice. That means you too, Anjelo."

Despite the concern for the dangerous ice beneath my feet, I still bristled. The commander hadn't bothered to address Cassandra.

Although I felt movement behind me, I knew neither Cassandra nor Anjelo had moved. The look on the general's face as he glared over my shoulder confirmed it. I didn't wait for the Wraith leader to demand that Anjelo leave. I tipped my head to the right and said, "Go, Anjelo. I'm sure the general has things under control here."

"Are you sure?" asked Anjelo, his voice still hesitant despite my request.

"Yes," I snapped, feeling all the more impatient, what with the general staring me down. "Go now, before you bring down this entire piece of ice and kill all of us in the process." It was probably unfair to bite his head off, but Anjelo should have heeded the general's command in the first place. I just hoped his stubbornness hadn't put me in more trouble.

At last, I heard Anjelo and Cassandra back away from me. Wren snorted as he watched them with disdain. I could see he had very little respect for Anjelo, especially now that my young friend had proved I was boss as far as he was concerned. It was a strange thing considering the general himself also answered to a female. I honestly did not understand him.

As Wren studied the ice again, another crack reverberated along the surface and through my legs. Suddenly I felt a little weak, as if my limbs were refusing to carry me any longer.

"Try not to move," said the general. He turned around and held out his hand. The Wraith who stood behind him handed him a coil of rope. The general took it and wrapped it around his waist. Then he nodded at the soldier who uncoiled another stack of rope. One end of it was tied around a hook, which he now fastened onto the rope around the general's waist. He then proceeded to walk away until the rope was straight but not taut. Then he tied the end around his own waist. Behind him, another Wraith repeated the whole process until the weight of three individual soldiers was evenly distributed across the safe area of the ice to support the weight of both Wren and myself.

"I have to be quite honest with you," he said to me. "It is quite likely that as we try to save you, you may fall into the water. Should that happen, the only thing I can suggest is that you close your eyes, nose, and mouth. Do not breathe in any of the water. Most non-Wraiths die almost immediately once they enter the water. The poisons enter through the skin itself, and death comes quickly."

I nodded and said, "I understand."

I couldn't decipher the look he gave me, but at this point, I didn't care. I just remained very, very still. Another sharp snapping emanated from the ice. I knew there was little time left for them to save me. I hoped they would get on with it before it was too late.

The general tossed the end of the rope at me. I held up my hand and grabbed it as it flew in my direction. I knew I couldn't step forward or lean in any direction to assist me in catching the rope. Fortunately, it landed safely in the middle of my palm and I grabbed ahold of. "Tie that tightly around your waist," the general said.

He stood very still, as if waiting patiently for me to complete his instructions, but knowing the general, he would have little patience for me. I ignored my thoughts and tied the rope around my waist, knotting it as tightly as I could.

As soon as I was done, he said, "Hold on to the rope in front of you. I'm going to walk back until it is taut. When I say so, you need to begin to walk across the ice. It will most likely be shaky beneath your feet, but try to keep your balance as long as possible." He stared at my face as if waiting for an answer.

"Okay," was all I was capable of saying. I cleared my throat as an idea occurred to me. "Would it help if I took off my cloak?" I asked.

The general merely nodded, his expression inscrutable.

A gust of wind slammed into me and I was aware that the chill of it had no effect on me. Strange the things you are aware of when you face the possibility of imminent death. I slowly untied the straps at my neck. As I prepared to remove the cloak, the general waved a hand behind him. A Wraith came running and halted beside him, awaiting instructions. "As soon as she removes her cloak and drops it to the ice, grab it and pull it toward you. Use one of the small grappling hooks. And work fast."

Immediately, the soldier felt for something inside the bag at his waist. He removed a small grappling hook and tied it to a piece of rope. He stood at the ready, his eyes on me, waiting for me to make my move. I had to admit it was a smart idea. They were being careful not to lose the cloak, and the method they used would not endanger them in any way.

It was a good thing too, because I preferred to have my cloak back when all this was done.

The general nodded, and I dropped the cloak slowly to the ice. As soon as it fell into a soft heap at my feet, the soldier beside him sank to his knees and threw the grappling hook. When the claws snagged securely among the voluminous folds of the fabric, he began to pull it slowly toward him. It was slow going, and I wondered if the general would, in the end, blame me for delaying the whole process. I tried to calm my breathing and remain still.

At last, the cloak moved off the small shelf of ice on which I waited. By now I could see a clear break, a crack that ran around me in a jagged circle. I didn't need to look behind me to know the circle would have completed at some point. The instability of the piece of ice was enough to confirm it was free-floating.

The soldier bundled the cloak in his arms and got to his feet slowly. The general waved him off, and he moved backward until he stood at least fifty feet away.

"Get onto your stomach. It will be a less precarious position and require less balance on your part."

I frowned but did as I was told. My first instinct would have been to make a running leap for the solid ice and hope for the best. But the way the general spoke, I sensed he had more than sufficient experience with black water ice rescues, and my common sense said I should trust him. I lowered myself to my knees, then spread out on the ice, keeping as still and straight as I could. I'd instinctively reached out in front of me, fingers forward. A part of me assumed that would be the best position in case I needed to grab for the stable ice shelf if mine tipped over.

Then Wren spoke and his voice echoed strangely on the quiet ice. "I will begin to pull you now. Try not to move. And remember, if you do fall in, we will pull you out as fast as we are able. Just don't breathe in any of that water. I'd suggest you shut your eyes as well. I believe you humans have very sensitive skin covering your eyes." I didn't bother to confirm that his species assumption was incorrect and that he was not conversing with a human.

Now was not the time.

He began to pull and I felt myself slide a foot across the ice. It creaked strangely and my heart twisted, but nothing happened. The general repeated the move. Another foot and still safe. My breathing was ragged with fear and nerves, and the entire front of my body began to ache with cold. Another pull, another slide a foot forward, and still I remained on the ice.

I was beginning to believe things would go well and that I would get out of this predicament without a dunking in poisonous water, when I heard another sharp crack, loud enough that even the general gasped. My heart began to race and I sucked in air way too fast. If I didn't control it, I wouldn't have the lungs to hold my breath underwater. So I calmed myself, forcing my breathing to slow down, forcing my heart to stop its rapid pace.

The general's voice echoed toward me, and I was surprised to hear the nervous timbre. "One more time. Are you ready?" His tone could almost be described as gentle.

Almost.

"Ready," I said, speaking as loudly as I could without raising my head.

He pulled slowly and I slid another foot. I chided myself when I discovered I was holding my breath again. Stupid.

But before I could do anything else but admonish myself for my own stupidity, the ice began to tilt.

And I knew one thing with absolute certainty.

I was going head first into the poisonous waters of the Black Lake.

CHAPTER 22

The ice shelf tilted, the end behind me rising high. It didn't stop until the entire section was almost vertical. I stared at the black, sludgy water in front of me, knowing it was inevitable I would soon sink into the dangerous icy liquid.

I slid forward, listening to the shouts around me. Someone tugged at the rope and I was pulled farther. But this time all it did was move me dangerously close to the water.

The soldiers were relentless. Another pull and I went sliding straight into the inky black sludge. The icy cold water hit me like a blow to the gut.

I forced myself to take a deep breath before the surface of the water closed over my head and the lake claimed me. Although I wanted to open my eyes, I remembered the general's warning.

Now sightless and breathless and slowly freezing to death, the experience was more terrifying than I had ever experienced. My heart threatened to stop, my lungs to explode. My mind was screaming at me. I was going slowly crazy.

I hung in the water, suspended in darkness, with my breath slowly running out, when I felt a tug on the ropes. I wanted to scream at them to hurry, but that would be another chalk up on my list of stupid.

My chest hurt with the effort to hold in my breath. I knew I could expel it slowly to remain comfortable, but I was terrified that letting go of one breath might open my nose to the liquid poison around me. So I continued to hold it.

My lungs rebelled, pulsing hard against my ribs, screaming for air. I ignored them. Someone tugged on the ropes, pulling me upward.

With my eyes shut, I had no sense of direction and I hoped I wouldn't slam head first into the stable ice shelf above me. More pulling and I rose a little farther.

Now lightheaded, I saw tiny specks of light behind my eyelids. My instinct made me want to blink, but I tamped down the urge.

Another tug and I was lifted a little farther. My chest hurt like the blazes, my neck muscles throbbed, and my head pounded worse than my usual headaches ever did.

I was suspended in the water, but something drifted to my ears. It sounded like a shout. *Dear Ailuros, let that mean I am close to the surface.* I spread my hands out, trying to push myself farther upward through the icy water.

Another shout above me confirmed I was very close to the surface. And the next moment, my head popped out of the water. The rope was taut and I felt myself being pulled farther along. I wiped at my face with my hands, felt no burning sensations, and was relieved.

Floating on the surface, I wiped hard at my nose and mouth and eyes, hoping to free it from the black poison, but I found that with my gloves on I couldn't feel a thing. I kicked hard to keep afloat while I tugged the gloves off. They'd sink, soaked as they were but I didn't care.

I wouldn't be able to use them again anytime soon unless someone produced a Wrythiin tumble-dryer. Fingers free I scraped away the water from my face as best as I could.

The level of noise rose around me, but despite my curiosity, I didn't dare crack an eyelid until I was certain I'd gotten rid of as much of the water as possible. The last thing I needed was to allow leftover droplets of poison to seep through into my eyes and kill me only after I'd been rescued.

At last, I was confident enough to open my eyes. And saw what had caused the shouts and commotion I'd heard while underwater.

My hands glowed bright gold, as if a light were inside my body.

I shivered as I floated in the water.

"Stop gawking and keep pulling that rope. Do you want her to die in that poison?" Wren yelled out, and suddenly the rope began to move and I was pulled along the surface so fast it took my breath away. I reached the edge of the ice and I held my hand out for someone to pull me up, but nobody grabbed onto it to help me.

Of course they wouldn't. My hands were still glowing gold, and by now the entire regiment would have known when my hands glowed, the Wraith I touched would die. It was silly because I knew it took more than just a mere touch to kill a Wraith.

The general was yelling and the group of watching Wraiths parted as he shoved them aside to reach me. He stuck out his hand, and I grabbed hold with both of mine, trying to be careful about where I touched him.

I wrapped my hands around the leather braces that were tied around his forearm. Likewise, he grabbed onto my forearm with both hands and I allowed him to heave me out of the water and drop me onto the ice. I coughed as I landed, then lifted myself. "Stay away. I'm still wet."

"I do not believe it is the poisoned water that frightens this lot." The general scoffed as he dusted his wet hands on his pants. I noticed he still wore his gloves. A smart man, he'd kept his gloves on the entire time, allowing him the confidence to touch me without fear of the poisoned water or the golden glow.

"They don't need to be afraid of the glow. It takes more than a mere moment of touching to kill a Wraith," I said as I pushed myself to my knees. And then struggled to my feet. My water-logged clothing weighed me down, but I bore the burden and kept my face free of any indication of my struggle.

The general's eyes raked me from head to toe, and I resisted the urge to shudder. "I would suggest dry clothes. We cannot build a fire on the ice, and you will need to get warm as fast as possible. We are still only halfway across." Then he turned and stalked off, yelling at his men to stop staring and get moving and that any man who straggled would be tossed into the black water. Wraiths scrambled and the sound of conversation died out almost immediately.

Cassandra and Anjelo hurried over to me as the column began to move, and we resumed our position in the line. Cassandra held my fur cloak out to me and asked, "Do you have dry clothes?"

I nodded as I swung my satchel around to my front. Then my heart fell like a stone. My bag was soaked and stained with black water. And everything inside was equally sodden. My spare set of clothes was soaked.

Thankfully, the first aid kit was inside a zip-lock bag. I sighed and grabbed the first aid kit, unzipping the bag and fishing around inside for the thermal blanket. I handed it to Anjelo, who ripped the plastic and dusted the blanket open.

I handed my satchel to Cassandra, then grabbed the cloak from her and proceeded to remove my wet clothes while trying to keep up with the moving line at the same time. It was tough going, and I almost fell flat on my face twice.

Upper clothing was easy enough, but my leather pants were soaked and difficult to remove, especially with having to remove my boots as well. By the time I got myself naked, I was covered in a sheen of perspiration from the effort.

Cassandra took my clothing from me one by one and wrapped them together before shoving them into my satchel. "I have a hoodie you can use once you're dry, if you like," she offered.

I gave her a grateful smile and said, "Thanks. That would be a lifesaver."

I maneuvered the blanket beneath the cloak and managed to wrap it around me. I'd kept moving, and it didn't take long before I began to warm up.

The only thing I could do nothing about was my sodden hair, soaked and heavy with the poisoned water. And then I stiffened.

"I'm still alive," I said softly. Both Anjelo and Cassandra walked closer, giving me strange looks. "What I mean is the poisoned water had no effect on me."

Anjelo shrugged. "It could just be that you closed your eyes and mouth and nothing got inside you."

I shook my head. "It makes no sense. Think about it. Water gets into your skin, everywhere. Ears, skin, nose even when you hold your breath. And I'm seeing no effect whatsoever."

"That must mean you're impervious to the effects of the poison," Cassandra said, nodding. "Perhaps it has something to do with your ability to kill Wraiths. Perhaps your power extends to Wraith world organic matter too."

"Exactly what I was thinking." She'd hit the nail on the head. I could kill Wraiths with my bare hands, and now Wraith poison had no effect on me. I frowned. "Anjelo? Have you ever gotten the dark water on your skin?"

He nodded. "Yes, on the last trek through this place, one of the soldiers slipped and I tried to grab his hand. Another soldier had managed to grab the guy's cloak as well, but both of us were splashed as the guy's feet hit the water. We saved him, but I got a few splashes of it on my neck." He lifted his hair to reveal a group of burn scars just below his left ear.

I winced at the sight; they still looked red and angry, but Anjelo seemed unaffected as he covered his scars. "It's fine now. Hurt like hell when I got the water on me." Then he fell silent for a moment. "But, Kai, that only means one thing."

"Yeah. I know. It's not a Walker immunity. It's just me." I sighed. What other abilities did I have?

"Seems like you have an immunity to anything to do with Wraiths. Have you tested it out on other demons?"

I laughed. "Yeah, did I forget to mention I can kill demons too?"

Anjelo's jaw dropped. "Demons too? Wow, Kai. You're way more powerful than we could ever have imagined." He sounded awestruck, and I understood exactly what he felt. I was pretty amazed myself.

I was warm soon enough and grabbed Cassandra's hoodie. I slid the blanket down and wrapped it around me like a skirt. I rolled it up around my waist and crossed my fingers that it wouldn't fall off. And when I looked up, I sighed in relief. We'd reached the other edge of the Black Lake valley.

The only problem was we'd also reached the Black Mountains of Wrygos.

And to my eyes, it looked pretty much unclimbable.

IN THE FAILING light of day, the regiment gathered at the base of the mountain and we were already beginning to feel the change in temperature. Or maybe it was just me, considering I was the only one bare-assed under my cloak.

But Anjelo's teeth began to chatter beside me, and he said, "We really need to get you some proper clothes. You can't get over the mountain wearing nothing."

I nodded and turned to Cassandra. "You think those clothes will be okay to wear?"

"Absolutely not. I dare say you will catch your death wearing them as soaked as they are."

Footsteps came hurrying toward us, and a Wraith soldier appeared from the crowd. "General Wren'do has commanded we set up camp. With nightfall, it will be too dangerous to attempt the climb." With that, he spun on his heel and disappeared into the mass of bodies.

I glanced at Anjelo and raised an eyebrow. "Either he really means for the regiment to rest, which is strange since the last time we also arrived in the dark and still climbed over the mountain, or—"

"Or the general doesn't want to be responsible for your death," Cassandra said happily. "I knew there had to be some speck of goodness to him."

"Why would you say that?" I asked, a little snappish.

"Because any creature capable of deep affection is clearly capable of deep emotion."

"You mean like serial killers?" I asked, still not ready to allow myself to be impressed with the general's decision.

Cassandra snorted and Anjelo let out a bark of laughter. "We'd better start helping with setting up camp before someone decides to kick us out." Anjelo tilted his head at me. "You can just wait to one side."

I huffed. "What the hell do you mean? I can help."

"Not unless you want to accidentally give our Wraith friends here an eyeful. The wind is beginning to pick up. Can you help pitch a tent and still hold on to your blanket at the same time?"

Seeing the wisdom of his words, I remained silent. I'd wanted to protest so badly, purely because I hated being the one to sit on the sidelines while everyone else was working, but Anjelo was making sense and I couldn't resist without looking childish.

I left them to it and moved aside to watch from a small alcove in the rock face. The sight of the Black Lake made me shiver again. And that brought me back to the one fact that didn't sit so well with me right now: I had General Wren'do to thank for my life. I would have been dead without him. I gritted my teeth and pushed out of the lee. Pacing suited my mood far better than hiding.

Soldiers were allocated one tent per six men, so we could be sharing with three other Wraiths. I wanted to laugh. Considering how afraid of me they were, I wouldn't be surprised to find we'd miraculously managed to get a tent to ourselves.

They made short work of the shelters, and Anjelo was already huddled over the fire before I made it to his side. I watched in silence as he swiveled a stick against a piece of wood. When I looked up, Cassandra was hurrying toward us. She crouched down beside Anjelo and held something out to him. I suppressed the urge to laugh out loud. He took a bright-red lighter from her and flicked the button. A flame sprang up almost immediately, and he grunted. "I often wondered how you were always among the first to build your fire."

She grinned. "Pays to have modern technology at your fingertips."

"Now, if only you could have brought your microwave over with you." He snickered.

She hit him on his forehead. "Don't be a smart-ass." She sprang to her feet and headed into the tent, hurrying back within seconds. Then she handed him a small bag.

"What is that?" he asked, a little worried to touch it.

"Don't worry. It won't bite. It's a microwave."

Anjelo's eyes widened. "No kidding?"

Cassandra was about to speak when a soldier came to stand beside our fire. "Your rations, Anjelo," he said, handing him a small linen bag.

Inside was what looked like a fresh chicken, some strange-looking spices, and a skin of water.

Dinner was on.

Cassandra instructed Anjelo on how to insert the fowl into the microwave bag. Then they fussed with the meal, deciding on how to spice it and how long to cook it.

While they kept busy, I dragged out my wet shirt and pants and set them on the rocks that bordered our little area. Each tent was pitched within a small crack in the side of the mountain, a naturally sheltered spot hugged by outcroppings of jagged rock.

Soon my clothes were drying and our food was ready. And after our meal, we found we had our tent to ourselves. Surprise, surprise.

I grinned to myself as I slipped into my dry-ish clothing, then crawled into the fur cloak, which doubled as a blanket.

I closed my eyes and waited for sleep.

As far as I was concerned, tomorrow couldn't come fast enough.

The troops were roused in the early hours of the morning, well before the first gray light of day began to bleed into the ebony skies. Within minutes, we broke camp amidst the darkness of predawn and began marching up the side of the mountain.

Every misstep sent loose gravel skittering down the path behind us and made my heart jump. I glanced up at the morning sky and huffed.

No surprise at all that there wasn't even a hint of golden sunlight. The dull sky seemed to hang low over our heads, and I suspected it meant snow. If not, then the skies of Wrythiin were certainly not to my liking if they were always this gray and cheerless.

The way over the mountains was faster than I suspected and within an hour, we were up on the ridge, huddled at the northern edge overlooking the Widd'en stronghold.

"What is this place?" I asked Anjelo, keeping my voice low. Every sound seemed to travel unnaturally far at the height.

"Widd'en's men have taken this castle. The castle and the grounds around it belong to a nobleman, a Wrythiin lord of the

North Plains. He's a representative of the king in this area, but obviously Widd'en's men no longer recognize the power of the king."

"What have they done to the lord?" I asked, afraid he would say the man had been beheaded and his head placed at the entrance of the castle on a spike. I gave a preemptive shudder even before he spoke.

Instead, Anjelo said, "He and his family were thrown out in just the clothes on their backs. Thankfully, they made it to a crofter's hut in the hills just to the east of here. They sent a message to the king, and that's how we heard Widd'en's men were here."

"Seemed a bit stupid to let the lord know who they were," I said.

"They didn't. They took over the castle wearing masks, but one of the children managed to catch sight of a sword. His description matched that of the hilt of the sword of one of Widd'en's generals. It was only by chance we knew they were here."

"So why did we have to wait for the mole's message when we already had intel that Widd'en's men were here?" I asked, irritated. Had Illyria just been playing us?

"Because we weren't sure if the army had split and went separate ways. If they had, we couldn't be sure where your mother was being held. Then a trek all this way would have been pointless." I listened and nodded. But though it made sense, I was impatient. I forced myself to relax and keep my edginess in check.

We were so close.

We waited on the ridge, shivering and silent. It didn't take long for the general to decide on his attack strategy, and a soldier appeared to advise us.

He kept his hood pulled well over his face, only a hint of shine within the shadowed cowl confirming he even had eyes. I disliked these hoods even more today than I ever did before.

The Wraith cleared his throat and stiffened his spine before speaking. "The general wishes for you to remain out of sight. He will come to see you once we are all in position. He wishes to talk to the ShapeChanger." With that he spun on his heel, his cloak flapping at his knees, and left us.

The line of Wraiths to our left shuffled, while the sound of boots and voices traveled up to us as the regiment began to move down the mountain. Below us, I could just make out the base of the north side of the mountain. It lay hidden from view of the castle by a small but thick forest of gigantic black trees.

Though they gleamed as black as soot, unlike the claw-like trees from the Dead Plains, I could see they were also alive; black and gray leaves covered the thick branches as they spread out around the trunk. I could swear they were very similar to the ash trees from back home.

We made it down the side of the mountain, our progress hidden by gigantic boulders and pillars of stone that guarded the pathway. I wondered where their sentries were.

Were Widd'en's men so confident in their hiding place that they didn't bother to watch the mountainside, or was this just an elaborate trap? I shuddered at the thought as we made it to the base of the mountain. I sank beside Cassandra as Anjelo left to speak to the other soldiers.

We hid within the shadows of the trees for a while, remaining silent while peering between the trees to study the specter of the castle ahead. Draped in early morning shadows, it gave off an eerie air. I suppressed a chuckle. It wasn't just my imagination running wild because I knew it was currently occupied by a bunch of murderous, soul-sucking monsters.

Anjelo took a while and we settled to waiting. Nothing moved on the grounds around the building, and it looked like the place was asleep. But experience told me assumption could lead to trouble.

A soft rustle in the bushes to our right announced the arrival of Anjelo and Wren'do, who looked neither happy nor triumphant at the status of our mission. He crouched down and addressed Cassandra.

He even looked at her face, which was a mile of progress right there. I decided he'd just moved up in my esteem. "What kind of strategy are you proposing once you enter the castle walls?"

Cassandra's expression was clear and businesslike, her accent so perfectly British it was almost amusing when considering she was conversing with a demon.

"I can either go completely invisible or I can assume the form of a few different people. Do you have a preference?" she asked.

He grunted, then looked at the ground for a moment as he considered his options. Then he glanced up, his eyes pools of darkness. "I would suggest the former of your strategies. That way you can search the castle and find the location of the Hunter, then return to us undetected. I might need your services once you return from the reconnaissance."

"Very well. I might need to take the form of another of Widd'en's men in case I need to pass a guarded door, but for the most part I will remain invisible."

He stared at her for a moment as if suddenly reminded she was there. Then he gave a curt nod and turned on his heel, disappearing into the shadows so fast I almost doubted he'd even been there in the first place.

Cassandra grunted. "Arrogant prick," she said, her accent making the swearword sound odd to my ears.

I laughed softly and glanced at her. "You ready?" She nodded, dusting herself off. She shrugged the heavy cloak from her shoulders and retained only the thin leather one we all wore. Then she smiled at me and disappeared into thin air. I felt the pat of a warm hand on my shoulder and then nothing.

She'd gone.

~

MORE THAN AN HOUR LATER, and just when I was beginning to wonder if she would make it back alive, a rustling sounded along the ground beside me. I sighed with relief as Cassandra took form. She sank to the ground, out of breath and shivering. I threw her fur cloak around her and she gave me a grateful glance, tucking the folds around her.

"Take your time and rest," I urged, even though I really wanted her to talk immediately.

She was kind enough to hurry up and rest. Moments later, she said, "I have her location. Perhaps we need to find the general."

"No need to go looking for me," he said as he walked up to us, his footsteps silent. I frowned as I looked up at him and wondered if he had someone watching us. "What can you tell me?" His attention remained fully on Cassandra's face.

The ShapeChanger cleared her throat. "Celeste is in the prison beneath the castle. There are twenty or so cells, all individual rooms with strong, thick doors. Celeste is located in the northeast corner."

The general nodded, then turned on his heel and left us standing there.

I gritted my teeth again and said, "That Wraith makes me want to do to him what I did to the charming Widd'en."

"And what exactly was that?" asked Cassandra, her voice prim and her expression curious.

She paled a little when I said, "Rip out his throat with my teeth."

CHAPTER 24

The general didn't linger too long before gathering up his men and sending word for us to meet him down the line. We wasted no time in hurrying over to him, practically following the messenger at his heels when he turned to leave.

I wanted to get moving fast, concerned more with the fact that the day was getting brighter and we wouldn't have shadows to hide our approach if we waited any longer.

Wren looked up as we arrived. He didn't wait to speak. "I have been instructed to allow you to go with us when we enter the castle. Although I do not agree, I am duty-bound to fulfill my orders. Thus, you will join us, but be warned. My soldiers are not here for your protection. You are to ensure you do not do anything to attract attention, to endanger my men, or to thwart our efforts to capture the castle and free the Hunter." I couldn't gauge his expression, but his words were cold enough for me to get his meaning.

We remained silent in the wake of his icy monologue, and he seemed to take our lack of response as agreement. Then he turned to face his men and, in one smooth move, gave the signal to head out. We crouched down and followed the line of men as they scurried forward.

When we paused, I dug inside my satchel, the leather still giving off a damp odor, and withdrew my bow. After a quick inspection, I was satisfied the mechanisms were all in working order and the water hadn't damaged anything. I had loaded the bow with Wraith ammo before leaving my apartment, so the weapon was ready.

I dug deeper for a second firearm, a Glock Tara had re-purposed for her special Wraith and demon ammunition. It too seemed to be functional. And when I popped the clip, it was dry and in good order. Satisfied, I turned to Anjelo and handed him the gun.

He raised an eyebrow but still took the Glock and checked the chamber and clip for himself. Then he readied the weapon, took off the safety, and turned his gaze back to the expanse of lawn between us and the castle.

Wren had decided to take only a dozen of his regiment, with the balance to enter in a second wave and only on his signal. Another smart move on the part of the surly Wraith.

We ran from tree to tree, using the wide black trunks to mask our invasion. Still, I got the distinct feeling it was far too easy.

As we neared the end of the small forest, the raucous sound of cawing suddenly rent the air. Birds flapped vigorously above us, staring down at the gathered interlopers and screeching so loudly it was sure to wake the dead.

They must have been disturbed by our movements amongst the trees. My heart sank and I wondered if the rowdy flock had drawn attention to our presence.

A shout sounded from the castle and a side door was flung open. Two Wraiths hurried from the threshold, heading straight into the small forest of trees. They ran at full attention, their heads swiveling from side to side as they scanned the trees.

Wren's men remained silent; none of us moved a muscle as

they approached. I hunkered down behind a wide-trunked tree and watched from between the trunks in front of us.

I saw two of Wren's men waiting to ambush the guards, probably about to slit their throats with consummate ease, so well not even a drop of blood touched the black soil. I didn't give them the chance.

I aimed and fired, the bullet releasing from the chamber in a whisper of sound. The poison cartridge hit the second Wraith in the neck, the wound almost invisible to our eyes.

The Wraith fell in mid-run, hitting the soft ground on his knees so hard his head snapped backward with a crack. One of Widd'en's men grabbed for the dead guard and eased his burden to the ground. The first guard was still hurrying through the trees, unaware his compatriot had fallen.

Within seconds of dispatching guard number two, guard number one received a bullet to the shoulder, giving a low grunt as his eyes widened. He didn't have time to look down at his wound in shock.

He crumpled to the ground, dead, amidst the men of Wren's regiment who were all ready to kill him but hadn't been given the chance.

Wren looked at me over his shoulder. He was hidden behind a clump of old trees and was staring at me with an odd expression on his taut-muscled Wraith face. His long white hair gleamed even in the dull morning light.

Then he turned back and waved for one of the men who were remaining behind. It looked like they were being given instructions to take the bodies as far back off the property as possible. Two missing guards would certainly confuse Widd'en's men.

The one thing the guards had done for us was leave a door open to grant us ease of access. Wren, who appeared happy enough to take advantage of the open door, pointed at the entrance and gave the signal to move out.

We followed the group in silence, reaching a low stone wall

that ran around what looked like a small kitchen garden. Dried plants adorned the black soil, and it was clear Widd'en's men had rooted out anything living long ago.

I called on my panther hearing and listened for sounds of movement, for hearts beating rapidly, for sharp intakes of breath that indicated the approach of the next wave of guards.

And I heard it. But I couldn't yell out to Wren's men to be careful. I aimed and prayed the bullet would hold true. A guard poked his head out of the dark doorway and, seeing nothing, strode into the yard, searching the trees behind us for his comrades.

Only when he'd gotten halfway between us and the door did I let loose my shot. The bullet hit him in the middle of his throat. I always aimed between jaw and heart, the best place to hit a demon and ensure the poisons worked fast.

In this poor guard's case, death came in the breadth of an instant. I felt Wren's gaze on me, but again he said nothing. Probably because I was making things easier for him. I glanced at Anjelo, who always remained by my side.

"Keep the gun only for the very last option. The sound alone will bring the whole castle down on us."

Anjelo nodded and pointed at the short sword at his waist. Then he gave me a quick thumbs-up and turned to watch the door again. His panther ears were peaked too, so I knew he was listening as well.

No sound filtered through to my super hearing and I nodded. Anjelo ran forward and I followed, reaching the doorway at the same time as the last of Wren's men.

They regarded me with strange looks, as if unsure what to make of me. Then they allowed us to enter first, which I found odd considering Wren's clear dislike of us. But then I saw the way they looked at Anjelo.

I hid a smile, admiring this boy who had been my sidekick and shadow, more now than ever before. Not that I gave a damn about Wraiths, but this was war, and these men were soldiers. And their respect for Anjelo meant he'd earned it, not by sitting on his hands.

Not by a long shot.

Up ahead, the soldiers swept through the passages in silence, the only sound accompanying us was the rapid trickle of water leaking through the gigantic stones used to build the formidable castle. We reached the end of another long passage, then turned.

Here the regiment split in half—Wren and his group heading up the stairs to our right while we followed the other half to the cellars.

Our way down was lit by the odd torch, placed well enough that we could see forward, but not too many to rid the way of all shadows.

We made slow progress down two flights, as the stone stairs were wet and slippery with a strange black moss. I hugged the wall, keeping one hand on it at all times despite the moist, squishy feel of it.

At the bottom, we faced two tunnels, one straight ahead and leading to the northeast corner and the other at our right. One Wraith took up a guard post at the entrance to the tunnel while the rest of us hurried forward.

I glanced at Cassandra, and she pointed up ahead, mouthing, "Last cell," at me. The Wraith in front of me held out a hand in warning and fury rippled through me.

He refused to allow us to follow them, pointing to us and then to the ground, ordering us to stay as if we were a pack of dogs. That got my hackles up.

Literally.

CHAPTER 25

*A*njelo placed a hand on my arm, his face apologetic but also urging me with a shake of his head not to do anything drastic. I gritted my teeth and looked away from him, down the tunnel at the band of Wraiths slowly approaching the shadowed end.

I glanced at Cassandra. "Guards?" I asked in a whisper. She nodded and raised two fingers. Then I heard two soft choking sounds that confirmed they'd taken out the guards.

I snuck forward, ignoring the Wraith's instructions, and hurried to within ten feet of the door to Mom's cell. I didn't dare call out to her in case it warned any of Widd'en's men who might be in the vicinity. My heart thumped with excitement. I wanted to see her so badly that tears began to film my eyes and I had to blink them away. I steeled myself against my rising emotions. Plenty of time later to be joyful.

Ahead of me the passage ran in front of a row of cells on the left, then it made a sharp turn to the right and went off into the darkness. I glanced at Cassandra and pointed in the direction of the passage. She shook her head, which I took to mean she had no idea where they went or if they might potentially be hiding more of Widd'en's men.

For now, I paid attention to Mom's cell as keys clinked in the keyhole and I heard the lock click open.

Just as the sound echoed against the stone walls, I noticed a movement within the shadows to my right. Someone was lurking in the darkness, watching and waiting. I pulled my panther sight through and the darkness shrank away, revealing the outline of a waiting Wraith, one of Widd'en's men.

I aimed my weapon, aware my sight was hampered by at least four Wraiths who moved around between me and my target. I controlled my breathing, easing my heartbeat into a slower, calmer rate. I saw the line straight through the crowd of Wraiths even before they moved.

And then I pulled the trigger.

The bullet flew through the air and with my panther sight, I watched it, watched the trail of air it raised in its wake, watched as it skimmed within a hairsbreadth of one Wraith's neck, another's cheek, and another's temple.

The bullet slammed into the waiting guard with a soft thud. He grunted, then fell forward out of the shadows and flat onto his face among the feet of Wren's men. They stared at the dead guard in shocked silence. Then they all turned to me simultaneously. I still had my bow aimed in their direction, but it didn't seem to bother them to be staring down my weapon.

The senior soldier gave me a respectful nod, then motioned for the Wraith at the door to keep going. The cell door swung wide on creaky hinges, and we were all hit with the blast of the stench of the room. The odor of urine and feces overpowered the stench of rotting food and moldy straw. Two Wraiths entered warily, their swords stretched out in front of them. The silence from the room was ominous, and my heart thumped louder and harder. I had to force myself to take a breath despite the stink, calming myself more important than the possibility of puking my guts out.

Then I heard a gruff sound and the Wraiths reappeared from the room, disgust clear on their faces. Disgust and disappointment.

The Wraith who'd warned us to stay put marched straight to us. Then he glared at Cassandra. "I thought you said northeast cell?"

She nodded. "I did. She was there. I even whispered her name and told her we were coming to get her."

"She isn't there," the Wraith snapped, and disappointment hit me like a blow to the gut. "Could you have made a mistake with the cell?"

Cassandra shook her head and snapped back, "No. No mistake. I am positive she was in that cell. Perhaps they moved her after I saw her." She held the Wraith's gaze, and he turned away, giving his men instructions to check all the cells. Soon Wraiths were walking up and down the passageways, peering into each cell and coming up empty. They'd just completed searching when the sounds of boot steps on the stairs filtered through to us.

Everyone froze, unsure for a moment what to do. Then we all turned together and headed for the only open cell. But we were too late. The soldiers bearing down on us were already at our backs and there was no point in running.

I swung around, my bow aimed at the oncoming Wraiths, ready to begin taking them down one at a time, but my finger froze on the trigger. I faced the rest of Wren's team, including the general himself.

And none of them looked too happy.

He raised an eyebrow at the bow aimed at his heart but said nothing. "What happened?" I asked, daring to be the impatient female, but the general seemed far too furious to be bothered by my outspokenness.

"It was a false lead." His voice rang out, grating on my ears. Then he rounded on Cassandra. "ShapeChanger, you confirmed the Hunter was in that cell. I can see that you too have come up empty-handed." His tone was almost accusatory, and I was not impressed.

But before I could tell him off, Cassandra moved ahead of me and said, "When I came through the castle, there were guards, plenty of them. And the cell was occupied. I spoke to Celeste and she answered me. It could have been no one else but her."

"Fuck," the general swore in response, and I couldn't help but raise my eyebrows. Swearing most certainly didn't suit any creature that didn't look human. "That means they knew we were coming. And they managed to get out before we came for her."

My heart sank as I realized we'd failed.

Mom was gone.

As upset as the general was, he was in no way as devastated as I was. I wanted to believe we would still find her, but something in the back of my mind kept telling me it was over.

We'd come all this way, followed intelligence gained by Illyria's mole in Widd'en's army, almost been eaten alive by wolves on the Dead Plains, almost drowned on the Black Lake. But it was all for nothing. And that led me to suspect one of two things. Either the Rebel army couldn't trust their mole, or I couldn't trust the leader of the Rebel army.

I trudged along behind Anjelo, following his footsteps, paying little attention to anything else. Once or twice Cassandra had tried to talk to me, but I'd ignored every attempt. I was in no mood for consolation or small talk.

Anjelo seemed to sense it would be a waste of time to attempt to pull me out of my fugue, remaining silent but watchful. What did he think I was going to do? Jump in a lake that wouldn't kill me with its poisoned waters?

I snickered to myself as I glanced around the frozen lake. Over to our left was the place I'd almost drowned, the area dark against the surrounding ice. A timely reminder of how fast things could change.

My thoughts steered me back to Illyria. I'd trusted her, and now my only hope was Lily was still safe. The last thing I wanted now was to return to the garrison to find Lily hurt or dead. But when I considered the respect the Rebel commander had for Anjelo, I had to admit I doubted she would betray him.

The woman certainly had her mysteries, but I wouldn't put it as far as hurting Anjelo unless there was something inordinately valuable to gain from it. That could only mean the mole was the problem. I made a mental note to ask Illyria if she really believed she could count on the mole.

On the other hand, this could be one giant coincidence. Maybe Widd'en's army had moved out just before we entered the castle, without knowing we were coming. Maybe they'd left before we even began crossing the grounds. It could be a plausible reason considering the birds hadn't roused more than two guards, who also happened to be part of only a handful of sentries within the castle.

I gritted my teeth as my hands curled into fists. I wanted to scream and shout out my rage. We'd come so close. From what Cassandra had said, it would have been an hour at the most between the time she'd seen and spoken to Mom and when we'd entered her cell.

That brought my mind back to the conditions under which Mom was being held. I glanced over my shoulder at Cassandra to find her eyes already seeking my gaze. She lifted her chin as if already aware I had a question.

"I'm sorry if I've been a little quiet," I offered, keeping pace with Anjelo. Then I cleared my throat. "When you spoke to my mother, how did she seem? Was she ill in any way? Did they treat her well?"

Cassandra frowned, as if knowing her answer wouldn't make me happy, but I admired her for answering. "I believe she was in fairly good health. She didn't appear to have been tortured, although the cell was squalid and she wasn't too clean herself."

I nodded, then looked forward, falling silent quickly, my thoughts pulling me into a seething morass of fear and self-blame. Cassandra's voice drew my attention once more. "If you will permit me, I do believe your mother is quite a strong woman. She seemed in good spirits and was very happy to know you were coming to get her out. In fact, she said she was quite proud of you even though you were too stubborn for your own good."

I laughed at that. I could just imagine Mom's face as she said the words. "Thanks, Cassandra. The only problem is she would have been horribly disappointed to find out she was being moved. Right now, she'd be furious with herself for not being there when we arrived."

Behind me, the ShapeChanger chuckled. "I believe I can see where you get your stubbornness." Then she paused for a while before saying. "I can also see a lot of Ivy Odel in you."

"You know my Grams well?" I asked, happy to get off the topic of my lost mother.

"Yes. She took me under her wing when I first came on board with Sentinel. I am happy to admit I am glad I was fortunate enough to have her as my handler. She's one smart woman."

"I'm assuming she chose you for this mission?"

"Yes. She said she wanted someone she could trust, someone she knew would lay down their life for her family, so she chose me."

"I'm glad she chose you," I said, glancing over my shoulder at Cassandra. "Thank you."

She waved the thanks off with a, "Pfft. Think nothing of it. I'm honored that Ivy chose me. Now if we can make it back alive, it might look good in my file." Cassandra winked, and I laughed before turning around to follow Anjelo.

And to sink back into my pain.

CHAPTER 26

The journey back to Illyria's stony garrison passed in a blur of depression and pain. I fought back tears the whole way, and though there were many moments I wondered why this failure was taking such a huge toll on my confidence, I still wasn't able to brush it off.

Being forced to move, to put one foot ahead of the other or be left behind was good enough incentive to prevent me from curling up in a ball and rocking myself to sleep. I was grateful for that at least, because I'd never been the type to feel sorry for myself. Action was always my answer in the face of failure.

Only this time action was hard for me because my hands were tied. I'd left Mom and Anjelo here in this dull, deadly land and went to save Greer instead. But in the end, that had been a waste of time because Greer had died.

In my arms.

Hot tears filled my eyes and I blinked them away. I didn't want the reminder, but Greer was part of my problem; she was part of this pain I felt, the sense of being useless and a failure.

I hadn't realized the line had come to a halt until I walked right smack into Anjelo's back. "Sorry," I said without making any stupid excuses. Both he and Cassandra knew I'd been struggling with my demons this past day, and they'd left me to it for the most part.

He turned and patted my shoulder then left the line and headed for the gigantic doors where Wren and Illyria were gathered with the other two generals, clearly having an unsatisfactory discussion.

From a distance, I had to admire the Rebel leader's attitude, not arrogant or superior, just commanding. Even when speaking to her generals, who were all at least a head taller than her.

I followed Anjelo and heard Cassandra do the same. Even though it may have seemed rude or presumptuous, I didn't care. I'd lost my Mom and I needed answers.

Anjelo was already talking with Illyria and her team when Cassandra and I drew level with them. When the Rebel leader turned to me, the first thing I saw was sympathy. Granted, I didn't want sympathy, but at least it was better than being told to mind my own business until they were good and ready to talk to me.

"Kailin. I am truly sorry this has happened. I thought our information was sound."

She'd given me the perfect opening. "Do you think your informant has been compromised?"

Her face fell and I knew she was already considering it a possibility. "Either that or we have a mole within our own regiment."

I shook my head. "How would your mole have transferred that information if not physically?"

Illyria glanced at her men, then back at me. Then she cleared her throat. "In Wrythiin, we have such things as portal reloops. They are like a normal inter-plane portal, only they loop onto each other, like a circle of sorts. It works only between two places and can be generated only by a Wraith with sufficient power." Illyria cleared her throat, the skin at her eyes tight with anger.

"This is the way we communicate with our mole. I do believe our own methods are being used against us."

I sighed. "Perhaps you need to test your mole to see if you can trust him. And also your men."

She lifted her chin, eyes gazing at me with curiosity. "What do you suggest?"

I glanced at all three of the generals, including Anjelo, and said, "Perhaps you and I should have a private word?"

For a moment she hesitated, then looked back at her generals. "No offense to any of you, but I think I will discuss this with the Walker in private."

She began to walk toward me with Anjelo in tow, when Wren said, "The Walker did ask for a private word, did she not?"

We turned around to see him glaring pointedly at Anjelo, whose cheeks went a tiny bit pink, whether with anger or embarrassment I couldn't tell. He looked at me and I gave a slight nod.

At first his expression filled with hurt, but then he looked at both Illyria and me, then back at her three generals who stood waiting for his response, and he nodded and stepped toward them.

The general's features tightened for a moment, and I wondered if Anjelo had disappointed him by not putting up a fight.

Too bad.

Then Illyria and I turned and headed inside the tunnels, leaving Cassandra, Anjelo, and the three generals to their own devices.

CHAPTER 27

Seated now in Illyria's office, I removed my fur cloak and partook of the glass of wine she'd poured. Something stiff and strong that had no effect on my senses, but which I drank because I was thirsty.

"So tell me what is this plan of yours."

"I'm afraid it's not all that ingenious." I laughed and set the glass back on the table. "Tell your mole one piece of information, tell your men another, and you should soon find your traitor."

Illyria sat back and smiled. She'd been about to sip her wine when I'd spoken and now seemed to have forgotten the drink in her hand. "Now, that is a brilliant idea."

I shrugged. "You would have come up with it sooner or later."

She frowned at my words, which were true. They would have figured on this very idea soon enough. She gave a slight nod, then said, "Perhaps. But at this time, it is your suggestion and I will do it."

She opened her mouth to say more, and I held up my hand. "Oh, and I don't want to know."

Illyria frowned and stared at me, an undecipherable expression on her face. I just met her gaze and said, "It's best to ensure my word isn't compromised in the matter either."

She nodded again. "You have thought of everything."

To that I shook my head. "I don't believe so. Had I thought of everything, I would now have my mother sitting beside me."

Before Illyria could answer, a knock sounded at the door and Lily entered the room.

"Oh, Kai, I'm so glad you're back," she said, throwing her arms around me even while I still remained seated.

I patted her arm and returned the squeeze. "Yeah, I'm back and still in one piece."

Then she gasped. "Yes, Anjelo told me you almost drowned in that lake. And your mom? I'm so sorry, Kai."

I smiled reassuringly at her. "It's okay, Lily. We just have to keep looking."

When I looked back at the Rebel leader, I wondered if she would be annoyed at Lily's barging into the room uninvited. Instead, I found her smiling at the lynx Walker, who said, "Thanks for sending for me." She smiled shyly at Illyria before turning to me. "I'll wait outside. Sorry for crashing in here like that."

"No, we're done. I think?" I glanced back at Illyria, giving her a questioning glance.

A smile curved at her lips and she got to her feet and said, "I will walk you out. I need to get this business moving. And, Kailin, I want you to know I have sent out all my feelers, probed all my contacts to try and discover where your mother has been taken. If she is in Wrythiin, we will head out the moment we hear of her location."

She held her hand out in the more human handshake, and I took it. I smiled at her, grateful for whatever she could do for me. Finding my mother was the most important thing right now.

And as I walked with Lily, listening to her chattering away, I realized why I'd been so upset with myself for failing to find

Mom. Because finding her was my job. It was up to me and only me. I couldn't put the responsibility on anyone else's shoulders, nor would I want to.

I was the only one capable, the only one with the necessary skills and abilities, and one of the few people with something to lose. And I believed that was a deadly combination.

And a combination that could have no other result but success.

I'd find my mom or die trying.

~

I WENT to the room we'd been assigned and threw down my satchel and my cloaks. Despite Illyria's assurances that she was looking for Mom, I sank back into a state of sadness. But it didn't last long.

The room was cold and I dove under the covers fully clothed and tried to get some warmth back into my icy body. A little while later, Anjelo and Lily arrived with food, the same unappealing mush as the last time, but now I knew it actually tasted a lot better than it looked.

"Thanks," I said as I sat up. I was so hungry I just about breathed in the food, and too soon the bowl was empty and all the bread gone. I sighed, although I wasn't fully sated. "That was good. Thanks for thinking of me, you guys."

"We suspected you wouldn't be in the mood for company," said Anjelo with a shrug. He tried to appear calm, but I could see the concern on his face. Concern for me.

I studied his face for any sign that he was hurt by what I'd done earlier. Finding nothing, I said, "I'm sorry about before."

"Before?" He stared at me, frowning. Then his expression cleared. "Oh, you mean the thing with Illyria and the generals." When I nodded, he said, "I totally understood why you did that. So what was your idea?"

"I told her I thought she should try to trick the mole or informant into passing the wrong information."

"Brilliant idea." He nodded, pursing his lips in approval of my plan. "So what is she planning on saying?"

"I told her not to tell me. She's meant to tell her mole something and also tell the regiment here something different. That way she can find out where her traitor is."

"It won't be easy, though. How many people is she going to tell different things?"

"I don't think she assumed it was going to be an easy task. I'd guess she'd start with testing her mole in Widd'en's army and her generals, then work down from there."

Anjelo nodded and Lily frowned as she contemplated the idea.

"Hey, Lily, how was it here without us? Everything okay?"

Lily looked up and smiled. "Yeah, it was fine. Better than I thought it would be. I admit I was pretty scared when you guys left, but Illyria was very nice and kept me with her all the time. I didn't even need to insist on staying with her. She seemed impressed when I said I wanted something to do that would make me feel useful. She showed me how to read the maps and identify which one is which. She even showed me how she sent her messages to her mole in Widd'en's army—"

"She showed you that?" I asked, my mouth hanging open.

Lily nodded and gave me a sly smile. "I suspect she did that thinking I would reveal how Cassandra called Sentinel for help, but I pretended there was nothing for me to tell. She never asked outright, so I guess she was hoping I would offer the information in good faith."

"She must have been disappointed."

Lily tilted her head as if it would help her recall the Rebel leader's behavior. "If she was, she certainly didn't show it. She just continued as if nothing had happened. Kept teaching me stuff, even arranged for one of her guards to start sparring with me. She said I should be well trained just in case."

"Okay," I said, curious as to why Illyria had kept Lily so close. I had assumed she'd be after Sentinel's communication method, but she hadn't even asked Lily for it. "Maybe Illyria wasn't up to anything, then."

"Disappointed?" asked Anjelo almost triumphantly. He'd backed the Rebel leader's honesty all along, and now it seemed her actions proved she was as trustworthy as he'd thought.

"No. Of course not. I wasn't sitting around waiting for her to prove she was up to no good. In fact, I quite like her, so I have to admit I am happy."

A knock on the door disturbed our discussion, and Anjelo rose to open it. A Wraith guard poked his head inside the room and said, "The commander would like to see you. She has urgent news." He withdrew his head and was gone before we could ask any further questions.

I threw off the furs and got my boots back on before grabbing my bow. I felt like I needed to be prepared just in case, and the feel of the weapon slung over my shoulder was comforting. We hurried to Illyria's office and entered through the open door. She waved us to be seated and didn't close the door. Someone else entered and I glanced over my shoulder to see Cassandra. She gave me a small wave and stood just behind me.

"I have information. It is from my mole, so be aware that I myself am taking this with my eyes open in case he turns out to be a traitor." Illyria spoke and I could tell she didn't like the idea of doubting her information, but she knew in this case it was the prudent thing to do. None of us replied, so she continued. "The intel we have suggests your mother was taken back into the Earth world."

"How can we be sure?" I asked, leaning forward, surprised at this turn of events.

"I'm afraid we cannot be certain. All I can say is we need to follow the lead to your world and try to pick it up there."

I nodded, feeling a tiny lilt of excitement run through me. We could get out of this place and go home to look for Mom. I did prefer home to Wrythiin in terms of territory in which to search.

I glanced at my two friends, then behind me at Cassandra, who were all looking at me and waiting for a response. "Well, what are you all waiting for?" I asked. "Let's go home."

CHAPTER 28

After farewell-ing Illyria, we headed to our rooms to grab our gear.

At my door, Cassandra paused. "I just wanted to let you know you are all welcome to use our transport to get out of Wrythiin."

I hesitated for a moment, unsure if that was a wise choice. Using Sentinel's transporter would undoubtedly mean we would be indebted to the organization, and I didn't trust corporations.

"I thought you would prefer the transporter instead of your portal key considering it's approximately midday in Chicago."

I scrunched up my face. "Broad daylight. Not a good time to appear out of thin air in a public place," I said with a wry smile. Cassandra had a good head on her shoulders. No wonder Grams respected her. "Thanks, Cassandra, I believe we will take you up on that offer." I didn't ask what Sentinel would expect in return, though I wasn't going to kid myself it would be nothing. Besides, none of us were in any mood to spend another eight hours in Wrythiin. It would be a waste of time.

"Very well, then, I shall only be a wee while." Then she headed off down the hall to her room.

Lily had packed quickly. And I was thankful we hadn't

brought much in the first place. I left the cloak and fur on my bed, feeling a bit bad that I hadn't thanked Illyria for her hospitality.

Cassandra and Anjelo returned together and we followed the ShapeChanger down through the tunnels. I paid little attention to the turns, as I had no intention of ever returning to Wrythiin. At last Cassandra entered what looked like a dead-end passage. We all walked to the shadowed, unlit end and paused, waiting for Cassandra's next move.

"What now?" I asked, trying not to sound impatient.

She glanced at her watch and said, "A few minutes, maybe five or ten. He's usually on time."

I frowned at her watch, knowing full well mine didn't work down here. "Does Sentinel have some super technology they aren't sharing?" I asked, taking the chance.

She did a small double take, concern filling her expression. "What do you mean?"

I gave her watch a glance and a nod. "Our timepieces don't work here."

Then she laughed, relief coloring her face a pale pink. "Oh, no, these are old world timepieces. They work with tumblers and cogs so aren't affected by plane transfers and electricity fields."

"Oh yes, mechanical watches, as opposed to our digital or electronic ones?" I said, and she nodded. "Interesting. I'm going to have to steal that idea."

She grinned. "Steal away."

Before I could say anything else, the air before us began to shimmer, as if losing its nothingness and transforming into some sort of liquid version of the ether. A man stepped out of the mercurial portal and stopped in front of Cassandra, his blue eyes bright with curiosity at the gathered group.

"Cass?" He frowned as he looked around at us, a question in his gaze.

"Larsson, this is Kailin, Anjelo, and Lily." Cassandra made

quick introductions. "They'll be returning with me. You up for the ride?"

"Of course," he nodded, giving me a quick reassuring smile. He impressed me with his red crew cut and muscles that looked like he'd do well lifting weights for the Olympics. Guns, those were called, and they put Anjelo's newly acquired muscles to shame. Larsson was polite and when he smiled, his teeth glinted enough to match the single diamond earring in his left earlobe.

After a quick introduction, Larsson transported us one at a time back to Sentinel headquarters, starting with me and ending with Cassandra, who acted as lookout just in case. The transporter took my arm and I held on a little tighter than I'd expected to. But this was my first transport if you didn't count Saleem's jumps in the Graylands.

Larsson deposited me in the middle of a small, sparsely furnished room that made my stomach turn over with worry. It looked far too much like those interrogation rooms you saw on the cop shows on TV. It even had the gigantic mirror window on one wall and was complete with a small metal table and two standard issue metal chairs.

I smoothed down my wrinkled and still-damp clothes, held tightly onto the strap of my satchel, and moved to the far wall to await the arrival of my friends. Larsson brought them through fairly quickly, taking only twice the amount of time to bring Cassandra back.

I felt the heavy weight of the portal keys in my jacket pocket, as if they were blaming me for not using them, but I was smart enough to prefer to move quickly rather than demand to move on my own steam just because I wanted to. I was often accused of being stubborn, and I would be the first to agree. But the one thing I knew I wasn't was stupid-stubborn.

So we had Larsson to thank for bringing us home. High Priestess Kira would probably not be impressed. My heart thumped a reminder of the blood promise I owed her, but I shoved the thought out of my mind and concentrated as Cassandra took shape out of the swirling pool of liquid air, her arm locked into the crook of Larsson's elbow as if they were about to head off to a ball.

Once Cassandra and the transporter arrived, she gave us all a quick once-over as if to check we were all in one piece. Then she turned and headed to the door. Opening it, she glanced over her shoulder and said, "Coming?"

I hesitated, then followed her out the door in silence, Anjelo and Lily slowing so I could go first. Cassandra led us out of the interrogation room, through a warren of passages marked by unlabeled, unnumbered closed doors, and finally to a set of glass double doors. She swiped a card and the door clicked open.

Outside was a bank of elevators, and Cassandra swiped her card again to call one up. She glanced at me, her head tilted a little as she studied my face. "Larson said Ivy was on a mission; otherwise, she would have met you."

I smiled, grateful she was thoughtful enough to think of Grams. "Thanks for letting me know, Cassandra. Grams knows where to find me if she needs me."

Cassandra nodded, and the sound of gears and metal grew louder as the elevator reached our floor. "Please call me Cassie. We have no need to stand on ceremony considering what we've just been through," she said. She was turning to leave when she stopped and spun back to face me. "Oh, I almost forgot. Do you need a tracker? We are happy to supply one. Just say the word."

"A tracker?" I answered, feigning ignorance. Seemed Cassandra was on the same wavelength. I'd been making a mental list of things to do when I left Sentinel HQ, and contacting a tracker was one of them.

"I would assume the best way to find your mother would be to use a tracker. I know of a reliable tracker if you wish me to give you a number."

I raised my hand. "No thanks, that is totally fine. I do know the perfect person. She's helped me before and I'm sure she'll be happy to do so again."

"Ah, yes. I almost forgot. You used Melisande Morgan on your search for your sister," said Cassandra. Then she paled as she realized she'd probably said too much.

My jaw tightened. But it wasn't as if I didn't know how Sentinel and Omega worked. Omega wanted me on board and Sentinel probably did too, though Grams was being subtler about it. I wondered, though. Was Grams passing information on to Sentinel or was Sentinel just keeping tabs on me? I preferred the latter of the two options. At least until I spoke to Grams.

Ivy Odel had some explaining to do.

The arrival of the elevator saved Cassandra any further embarrassment, but I accepted I couldn't blame her for doing her job. We filed into the lift, and I gave her a reassuring smile. "Thank you for everything, Cassie. I'm pretty sure words aren't enough, so please, if you ever need my help, just call."

The ShapeChanger smiled gratefully, then waved as the doors shut and the elevator sank toward the ground floor.

THE ELEVATOR DOORS opened into the lobby of the building, all aluminum and glass with a security guard's desk in the middle. Sofas and plants dotted the perimeter of the open space, along with a set of escalators leading to what looked like a coffee shop or cafeteria. The scent of fresh-brewed coffee drifted to us, and I could hear both Anjelo and Lily inhaling the smells.

Nice.

Sentinel's HQ was certainly more than I expected. We walked warily through the lobby, the guard glancing up from his monitors to watch us as we passed. I tensed under his scrutiny, expecting to be hailed, but he let us walk on to exit through the automatic doors into the sunshine.

The three of us stood outside a moment and basked in the warmth. Suddenly, I was looking forward to going home, especially since my pants had never actually dried in the crotch seams and had continued to chafe my thighs raw all through our travels.

I hadn't paid much attention until now, when the adrenaline had run its course and the attention was finally on the here and now. And now it stung to high heaven.

I winced and said, "I'm off home. I think you two need to head off as well. Get some rest and meet me later. I'll give the tracker a call and arrange a meeting as soon as possible."

We parted ways, and I reached into my pocket for my cell phone. My stomach tightened as I pressed the button to turn it on. It sang its little welcome ditty, and I swiped my thumb across the screen, mentally crossing my fingers and hoping it hadn't been destroyed when I'd gone for a swim in the poisonous Black Lake.

The battery was low, but the phone was still working, which was a plus. The icky black water had seemed thicker than Earth water, so perhaps it had been too gloopy and thick to enter the mechanical parts of the mobile phone.

Small mercies.

A good thing too, as I didn't have time to mess around looking for a replacement. I sent three texts in quick succession. One to Grams and one to Logan, because both had to be brought up to speed and at least be aware that I was back home. The rest of the family would be informed in due course. Besides, I really couldn't wait to see Logan's face again. A spike of longing stabbed my heart and suddenly I missed him terribly.

The last text was to the tracker, Mel Morgan. I hadn't expected to need her help so soon, but I hoped she'd make a little time for me. All communications sent, I strolled home, every so often lifting my face to the sun. The day was warm and such a pleasure to return to, especially when coming from the arctic conditions of Wrythiin.

The sun was hot on my head, and I relished the feel of it. But more than that, I would relish the feel of a hot shower, not to mention some decent food.

I sighed as I pushed open the door to my building and climbed the stairs. As I reached my landing and my front door, I let my panther senses free to roam the apartment, searching for odors and heartbeats and anything that could be a threat. They came up empty.

Piping hot shower, here I come.

$\mathcal{I}$'d probably stood under the stream of steaming hot water way too long, because when I finally forced myself to come out, the skin on my fingertips was all wrinkled and prune-like. I didn't care that the water had stung the scar on my face. I'd turned up the heat as high as I could stand, despite already accepting it would do nothing to alleviate the ice that seemed to have settled in my bones.

Even when I turned off the water and dried off, I still felt cold. It called for PJs and thick bunny slippers and an oversized fluffy gown, but that wasn't possible. I pulled on jeans, a turtleneck, and a thick wool sweater and eyed the disused fireplace in the lounge. I'd only ever lit the thing a few times, and I wasn't so sure the weather called for a fire.

Still, I couldn't shake this chill.

I puttered around, then decided maybe a cup of hot chocolate would help warm me up. I checked my phone while waiting for the kettle to boil. Nothing from Grams, but a message from Logan brightened my day a little.

He was on his way.

Still no response from Mel, but I hadn't expected an immediate answer. The tracker probably had a busy enough schedule without me sticking my nose in and making it worse.

When the kettle switched off, I listened to the silence of the apartment. Everything was still. The wood of the floor smelled warm and comforting, heated by the sun streaming in through the kitchen and dining room windows. Somewhere in the apartment, a clock ticked away, signaling the steady passing of time.

Then the fridge kicked on and the beauty of the silence was gone.

Moments later, while I sat feet up and curled on the sofa, sipping my hot chocolate, I heard a key rattle in the lock. I stiffened and placed my cup on the coffee table. Standing, I approached the door, aware that the intruder could be any number of people welcome in my home.

On the other hand, past experience told me that wasn't always the case.

Before I could call on my panther senses to check out the trespasser, the door opened.

Logan, bearing coffee and pastries.

The sight of Logan caught me off guard—navy Henley, low-slung jeans, sexy smile. And all I could do was swallow hard and try to maintain control over a sudden need to grab him by the shirt, shove him against the door, and kiss him senseless.

Rightly so, I decided against it, at least until he got the food and coffee out of his arms.

"You are a godsend," I sang out, grabbing the bags and taking them to the coffee table in the lounge. I was still in the mood to relax and be comfy.

"Good to know where I stand," he said, grinning that incredibly sexy smile of his. I narrowed my eyes at him and handed him a coffee, deciding right now it would be better to have his hands occupied with coffee and pastries than with me.

He glanced at my face, eyes darting to the thin scar that

marked the side of my face. He didn't ask any questions, just raised his cup to his lips, a touch of fury flickering in his eye.

He sipped, I sipped, and then I gobbled down pastries and swallowed the coffee as if I hadn't eaten in days. It was on the heavenly side of enjoyment considering the quality of standard Wrythiin fare.

"Hey, slow down. You're going to die choking." Logan laughed as he set down his coffee and picked at the mangled remains of a cinnamon bun.

"Not a bad way to die considering what I had to eat these past few days," I said as I sat back and sighed with pleasure. Pastries had never tasted that good in my life, and I hoped I wasn't going to regret my gluttony.

"Which was…?" Logan asked as he put his arm around me.

I licked my fingers and settled against him, resting my head on his shoulder. "Wraith food. Icky, gray soup and gloppy, oatmealy gunk." I made a face even though I knew he wouldn't see it.

"Mmh. That doesn't sound in the least appealing." He was trying his best to sound serious, but I could tell he was near to bursting out with laughter.

"I shouldn't knock it," I said, trying to be objective. "The soup was edible and at least wasn't disgusting, but they definitely need a cooking channel in Wrythiin."

Logan chuckled and the sound rippled through his chest and against my cheek. I was reminded again how safe he made me feel. Then he pulled me closer. "So tell me what happened."

I smiled and settled against him, launching into the quickest yet most informative roundup of our trip to Wrythiin.

I ended with our failure to find Mom, and suddenly I needed to be away from him. The proximity to his comforting body made me want to cry the pent-up tears that sat at the base of my throat. I pushed away from Logan and walked stiffly to the kitchen as frustration and disappointment began to overwhelm me. The retelling was enough to bring back all my dissatisfaction and all the recognition of my failure.

Sofa springs twanged as he jumped off the couch and came after me. "Hey, hold on there a minute," he called as I entered the kitchen, my socked feet sliding a little as I stalked to the counter. I refused to turn around as I struggled to blink back the hot tears that stung my eyes.

I filled the kettle, more for the need to do something with my hands than the desire for something to drink. Logan drew alongside me, placed a hand on my shoulder, and turned me to face him, uncaring that the tap was still running in a cool stream, straight into the kettle that was now full and overflowing. He glanced over to the sink when the sound of rushing water penetrated his intensity.

He turned off the faucet and took the pot from my viselike grip. Only after he'd set it on the counter did he face me again. His lips curved into a sweet, tender smile as he cupped my face with both his warm hands, thumbs lingering on the soft skin of my cheeks. "The worst thing to do is ignore how you feel right now. I know it hurts. Failure always does. But you have options. You will find her."

Then he drew me into his arms and I was enveloped by his scent, his breath, his body. His comfort. "Thank you," I whispered against the smooth skin of his neck. Then I lay my head on his chest and closed my eyes, the sound of his heartbeat thrumming against my cheek filling me with peace.

He gave me a tight squeeze and said, "Oh, and there is one more advantage."

"And what's that?" I asked, smiling at the smile in his voice. I didn't have to look up to know he had a cheeky grin pasted across his face as he played with the hair at my temple.

"Now that you have me right beside you, I'm here all the way. I'm not leaving you even if you insist on it. Wild horses, blah, blah."

I craned my neck back to look at his face. His eyes were dark and serious as he looked into mine. "I wouldn't dream of insisting on it," I said, my voice suddenly husky, breath suddenly short from the proximity of our bodies.

His fingers curled into the hair at the back of my head, pulling a little harder to expose the curve of my neck. I gasped softly, then breathed in the scent of his skin as he hovered over my mouth, his lips just inches away. All I needed was to stand on my toes to force him to kiss me, to force him to place those delectable lips on mine, but I didn't. Not yet. I sucked in a breath as heat pooled within the core of my body, sending sparks flaring through my veins.

He lowered his mouth, and I almost sobbed, but instead of giving me what I wanted, he placed his lips on the skin below my ear, then trailed heated kisses along the curve of my neck. I inhaled sharply as he nipped at the skin in the arc of my shoulder.

When he brought his face back alongside mine, I shivered, electricity pulsing all the way down my spine. My breathing turned from short, sharp, and urgent to hot and screaming with need.

Then he turned his head the tiniest fraction, his mouth almost touching my lips, and said, "Welcome home." His words entwined with his heated breath as it entered my mouth. And then he kissed me, claiming my lips with a desperate passion that spiked my need so high I felt faint.

His tongue slipped against mine, driving me insane with the need for more. I threw my arms around his neck and pulled him closer. And when he slipped his hands under my jumper, I realized I was no longer cold. Logan had managed to banish the iciness from my bones just with the mere touch of his mouth.

I shuddered with need as his kiss deepened with wild, unadulterated desire. In one smooth move, he lifted me off the ground, his hands cupping my rear. Instinctively, my legs wrapped around his hips, and I had to close my eyes as he carried me through the kitchen into my room.

When did this need for Logan reach such an impossible level? I wondered as he bumped the door with his hip and it gave a satisfactory thud as it closed.

My thoughts remained on questions for only a second before they became entirely Logan's domain. I swallowed hard when he lowered me to the bed and dragged off my upper clothing in one sensual, impatient move. I gasped when his warm hand claimed my breast and moaned when he squeezed softly. His thumb flicked over sensitive skin, sending pulses of electric fire scorching through my veins, straight to my core. I arched toward him, then grabbed for his shirt, the need to give as good as I got almost taking over me.

Bare-chested, Logan's smile was truly wicked. He stared at me, his eyes hot and need-filled as he pushed me onto my back and took my mouth with a hard, deep-seated passion that left me breathless.

And wanting more.

I'D FALLEN into a deep sleep, half comatose from the events of the last few days, with my most recent exertions probably tipping me over the edge. I sighed, wriggling on the soft mattress, and wondered what had disturbed me enough to draw me from such a dead sleep.

Then I heard it, a moan that was more of a yearning lament. Logan tossed beside me, struggling with whatever dream seemed to bother him so much that it resulted in a full physical response.

Soft words slipped through his lips, and I could make out what sounded like, "Where is she? She's supposed to be there." And then a few moments later, "Something isn't right. It's all a lie."

My attempt to listen to his words brought my face closer to Logan's. And that was when I felt the heat that flowed off him in waves. A tentative touch to his bare chest confirmed what I'd suspected. Logan's body was so heated he felt like he had a raging fever. But I knew better.

It was his fire, surging through his veins. Which meant he had to wake up for his own good.

I reached for my panther strength just in case I needed it, then shook Logan's shoulder. I gasped at the scorching heat that emanated from his skin and instinctively let go, fingers stinging. I wasn't planning to be rash and keep hold of him if it meant I'd be burnt. I grabbed the comforter, threw it over him, and shook him again.

He grunted, then ran a hand over his eyes before lifting his head to look over at me. I'd shaken him, then sat back on my heels to get out of the way just in case. From his thrashing, he looked quite likely to swing a left hook and not know a thing. I thought it best to stay out of the way.

"Are you okay?" I asked, taking in his groggy, sleep-swollen face.

"Huh? Yeah. What happened?" His voice cracked sleepily.

"You were calling out for someone. Sounded like you were really upset."

"Oh," he said, then dropped his head back on the pillow.

"And you're burning up. I thought you'd want to get up before you either smoked yourself or the bed." I gave him a smile to soften the words, more worried about his emotional state than my furniture.

Logan sighed, resting one arm over his eyes. The sun was still bright but a little lower in the sky as it crept past mid-afternoon. We'd been asleep only a couple hours. "I'm sorry," he said softly.

"For what?" I asked as I ran a hand down his well-muscled arm. "It's not like you hurt me in any way."

He chuckled. "I should hope I can be trusted not to hurt you in my sleep."

"Well, you did get pretty wild there for a moment. And you were so hot." I narrowed my gaze at him, frowning. "Is everything okay? You know you can talk to me, right?"

He nodded, watching me with his sleepy gaze. "Yeah, I know. These dreams have been bothering me for a few weeks now."

"What are they about?" I asked, lying back down and propping my head up on my hand.

He scrunched up his forehead as if trying hard to probe his dreams. "Lately, I feel like someone's messing with my mind." Then he laughed. "That's ridiculous, I know, but it's weird. I have these memories or thoughts that seem to pop into my head, and I feel like they're real, but then it's something so against what I know to be true. I'm a bit of a head case lately."

"So what are these new memories telling you?"

He snorted and stared up at the ceiling. "They tell me that what I remember to be true about my past isn't really the truth."

"Which is…?" I urged him to open up and crossed my fingers, hoping he had it in him to trust me with this intensely personal part of him.

He shifted so he was facing me, then placed his hand over mine and squeezed. "I'm an only child. These dreams are telling me I have a sister."

That brought me up short, but I asked the next question waiting on the tip of my tongue. "These memories, are they replacement memories or the old ones but just different?"

He frowned and nodded. "Old ones but just a little different. A table with two milkshakes instead of one. Waves crashing on my feet, but there's another set of toes beside me, all sandy and wet. It's not as if I've seen her face. It's more like I sense she's there."

"How do you know it's a girl?"

He gave me a wry smile. "The badly applied nail polish did it for me. Oh, and bright-red hair, long locks. I keep seeing it backlit by the sun so it's almost rust." He sighed and squeezed my hand again. "It's not like it makes much sense to me. It's like a movie, but someone's fiddled with the images and inserted her into my past. But only bits and pieces."

"That doesn't sound like it's easy to process or accept," I said, feeling a deep sadness wash over me, sadness for him and for memories that were lost or different.

He lifted his hand and cupped my cheek, tracing the line of my jaw. "Thank you," he whispered. "Thank you for asking and for listening and for not looking at me like I was nut-house-ready."

"Don't worry, dear. I'll commit you myself if you show any such indication," I said sweetly.

He just snorted, then put his arm around me to pull me onto his chest. I snuggled close, my hand still trapped within his, placed near enough to his heart to feel the steady beat. I listened to the regular thump, to his regular breath, and soon I was asleep again.

C H A P T E R 3 0

J rolled over, pulled from my sleep by the ping of the cell phone, a text from Mel saying she has time to meet me at O'Hagan's. I lay on the bed a moment before realizing the other side of the mattress was empty. Although I felt a smidge of disappointment, I accepted we both had jobs to do.

Sighing, I dragged myself into the shower, dressing in my black turtleneck and an old leather jacket and my usual leather pants, this time a pair that was dry and didn't chafe. The pants I'd worn during my Black Lake swim weren't faring so well. I grabbed them from the foot of the bed and shook them out, but they were still too damp in the seams and would need time to dry before I wore them again.

If I ever wore them again.

I bent and lifted my still-damp jacket in my hand and felt the weight of the portal keys in the pocket. Removing them, I sat on the bed to study them for a brief moment. I compared Mom's key to mine and found no difference besides the natural oddities of being handcrafted. Otherwise, they would be carbon copies of each other.

I slipped Mom's key into my pocket, then buried mine

beneath a stack of envelopes and notepaper that littered my bedside drawer. For now, I could do without thinking of portal keys and blood promises.

I ran a brush through my hair, then headed out the door. O'Hagan's was just a few blocks away and known for their amazing burgers, so I was quite looking forward to ordering one. The glass door swung inward and I entered, only to be smothered in the delicious aroma of food laced with a hint of the yeastiness of beer and Guinness.

The booth I chose sat against the left wall, far enough from the door for privacy but close enough that I had a good line of sight to the entrance. I ordered and hoped I'd be able to eat before Mel arrived. Then I laughed to myself, wondering when I'd become so focused on food. Oh yeah. It must have been when I'd gotten stuck in the Wraith world without decent sustenance for miles.

I relaxed against the cushioned booth seat and listened to the soft rock the bar was playing. The place was busy enough, lunch crowd light, with the dinner clientele slowly filtering in. My order arrived faster than I expected, and soon I was enjoying the best damn burger in town. Not to mention the best fries.

I finished off my meal and wiped my lips, then crumpled the towels and threw them into the basket that had so recently held the fries. I was about to call for Beth, the waitress, to clear my plate when the door opened and I stiffened.

Samuel Collins walked into the bar and gave the place a cursory inspection before his gaze landed on me. His features twisted in what I could only interpret as distaste. My esteem of Collins had been pretty low to begin with.

Now it just sank lower.

He wore dark clothing, grubby white shirt and a long black coat. Collins belonged to City Deep, a clan initiated by my Immortal friend Storm, in the hopes of bringing the clan-less into one familial group. It would have worked well if only Pastor

Sam would quit stirring up trouble. I wasn't sure why he even belonged to City Deep if he had such a hatred for Walkers and other non-human species.

He kept his gaze trained on me, not caring to appear in the least bit friendly. Collins closed in on my booth, then paused beside the table. He'd seen me looking at him, so I couldn't pretend he wasn't there.

"We need to talk," he said in a voice that sent arctic chills down my spine. He had his hands on the edge of the table as if already laying claim to his right to sit if he wished. When I did a double take, I tried to control my movement. I raised my eyes to his face, the thought of what I'd seen beneath his fingertips making me sick to my stomach.

"Why do I care what you have to say?" I asked, matching the chill in my voice to his.

"You will care when you know your mother's life is at stake," he snapped. Then, without waiting, he slid into the seat opposite me. Collins leaned against the back of the booth and stared me down, the wrinkles at the corners of his pale eyes more prominent, the bags below his eyes looking like they may well need a nip/tuck.

But then, considering his situation, he probably wouldn't be needing it. My heart thudded as I saw, again, his fingertips wreathed in coral, the sign of the possession of a Wraith.

I sat with my own back stiff, my stomach churning. I didn't want to be sitting here, directly opposite a possessed human with a Wraith's eyes staring back at me. He knew how to play his cards right. Mentioning Mom certainly got my attention.

Now I stared at him, waiting in stony silence. No reason for me to ask him what he wanted. He'd come here to say something; otherwise, he wouldn't be wasting my time, or his for that matter.

He lifted his chin, meeting my eyes. "We have a proposition for you." Then he fell silent.

"Okay. If that silence is meant for dramatic effect, it's not working. You have something to say, then say it. I don't have time for games." I kept my tone as emotionless as possible, not wanting to give away the fact that my heart was beating so fast I'd soon pass out, not wanting to let on that my stomach was churning so wildly I was probably about to chuck my dinner all over the table.

I was afraid; that much I had to admit. They had my mother and now they wanted to bargain for her. I waited for him to speak, wondering what his proposal would entail.

He leaned forward until his thin waist pressed into the edge of the table. "We have your mother. We suggest you stop looking for her. We don't intend to harm her, so you need not worry. Just stay out of our way and she will make it through this alive." Then he sat back, sinking against the cushions as though the very strength had drained from his bones.

I knew that stage. The Wraith had finally taken over his body, the possession gone just past the point at which the demon would be able to release the body, leaving a living person behind. But for Collins, it was all over. And I wasn't sure I felt sorry for him anyway. Not that I wished him dead. I just wasn't in the mood to feel sympathy for someone who'd done nothing more than cause dissension and tension within City Deep.

Out of the corner of my eye, I noticed Mel enter the bar. She took a step toward me but stopped in her tracks when she saw my face. I was sitting toward the outer end of the booth, able to wave a hand below table level so she could see I wanted her to stay away.

She slipped into a booth by the door and gave me a worried glance as I turned my gaze back to the Wraith. "So what if I refuse to cooperate?"

"Well then..." He spread out his hands in front of him, placing his palms on the table, leaving little trails of coral dust all over the tabletop. "If you refuse, we will have no choice but to kill your mother."

The breath rushed out of my lungs in a whoosh.

The words were like a punch in the gut. But I didn't react. Just watched his gaze waver, just the tiniest movement to the left. I decided to challenge him. "If you didn't need her for some reason, you would have killed her by now. And I know you haven't kept her alive just so you can convince *me* to stay off your back."

The Wraith tilted his head and stared at me. He knew I had him, but he was pretending otherwise. "Very well, then. If you wish to be difficult, I will have no choice but to terminate the Hunter. At least that will remove one particular threat from the equation."

"What threat?"

He laughed. "My dear girl, do you not know who and what your mother is?"

I shook my head, pursed my lips. "She's my mother, a Hunter. Not sure what else you mean?" I tried to imbue an attitude of nonchalance to the Collins-Wraith.

He leaned forward, his lips lifting in a cold sneer. "You, ignorant Walker, have no idea how powerful your mother is. She is the greatest Hunter that has ever lived. She is the bane of our lives, and as the only creature capable of killing our kind with such ease, it will be my pleasure to be the one to end that life and free us from the threat of her existence."

I snorted and folded my arms.

"What is it you find so amusing, Walker?" Collins poked out his head in question, the loose skin on his neck making him look more like a turkey than a human.

"You have your wires a little crossed. If you think Celeste Odel is the Hunter, you are mistaken."

"You may simply deny it. That is your choice. But heed my warning, Walker. Stay away and she will live."

I shifted forward in my seat. "Let me give you a little ultimatum of my own." He lifted a weak brow and waited. "You hurt her, ill-treat her in any way, I will hunt each and every one of you down and kill you with my own bare hands."

His nostrils flared, a lip curled in arrogant disgust. "We are not afraid of you, little Hunter."

I leaned forward almost halfway across the table. I got so far across that Collins leaned away from me. "Let me tell you a little something, Wraith," I said, inflecting the word Wraith with as much reverence as I would crap on the bottom of my shoe. "You have one very important piece of information wrong."

"And what would that be?" he asked, tilting his head, trying to retain the cocksure mien he'd worn upon entering the bar.

"You may have a Hunter as a captive. But you have the wrong Hunter."

"How the hell would you know?" he snapped, clearly losing patience.

"Because *I* am the greatest hunter that has ever lived. *I* am the bane of your lives, the only creature capable of killing your kind with simple ease. And let me tell you this. It will be *my* pleasure to be the one to end *your* life and free all humanity from the threat of *your* existence."

He sat so still it didn't even look like he was breathing. I studied his body for a sign of life, then realized there would be none. The husk of the Wraith would be dead by now.

Then he shifted, moving sideways along the seat, sliding out of the booth.

"Oh, and Collins?" I called out, forcing him to turn to hear my parting words. "Touch one hair on her head and I will make your death worse than you could ever imagine.

CHAPTER 31

Isat in the booth for a moment, my body cold, wondering if I had just signed my mother's death warrant. But no, he'd go back to whatever hole he'd crawled out of, investigate the truth of what I'd revealed. At best, he would believe me and take good care of Mom, fearing for their lives. At worst, they wouldn't believe a word I said. I was confident Mom was too valuable to them or they would have killed her by now.

Or so I hoped.

Something moved in my line of vision, and I noticed Mel Morgan striding over. She was about to slide into the seat just vacated by Collins when I stood. "Let's sit somewhere else."

Her gaze snapped to me, her eyes questioning. "Sure, the booth by the window?"

I nodded and grabbed my satchel, following her to the seat in which she'd waited for me while I was speaking to the Wraith. When we were both seated, she leaned forward. "Kailin, are you okay? You look like you've seen a ghost."

I snorted. "I have, in a manner of speaking."

"Who was that guy? He looked a little creepy." She gave an

elegant shudder, but the look she sent me made me wonder if she was in doubt of the company I kept.

I sighed. "That creepy guy wasn't a guy at all." I pressed my fingers to my forehead, feeling a headache coming on. "Chicago is in the midst of a Wraith infestation. That was one of them."

Mel's silver-gray eyes went wide. "What the hell was he doing talking to you?"

"Giving me an ultimatum."

The strained silence that followed was interrupted by the waitress who came by and offered Mel a menu. Beth gave me a wink and said, "I don't think you're ready to order again, are you?"

"Not by a long shot. I'll just have an iced tea, Beth." She scribbled the order on her little notepad, then did the same for Mel as she ordered the burger and a soda. With Beth gone, I sank into the soft cushion at my back. "I'm sorry for the spy-subterfuge thing. I just didn't want you to run into him. The less he has against me the better."

"So what did he want?" she demanded, and I hid a smile. She was already beginning to sound like Tara.

"He was threatening my mother. Said I needed to stay away from him and his kind or they will kill her." The words left my mouth, but I didn't feel even a spark of emotion. I quite liked the vacuum I was in, but I knew it wouldn't last long. Mel paled, and I shook my head. "I think it's bluster. Mostly. They assumed she's the Hunter they're looking for, but they're wrong. And I told them as much. I will slaughter every single one of them if they hurt her in any way."

"How can you be sure they won't hurt her?" asked Mel softly, her face dark with worry.

My shoulders fell. "That's the kicker. I can't be sure. I'm just hoping they won't. And that's what I need you for."

She nodded. "To track your mom?" When I nodded, she asked, "You have something I can track her with?"

"Yeah, but I forgot to put it into some sort of protective case."

"What is it?"

"It's a portal key. It's got her blood in the crevices of the carvings. It was the only thing I had on hand in the apartment. If you need something else, I'll have to go home for it."

But Mel was shaking her head. "That's totally fine. It should work. I don't see any reason why it won't."

"Good." I sighed, hoping she was right. The thought of a visit home was not in the least appealing considering I would be going there without Mom. "I really want to get this done as soon as possible."

"Right then. As soon as I'm done shoveling food down my throat, we can go back to your place and I will track her for you."

I stared at her quizzically. "No appointment, then?"

"None at all. I have a little time, so what better moment than right now?" She met my eyes, and I was taken aback by her generosity.

"And about your fee?" I'd almost forgotten about payment.

She waved her hand at me, but something in her eyes made me accept her decline of payment. "No fee. Except I may call in a favor sometime in the future."

"Sure," I said, now curious, and happy too. I would be able to return the favor and that made me feel better. I disliked unpaid debts. "Anything you can talk about right now?"

She shook her head, her expression far away, as if already delving into the details of her case. "Well, yes and no. I don't have all the information. It's just a suspicion at this point. When we have something more to go on, then I'll call you."

"No problem. Just text me. And if I don't answer, call Logan. He'll know if I'm alive or dead."

She laughed mid-bite. "Very optimistic of you."

"Hey, I'm just calling it like I see it. Wraiths are unpredictable. And the more powerful they are, the more my life is at risk." Just saying the words made me feel bone-tired.

She looked at her plate for a moment. She seemed far away again, and I left her to it. She chewed, swallowed, sipped, and then asked, "So can you tell me something?"

"Sure. Shoot."

"Okay, so when you track the Wraiths, what is it you look for?"

I sipped my tea, then set the glass back on the table. The ice cubes clinked, and I thought about how simple life is for some people. The guy at the bar, kicking back scotch after scotch because his wife was nagging him to find another better job. He didn't know how good he had it. At least his wife wasn't part of the walking dead, possessed by a Wraith, with no hope of living if the demon ever decided to vacate her corpse.

"One of my skills is the ability to see the tracks they leave. Everything they touch is colored by a fine dust. To me, it appears as a glowing coral powder. I can see it anywhere, on people, on furniture, anywhere a Wraith touches."

"So the ability to see these coral prints has allowed you to successfully track them?"

I nodded. "I guess you could compare them to a snail's trail rather than fingerprints." I shrugged, just wanting to get as far away from Wraiths as possible. But that wasn't going to happen anytime soon.

My cell phone pinged with a well-timed text from Logan announcing he'd be home later to see me. Mel had finished off her burger and was slurping up the dregs of her drink. I did the same, and we hailed the check. Which I insisted on paying since I wasn't going to pay Mel for tracking Mom. She argued a little but eventually gave in, shaking her head at my bossiness.

Post check payment, we walked home, enjoying the Chicago streets as the sun went down and the nightlife took over.

CHAPTER 32

We headed to the dining room table as soon as we entered the apartment. Mel was ready and I didn't want to take too much more of her time. I dug the portal key out of my pocket and laid it on the table in front of us. "Is it okay that I touched it?" I asked, wondering if I'd just mucked up the mojo.

She nodded. "It should be fine. I need DNA, and I don't usually have a problem with epithelial DNA causing interference."

I watched as she reached for the portal key, my heart thudding in my chest. She must have sensed my nerves because she leaned forward and placed her hand on my arm, the expression in her eyes warm and encouraging. "Hey, I'm going to do a projection first, so I'm not going to disappear or anything. I'll project, get the lay of the place, then come back and tell you what I know." She only let go of my arm when I nodded.

Her bright gray eyes were soft as she gave me a reassuring smile. Then she turned her full attention on the portal key. She dusted her hands out, then took a breath, whether to calm herself or draw on her ability I didn't know. All I did know was her inhalation made me do the same and it forced me to relax a little.

She settled into her chair and then took the metal disk into her hands. Then she stiffened and fell silent. I felt my own muscles tensing as I watched her and had to force myself to calm down. My gaze remained on her face, as if any change in her expression may hint at what was happening in her projection, but her expression remained serene.

The silence in the room kept me company. Even the refrigerator didn't disturb Mel as I waited in silence. Soon she moved again, the slightest shift of her eyes beneath closed lids. Then she blinked and was back. I leaned toward her, studying her face. "Are you all right? Do you need anything."

She held out her hand and gave me a strained smile. "I'm totally fine."

"Did you see her?" I asked. I was probably moving too fast, but Mel nodded and swallowed hard. "Is she okay?"

Mel shook her head. "I'm not sure. I arrived right beside her. She's conscious, but I think she's been injured or maybe... I'm not sure... I think she's being bled. There were soiled bandages around her arms. And she looked thin, emaciated. I'm not entirely sure what they're doing to her."

I gritted my teeth, a spike of fear stabbing straight through my heart. Poor Mom. "I think I know."

"What is it?" Mel was shaking her head, her eyes filled with the turmoil of what she'd seen.

"They probably know about the glow." I couldn't get my mind to focus. I fell silent as my fears built up into an inaudible scream inside my brain.

"What glow?" Mel's tone was a little high-pitched with concern, but she rested her hand on my arm and waited for me to answer when I was ready.

The words felt like they were stuck in my throat and I had to swallow hard. "It's my fault. The Wraiths know about the glow. It's what happens when my killing power comes into play. My hands glow golden and the Wraith I'm touching dies."

"That sounds cool in a gross way." She made a face some-where between impressed and weirded out. "So you're saying the Wraiths found out about this glow and think your mother has the same power because she's also a Hunter?"

I nodded, the movement jerky and painful. The headache was returning with full force. "And it's my fault. They never would have learned about it if I hadn't told Illyria how it works." I felt sick to my stomach for the second time in one day. Had I confided in the one person who had passed that information on to Widd'en's army? Was Illyria the mole?

Then I shook my head, recalling that the generals knew as well. What if one of the generals was the traitor? I had to let Illyria know. And I had to save Mom.

Now.

I blinked away the thoughts that crowded my head and gazed across the table at Mel. "Tell me, did you manage to get a good idea of where she's being held?"

Mel nodded. "I got a feel for the room, then did a little explor-ing. She's in a warehouse by the docks somewhere. She's being kept in a disused commercial refrigerator. It's fortunate I can project through anything, even metal. Or else I won't be able to get her out."

"I thought jumpers couldn't pass through lead and… What was the other metal…? Silver?"

Mel grinned a little too triumphantly. "Metals are no match for a Master Teleporter. I can get her out."

"Can we go now?" I asked impatiently. Every moment we waited was an extra moment in which they could hurt Mom.

"We can, but just because I can project in doesn't mean I can jump in. So be aware that it might not work on the first run." I nodded, feeling disappointment well up in my gut. I'd hoped it would be a quick in-and-out to bring Mom safely home. Then Mel spoke again. "There could also be another problem. Some-times I can jump in, but I can't bring the person through."

"Why would that be?"

"Many reasons. Blood magic preventing the person from moving through the Veil. Or the person could be too weak." She looked at me sadly, and I knew where she was going with her line of thought. My heart sank.

"You think Mom will be too weak for a jump?"

"I'm sorry, Kai. I'm almost sure she's too weak. She's pale and she looked very undernourished. A jump could kill her."

My shoulders slumped. I hadn't been prepared for disappointment.

"We can still go in, Kai. We just need be well prepared."

I nodded, swallowing a little of the disappointment. We could still save her. It just wouldn't be that easy. And when had anything I ever did been easy? "Will we need backup?" I asked, strengthening my resolve. I had to regroup, be strong in mind and body. These Wraiths were not going to beat me. I wouldn't allow them to.

"Yes, I usually don't go anywhere without knowing what I'm up against. I don't always have the luxury of backup, but when I do have it, I take it, no questions asked. It's always better to go in with company."

"I can arrange a few people," I said, my brain already listing all available bodies.

"I can wrangle a couple as well if needed," she offered. She looked ready to tackle anything, and I was glad. She may look all feminine and fragile, but Mel was tough as nails and I appreciated that.

"That depends on what you saw. What are we up against? How many Wraiths in the building? How secure is her prison?"

Mel fell silent as she sank back into the astral projection. She returned within a few minutes. "So there are two guards on each corner of the building, two at the end of the drive. Inside, spread along all three floors, there are forty odd Wraiths, and they have weapons."

"Weapons? Not spears and swords?"

She shook her head, looking more worried than before. "No, they have guns, revolvers and rifles."

"Looks like they've upgraded." I gritted my teeth. Seems the Wraiths had smartened up, and I didn't like it one bit. "So it means we have to amp up our ammo as well."

"Do you have sufficient Wraith ammo?"

I pursed my lips. "I'm not sure. I wasn't planning on an all-out war. And with Tara gone, I can't commission more ammo." I sighed and rubbed my forehead. Determined to see this through, I said, "Right. Are there guards where they're holding her?"

"No. They have her sealed from the outside, in that commercial fridge. There are vents near the ceiling so she does have air. But she's weak, hooked up to what looked like an IV. She'll need to be carried out."

I nodded. "Okay. What about other jumpers?" I asked.

"The more jumpers the better, I say." I was glad to see she wasn't the territorial type. Must be the fact that she was a Master Teleporter. From what I knew, there were only a handful in existence.

"I think I can round up one or two," I said.

She smiled and looked like she was about to say something, then closed her mouth, having thought better of it. I was curious, but I didn't have the time to get sidetracked. Then she said, "Okay, so how much time do you need?"

"Half a day? A day at most?"

"So tomorrow, sundown?"

"Yeah, if we could time it to the instant the sun sets, we have an advantage. They are at their weakest at the change of light."

"Okay, so sunset and sunrise make them weak. Are they stronger at night?" When I nodded, she said, "I thought so. Too late for an early morning raid, unless you can round up your people that quickly?" She looked at me, the question clear in her face.

I got to my feet, more determined now than ever. "Let's aim for sunrise," I said, pulling out my phone.

She got up too and started dialing as I did. Soon we were talking and dialing, calling in favors and calling up our backup.

Within half an hour, Lily, Anjelo, and Cassandra had all called back. I arranged for them to meet me at the apartment at four in the morning. Logan was harder to track down, and I set the phone down a little too hard. That got Mel's attention. "What's wrong?"

"I'm trying to get a hold of Logan, but he must be on a job. He's not answering." I knew I sounded more frustrated than he deserved, so I took a deep breath.

"I'm about to call Saleem. Do you want me to ask him if he knows where Logan is?"

I raised my eyebrow and her cheeks turned pink. So that's what she'd been holding back. Mel and Saleem. That was a happy little surprise. She gave me an impatient glare, then began dialing.

Not ten minutes had passed when my phone began to ring, with Logan on the other end of the line. "What's wrong, Kai? Saleem said he got an urgent call from Mel. And I see you've been trying me?"

"Yeah. I need you here stat. Mel's found Mom and we want to go in at dawn. They have her at a warehouse on the docks. Mel's got the lay of the place, but we need manpower."

"Right. I'll see what I can do." His tone was all business, serious.

"Oh, and, Logan?"

"Yeah?"

"I have a couple of Sentinel people on board for this. Is that going to be a problem?" I'd been worried that throwing opposite organizations into this mission would cause undue friction, so it was important I remained upfront with everyone.

Logan answered immediately, no hesitation whatsoever. "Not

a problem at all. I'll be there in a couple hours. You need weapons, of course?"

"Yes. Mel said they have revolvers and rifles. Not sure what else they have up their sleeves."

We rang off and Mel was already moving toward me. "I have to go home, but I will be back soon. I'll come back with my car and hopefully with my partner. I'd rather not do too many jumps right now. Not until it's necessary."

She gave me a quick smile, then disappeared into thin air.

I was never going to get used to that.

CHAPTER 33

I was left to my own devices for a while, and although I knew I should probably be resting, instead I paced. I tried Grams again and got no answer. Then I texted Iain to keep him in the loop. Something made me think he would want to come with us on this mission. I wasn't sure how connected Iain was in Sentinel, or if getting Cassie and her jumper friend involved would mean the Sentinel hierarchy would also be aware of the mission, but I hadn't told anyone that this was meant to be super-secret, so nobody had any need for silence.

Illyria and her mole still bothered me, and I wondered if there was a way to get the information over to her. Despite the possibility that she herself could be the leak, I still felt like I owed her my trust.

Thinking about the Rebel leader made me text Cassie with an idea.

The phone rang within seconds. "Hello, Kailin. Are you sure you want to do this?" she asked, her voice still holding a touch of disbelief. Even I couldn't believe I'd asked her to send word to Illyria.

I nodded. "Yes, we have to take the chance that she is trustworthy. She should know what Widd'en's men are up to here in Chicago. As she herself said, we have no idea how widespread the infiltration is. Chicago could be just the tip of the iceberg."

"Fine. I cannot say I like the idea, but I do see where you're coming from. Perhaps you're right. So what is it you wish to tell her?"

"Where Widd'en's men are holed up. That they have resorted to using human weaponry and they're experimenting on my mother."

"What?" Cassie's shocked voice leaped through the phone. "How do you know this?"

"The tracker saw it. They have her in a warehouse on the docks, and she's been drained of her blood."

"The glow," said Cassie softly. She too had made the immediate connection. "But how did they find out? Surely the Wraiths who saw your hands glow would have been pretty dead minutes afterward. No chance to go back and report to their commanders."

"Exactly what I was thinking. The only people who knew about it were us, Illyria, and her generals."

"And don't forget her personal guard."

"That's one of the reasons I need to take the risk. If she is the mole, then this is a waste of time. If not, her life may very well be in danger."

After a moment of dead air, she responded, "Yes, that is a distinct possibility. I will have a message sent to Illyria. In fact, I may make the trip myself."

"Thanks. You and Larsson will be here by four in the morning?" I asked, knowing I was being pedantic, but I asked anyway.

"With bells on," she said, then rang off.

LOGAN ARRIVED at three with Saleem in tow. I opened the door to the two men who were weighed down by four large army-issue bags. From their bulk, I was pretty sure they'd brought enough weapons for an army. It took my mind back to Tara and her absence. I hadn't expected it to affect me so deeply, but I did miss her, and not just for her amazing weapons.

Logan dropped his bags to the floor and slung an arm around me. Kissing me on the top of my head, he asked, "How you holding up?"

I nodded. "I'll survive."

Then I laughed as Saleem pushed away Logan's arm and wrapped me in a big squishy hug. "How is my favorite feline feeling today?"

"I'm fine. And if either of you asks me that question again, I will have no choice but to kill you." I glared at them, but both ignored me as they unzipped and offloaded their bags and began stacking weapons on Grams' dining room table. "You guys better be careful with the wood or you'll have Grams to deal with."

"And she will enjoy every second of it," said Grams from the open doorway.

I spun around in shock as she grinned and closed the door. "Where have you been? I've been texting you for hours." I couldn't keep the hint of accusation out of my voice.

"I'm sorry, dear. I was off-world," she said as she paused to study the array of weapons spread out on her dining table. "I saw your texts when I arrived, and in fact, it was young Larsson who brought me home. He said to tell you he and Cassandra are coming over soon." Grams spoke but still stared at me with a question in her eyes.

Then she crooked her finger as she strode to her room. I followed obediently, giving the boys a glance over my shoulder. Saleem was staring at Grams and I knew exactly why. His expression was saying, "The hottie is your grandmother?" I just shook my head and shut the door behind me. Just in time too, as Grams began undressing for her shower. I sat on the small stool outside her shower door and brought her up to speed on everything from the trip to Wrythiin, meeting the ShapeChanger, and having Mel track and find Mom.

Grams stepped out of the shower wrapped tight in her towel, her wet hair hanging over her pale shoulder. She leaned against the sink and ran a comb through her hair, her blue eyes watching me in the mirror. "Are you going into this with your eyes open, Kai?"

"What do you mean? We have the firepower, and the agents. We can get in and retrieve Mom easy enough."

"And what if bringing her home isn't enough?"

I stared at her, then opened my mouth to respond. But I closed it as I realized exactly what she was saying. "You mean with Mom being hurt? That she could be dying?" Grams nodded and my shoulders slumped. "No, it never even crossed my mind." I sighed, already defeated by the mere thought.

Grams crouched beside me. "That's what so amazing about you, dear. You go in guns blazing and you always think positive. But sometimes you need to prepare yourself for the worst. Just in case." She patted my cheek, then stood up. "Come. Let me get dressed. Then we can plan this invasion."

I left her to it and returned to find that Lily and Anjelo had arrived and were standing over the cache of weapons. "So what do we have here?" I headed to the table and joined them. All were standard-issue police weapons, except for the small modifications for specialized ammunition. Seemed Omega thought a lot like Tara when it came to paranormal weaponry.

Logan ran through the guns and each of their capabilities. I merely nodded, pretty sure I had all the firepower I needed. That reminded me. I needed to get them all out and give them a good once-over, not to mention take stock of my ammo. As soon as Logan was done, I said, "Well, I guess I'll leave it to you to divide this lot among the team. I'm not sure if the Sentinel people are bringing their own weapons either."

"They probably will," said Grams as she entered the kitchen.

"Anyone for coffee or tea? Or should we order in something a little more substantial?"

The thought of food just turned my stomach, and it seemed from all the "No thanks" and "I'm fines" everyone felt the same. I headed to my room, tugged my closet door open, and pressed the back panel behind the hanging clothing. The wood popped and the panel slid away to reveal the weapons I'd stashed away, the ones I didn't always use.

I dragged them all out, spread them on the floor, and sorted through the pile, taking only the ones that used Tara's demon bullets. My bow and a few handguns should be sufficient for me, especially since my hands were weapons themselves.

Footsteps made me glance up, and I smiled at Lily. "Hi. I wanted to remind you that I have your second bow."

"That's fine. You keep it. Are you confident enough to use it in a fight situation?" I asked her, keeping my eyes on her face. She nodded and didn't seem to be in any doubt of her proficiency with the bow. "I know you've been practicing, but you need to be sure. It's going to be super stressful, running and maybe even hand-to-hand combat. Take the bow only if you're sure."

She still nodded. "I'm sure. It's all I've been using these past weeks."

"Okay, then. Check in the closet in the back panel. You should find a box of Wraith bullets designed for the bow. Take those. Remember, only fire if you're sure of your target. Don't waste them."

"Okay, got it," she said, her voice muffled from inside the closet. "I think I'll take a couple handguns, use those for far-off targets, and keep the bow for when I'm in good range."

"Now you're talking." I grinned and nodded.

"Thanks," she said, falling into a cross-legged pose beside me. She pulled a gun forward and began to take it apart to clean it.

"For what?" I asked without looking up.

"For allowing me to figure that out myself instead of spoon-feeding me. I do have to thank you, you know. You've helped me, trained me, and all that even though I used to be such a grade-A bitch toward you."

"Used to be," I repeated and winked at her. We settled into a rhythm and cleaned quietly until the doorbell sounded.

Cassandra and Larsson were walking inside when I hurried out of the room. They also carried heavy bags on their shoulders, and I grinned. "Thanks for coming."

Cassandra shook my hand and so did Larsson. After a quick round of introductions, I barely took a breath before the doorbell pinged again. A glance at my watch confirmed it was four in the morning. Everyone was on time and ready to roll.

I opened the door to Mel and her partner, who turned out to be a totally sizzling hot paranormal. I wasn't sure what he was, but where Saleem used a little bit of glamor to hide the majority of the markings on his face and body, this dude emanated glamor.

"Hey," Mel said. "This is Drake. Don't mind him if he's surly. He likes his sleep."

He glared at her, but I could tell there was more affection than annoyance in his expression. "Pleasure to meet you." He shook my hand and the glamor magic sizzled up my arm. The look he gave me was appraising and appreciative, and I had to maintain control of my smile. Somewhere in the room, Logan would be watching.

No sooner had I thought his name than he appeared at my side. Mel made the introductions and we all gathered around the table again. This time Grams came too, then slipped away for a moment. She returned with Iain, who slid in beside me and gave me a quick, albeit bone-crushing, hug.

I cleared my throat. "So our army of eleven against... What did you say, Mel? Over forty Wraiths?"

She nodded.

"Make that thirteen, although I do believe that is meant to be a bad omen for humans," said a voice behind us. I spun fast on my heel, ready to fight, then calmed when I saw only Illyria and General Wren'do standing behind me.

"Please forgive me for the intrusion into your home. I felt it would be more prudent to remain out of sight." Illyria spoke softly, tilting her fair head, her pale-gray skin gleaming. Today her eyes looked strange, all black, no pupils, and I found it unnerving.

I waved away her apology. "Don't worry about it. That's fine."

"Just don't make a habit of it," said Grams, arms folded as she stared at the Rebel leader. I'd omitted telling anyone besides Cassandra that I was expecting a Wraith to the party, and only Anjelo and Lily looked accepting of the white-haired Rebel and her companion.

I sighed.

"Even with thirteen, this isn't going to be easy."

That was putting it mildly.

CHAPTER 34

Although the tension had risen a little in the apartment since Illyria had arrived, I ignored it. Mostly. The only person I took aside to talk to was Grams.

"What's wrong? It's not like you to be so judgmental, Grams." I stood in front of her, giving the closed door of her room a glance. I'd brought Cassie with me, seeing as she was Sentinel and she was also Grams' trusted friend.

"I just don't like Wraiths," Grams snapped, her eyes broiling. Then she sank onto the bed and folded her arms.

"Funny coming from a Walker. That's like saying you don't like Asians because one Asian killed your cousin in a hit-and-run." I knew the words were coming out critical and a little rude, especially since they were directed at my grandmother. But I couldn't afford dissension. I needed to know everyone was on the same page.

"Look, Kai. I know what your mother went through in her life. I know what she had to deal with. These Wraiths were constantly out to kill her."

"Of course they were out to kill her, Grams. She was offing

their people left, right, and center. That they were here illegally is irrelevant. She was just part of the cycle."

Grams looked at me, giving her shoulder a helpless shrug. "You just can't see it, can you?"

"I see it well enough. I'm not going to deny that the whole race gives me the chills. But that's like admitting ShapeChangers give me the chills. Or Trackers. We are all paranormal, Grams. And Wraiths were part of our world once."

"I understand what you're saying, Kai. It's just hard for me to be in the same room with one of them."

"Why, Grams?" I watched her face. I was beginning to suspect there was more to this Wraith hatred than I was aware of.

When she didn't answer, Cassie said, "Ivy, I can assure you that the Rebel leader is trustworthy. She looked after us, and even when I was undercover, I never heard a peep about her ill-treating her soldiers or being in any way untrustworthy. She's well respected and powerful."

"She's still a Wraith."

"Grams," I asked, folding my arms and deciding to get to the point, "what are you not telling me?"

Cassie looked at me, then back at Grams for a moment before frowning. She knew something that Grams wasn't telling me. Hurt flooded my heart, singeing my blood like molten lava.

Then Cassandra sighed. "Ivy, if you don't tell her, I will." There was a note of iron in Cassie's tone as she tossed her pale hair over her shoulder.

Grams sank onto the bed and stared at me sadly. She didn't respond to Cassie. Just stared at my face so sadly and so tenderly that I was slowly beginning to understand that her issue with the Wraiths was bigger than me and my problems.

I knelt beside her and took her hand. "What is it, Grams?" I knew I could demand an answer, but for such a strong woman, she seemed so fragile, like a spider's web sparkling with morning dew, so strong yet so easily destroyed.

She sighed and cupped my cheek, her skin warm and smelling of jasmine. "What it is, is that Clan Odel keeps too many secrets from their own." Her hand fell away and she got to her feet. She moved to the window and leaned against the casing, staring out into the black morning. "Your grandfather Mason was killed by a Wraith. Celeste had just come into the family, was still fighting them on the streets, and they organized, came after her. They got Mason instead, and Celeste never forgave herself. So many things she never forgave herself for."

"Grams," I whispered sadly, unable to form the words to voice my feelings. My heart splintered into a million shards. I'd never known Grandpa Mason had died of anything other than natural causes. Nobody had ever spoken of it. "When?" was all I managed to ask.

"Before you were born, dear. Your mother was in confinement, waiting to welcome Iain into the world. But her time away from killing must have given the Wraiths the opportunity to plan. They knew she was vulnerable, so they came for her."

The Wraiths came to kill Mom? And in Tukats? I couldn't get my head around it. "Tell me what happened," I urged, hoping she wouldn't deny me the right to hear the truth at last.

She laughed softly, the sound like a knife cutting into bare skin. "Mason tried to protect her, and he was killed. That's all there was to it. He defended his daughter-in-law and unborn grandchild against a horde of Wraiths, and they killed him." Then her head fell forward and she seemed to shrink into herself. This would have been over twenty-two years ago, yet the wound was still raw, the memories still clear. I could see now why she felt so strongly about the Wraiths.

I wanted to say I was sorry, but that would sound glib. Somewhere in the last few minutes, Cassie had left us alone, and my heart swelled at her thoughtfulness. I walked over to Grams and wrapped my arms around her. "Why didn't you tell us?"

She sniffed. "And give the three of you another reason to hate your poor mother." She shook her head almost violently. "No. I wouldn't have allowed anyone to do that to you. Not after losing your mother."

I held her close and nodded, admitting to myself that I probably would have done the very same thing had it been me. We'd missed Mom all our lives, missed her, hated her, ached for her. The knowledge that Gramps had died because of her would have messed us up more than we already were.

"I know how you feel," I said, realizing in that instant that I didn't. Not really. "Okay, maybe I don't know what it's like to lose a lover, but I know how I feel when I even contemplate losing Logan. I know I won't be able to handle it. But right now, I need you, and Mom needs you. The Wraiths out there had nothing to do with Gramps' death. All they want is to stop Widd'en's men from destroying any hope they have of being allowed to return to the Earth world. They are fighting their own battles. And Anjelo, Lily, and I owe them, for shelter and for our lives. And for so many attempts at saving Mom. They haven't stopped trying to get her back, not once. Even while I was here wasting time, they were looking for her, trying to get her out." I swallowed hard before continuing. "I know it's hard, but they came to help us. Against Widd'en's men. That should count for something, right?"

I came to a sudden halt, my monologue ending in an awkward, stiff silence. I hoped she would listen to reason, anything to make things easier to handle over the next few hours. I could only hope.

I let go of her and stepped away, intending to leave her alone with her thoughts, but then she called out, "Kai?" Her voice wavered, tears and emotions playing with her tone. When I turned to face her, she gave me a weak smile. "I heard everything you said, dear. It's just a lot to process. I promise I won't be antagonistic. But I can't promise I'll make friends."

I smiled. "No need for friends, Grams. We just need to be sure none of us is out to kill each other while we're trying to free Mom."

Grams gave a snort, the sound wet and amused. "I promise I won't try to kill anyone of our team."

With a soft laugh, I said, "Thanks, Grams."

~

WHEN I LEFT THE ROOM, Illyria handed me a gun. "Oh, thanks. But I already have plenty of weapons."

She shook her head and smiled. "It's not the gun you need. It's the ammo."

I raised my eyebrows, already guessing what they'd done. "You did it?" I asked, almost breathless.

She nodded, grinning widely at me. The expression was odd, especially when it made the little wrinkly lines at the outer edges of her eyes widen and resemble vents.

"That's incredible. You must have an amazing scientist." Illyria hesitated, then looked from her general to me. It felt like she was about to say something, but I watched the exchange between her and Wren closely. He gave a slight shake of his head as if to say no. Then she fell silent, her expression a little odd. I had to admit I was disappointed. I'd thought they could be trusted, but they were holding out on me, and I didn't like it. "What are you not telling me?" I asked, my tone a little frostier than a minute ago.

The Rebel leader smiled apologetically. "I'm sorry, Kailin. We just need to be very sure before we take the risk of revealing the identity of our scientist. What you need to know is he is efficient and very dedicated to our cause and to protecting humanity. I just wanted you to know he worked long and hard on cloning the ammo." Her speech was well thought out, but something didn't click about it. Why did I care who her scientist was?

"Have you tested it?" I asked, changing the subject.

She nodded. "We have used it in two raids since you left, and though it's not deadly, it incapacitates long enough for the Wraith to be taken prisoner."

"It doesn't kill?" She shook her head. "But my poisons are deadly," I said, finding it strange they hadn't been able to fully clone the poison.

She shrugged. "It must have something to do with the cloning process. Your poison is deadly, but the cloned version only dulls the senses for a short period of time. Whatever the case, we are satisfied. It gives us an upper hand in the raids."

I snorted. "As long as the technology doesn't get fed to Widd'en's men, you mean?"

"What do you mean?"

"Widd'en's men have been bleeding my mother. No other reason to do that unless they know about my glow." I stated the words a little too coldly and cursed myself for the lack of control. But it was my mother I was talking about, so I didn't give a fuck about control right now.

Illyria's eyes widened even when it seemed it wasn't possible, her eyes being already unnaturally large. "I have been working on discovering the mole. I'm not very far from receiving the notification." She was trying to give as little information as possible, and from the ripple of anger that ran across Wren's expression, I knew why. He didn't appreciate being on her list.

Too bad, dude. If you're our man, you just better hope you aren't found out, I thought.

Then Illyria continued. "Thank you for letting me know. I'm sorry your mother has to bear the brunt of Widd'en's destructive goals."

I gave her a sharp nod, then turned and strode to the table. Four thirty. Sunrise in just over an hour. To Logan, I said, "So are we ready?"

He nodded and handed me a walkie-talkie like no other. I raised my eyes and examined the device. It looked like a smartphone, no antenna, no bulky speakerphones. Then he handed me a tiny earpiece, which I stuck in my right ear, followed by a tiny microphone, which I pinned to my collar. I certainly couldn't fail to feel very FBI.

"We are all in contact. The frequency has been programmed and the lines are tested and in good order."

I nodded, glancing around to see everyone else already wired, including the Wraiths. "Do we have a plan of attack?"

Logan studied my face and said, "I was hoping for your input before we decided firmly on anything."

I cleared my throat, thrown off balance by Logan's deference. I had almost expected him to take over, but I also did relish the idea that the mission was mine to lead. A little voice inside my head said, *Mine to fail too.* I tried not to listen, but I couldn't deny that the doubt sat thick in my gut, like a layer of poisonous oil on a clear ocean. I stared at the sketch Logan had drawn on a large sheet of paper, a map of the warehouse area. "When did we get these?" I asked.

"Saleem and Cassie went out and did a little recon." I glanced at them and gave them a grateful nod.

"Okay, I think we should break up into at least five smaller groups. One to take out the guards at the front gate, the other four to simultaneously dispense with the four sets of perimeter guards."

Logan nodded approvingly. "Exactly what I was thinking."

"So Lily and Anjelo, you two get as close as possible outside the gate and wait for our signal. You can use the long-range rifle and the bow to finish them off. How many were there?" I glanced up as two voices said two, both Mel and Cassandra. "Okay, so you guys pick your poison and your target, finish them off, and get over those gates." The couple nodded, their faces both so deadly serious I wanted to smile.

"So the other four teams… I suggest a jumper with a non-jumper." I studied the map markings that showed three guards on the rooftop. Tapping the little red circles with my finger, I said,

"Grams, Larsson can jump you and Cassie to the rooftop. You guys eliminate those Wraiths, then leave Grams there to keep a lookout. Larson and Cassie will take the north corner. Mel and Drake east. Illyria and I will take south, and Saleem and Iain west. Logan and Wren, time your entry to after the outside guards are eliminated."

Logan nodded. "A simultaneous entry would be stronger. All outside guards eliminated. We enter together for maximum effect." I nodded. Looks like I didn't do too badly with strategy. "The warehouse had three floors and the refrigerators are on the ground floor at the east end of the building. First team heads directly for Celeste. Kai, you head to her. Mel and Drake will meet you there. The rest of us will spread around the building. I think we have enough of a surprise factor with the jumpers to allow us to catch them off guard. But just be careful."

"Yeah, they're using human ammunition, so be extra careful. I want everyone out alive, please." Nods all around. I guess they all wanted to get out alive too.

Logan went on to cover plan A and then plan B for the rest of the team. My team, though, had only one mission. Get Mom out of there.

Fast.

CHAPTER 35

Everyone moved together, the jumpers taking us all to the site in small batches. Although weighed down by my old, ratty satchel filled to the brim with ammo and weapons, I moved fast, light on my feet. I drew on my panther senses, allowing night-sight to filter through, ignoring the burn of the physical change.

The chilly early morning air created visible clouds as I exhaled. I tried to breathe out into the crook of my elbow and noticed Illyria doing the same. She didn't seem at all annoyed with being split up from the general. We'd been deposited outside the building, near the fence, and hid behind stacks of wet wooden pallets. Rain had moistened the tarred ground between us and the south entrance, which happened to be a solid metal door with a giant metal padlock looped into the catcher. Two Wraiths guarded the door, taking turns walking the length of the building and then returning.

Hooded and shadowed, we couldn't make out their faces, not even in the reflection of the lights on the puddles dotting the ground. The warehouse itself was a giant building constructed of brick and large multi-paned windows. Here and there, a pane was shattered, probably street kids chucking stones, but mostly the building looked intact. Lights were on inside, and every so often, a shadow passed over the sodden road as a Wraith guard paced his station inside.

Illyria and I crouched and watched the guards, waiting for Logan's signal. We'd set our watches, but he planned to give the signal over the wireless feed just in case. I met Illyria's gaze and pointed at the guard on the left, then to me. I'd take him down when the time came. She nodded.

A few minutes later, the guards swapped position and now my target was sitting while Illyria's was pacing up and down, splashing in the pooled water. So much for well-laid plans. I looked at her over my shoulder and found she'd focused on the guards, her eyes flitting back and forth between the two.

I lifted my bow, aiming left, while Illyria aimed her pistol right. Just when I thought it was past time to move, Logan's voice sounded in my ear. Call for attention. The pacing guard was inches within my sight. I pulled a veil of calm over me, listening to my heartbeat as it slowed. Finger on the trigger, getting the guard in my sights. Seconds later, my phone vibrated softly in my jacket pocket. Sunrise. And Logan's voice whispered, "Now." I adjusted my aim and pulled the trigger.

The bullet hit the Wraith's neck with a soft thud, no louder than the tap of a heel on a carpet. The guard dropped slowly to his knees, then slumped forward, his hand hitting a puddle of water with a flat splash. I winced and ducked down behind the pallets, not waiting to see his final demise. Peering over at Illyria's target, I saw a Wraith leaning against the door, his head hanging forward as if he'd just fallen asleep. Seconds later, he began to disintegrate, his body breaking into tiny little particles of solid blackness. The shadows danced around him as his body began to deflate, the Wraith cloak suddenly all that was left of the guard. I watched the cloak fall straight to the ground in a silent splash of fabric.

The Rebel leader turned her eyes to me and grinned, then gave me a quick thumbs-up. I smiled in response, wondering how it was that she remained unaffected after watching the death of a fellow Wraith. Even if Collins were dying at my feet, I'd feel something to mark his death. Maybe her lack of emotion was because she was a woman bred of war, had probably spent most of her life in the midst of battle.

We counted down the seconds to the next phase of the mission. Moments later, Logan gave the go-ahead, and Illyria and I scuttled across the wet tar and pasted ourselves against the wall beside the dead guard.

I rifled through the cloak, grabbed the weapons, which amounted to three pistols, and snatched up the fat key that had hung on a thick chain around his neck. All done, I handed the key to Illyria and kept a panther eye out while she jiggled it in the lock and snapped the padlock open. She slid it out carefully, then dropped it onto the pile of fabric that had once been a Wraith.

She pulled the door, the slit of light growing ever larger as she opened it wider to slide inside. After a quick, "We're going in," to Logan on the wireless, I followed her through the slim opening, then pulled the door shut behind me as gingerly as I could.

The door snapped closed with a click that sounded deathly loud to my oversensitive ears. When no guards came running, I figured we'd bought ourselves some time. The layout of the warehouse was simple. Three floors with two stairwells, each on the north and the south ends.

Illyria and I ignored the stairs and headed right, toward the refrigerators. Inside, the warehouse appeared abandoned, but that was probably only the appearance of the ground floor. The building looked like it had been abandoned a while back, the distribution floor empty except for a few broken pallets and some empty cardboard boxes strewn about.

Nothing moved.

Illyria and I tiptoed slowly, silently across the floor toward a large set of double doors. The doors were set with frosted glass that annoyed me. But Illyria seemed unaffected, just vanished through the wall beside the door, then reappeared to give me the okay.

She also gave me the chills.

Seeing her pass through a solid wall, even knowing she was a Wraith, made my stomach turn. I refocused my attention, dialing up my panther senses. My inner feline seemed to sense the urgency of the situation and clawed at me to let her free. It was strange that suddenly she had the urge for freedom, but now was not the time.

Illyria was about to open the door when I put my hand on hers and keyed up my hearing. There, I knew I'd heard something. The soft fall of a heel on concrete. The hiss of breath, almost silent, but not to my ears. I lifted a finger to my lips and moved away from the door, crouching beside a wall that I hoped was far enough away that the guard wouldn't see me the moment he came through the doorway. I didn't want to use my guns yet, and the crossbow's silence was perfect. As soon as the door opened, I let loose the arrow. Only afterward did I consider that the Wraith might actually have been Wren'do.

Logan hadn't told me when he and the general would be entering the building. As the Wraith guard sank to the ground, I lifted my collar, holding the microphone to my lips. "I just took down another guard. Please tell me Wren'do isn't anywhere on the ground floor."

"You're clear," was all Logan said.

Satisfied that the tendrils of smoky blackness disappearing into the ether didn't belong to Illyria's right-hand man, I followed her through the doorway and left, down a short passage that from memory should run straight down the middle of the last third of the ground floor. At the south wall, we should reach a bank of commercial fridges.

We moved forward, me in the lead with my bow aimed

straight ahead, Illyria behind, ready to flit away if required to perform a silent kill. We reached the passage and I hugged the wall before peeping around the corner. It looked clear, but I still used my panther senses to see if anything alive was lurking around the place.

Nothing.

Seemed too easy.

I slipped around the corner and hurried along the corridor. I could make out the gray gleam of the metal refrigerator doors up ahead. Numerous doors led off the passage, all closed and everything deathly quiet. My heart slammed against my chest, screaming that something was wrong. I slowed and stood against the wall. Tilting my head, I whispered, "Something is off. Everyone stay alert."

"Any specifics?" asked Logan. The line was so clear I had to look beside me to make sure he wasn't standing right there.

"Just that it's been way too easy. Widd'en's men aren't stupid or sloppy."

"Okay, everyone on alert," Logan whispered, then fell to silence.

I edged forward, feeling Illyria move slowly with me. We'd reached the end of the corridor and now faced the bank of fridges. The path in front of them was empty, no guards, not a Wraith in sight.

I held onto my microphone and said, "Mel, which one?" I hoped she would know what I meant without me having to give specifics over the wireless.

"Third from the left," her voice whispered in my ear.

I followed her instruction, motioning for Illyria to follow. She kept close as I hurried to the door. I grabbed hold of the large metal handle and pulled hard. The door released with a soft whoosh, and I swung it open and rushed inside.

Maybe I should have entered slowly or looked around the square space with more care. Had I done that, I would have seen the empty bed, straps hanging off the sides, the IV stand sitting bare beside the bed. I stopped in front of the bed so suddenly that Illyria would have had to step sideways to avoid hitting me in the back.

Instead, she slammed straight into me, pushing me forward so hard that I fell forward onto the soiled mattress. "Illyria? What the hell?" I managed to get the words out, a strangled cry of disbelief and rage.

CHAPTER 36

She spun me around to face her, but I didn't register her
face. Instead, pain screamed up my side, and I gasped,
my hand lifting to my abdomen. Illyria stared at me as she shoved
her knife deeper. Her lips curled into a cold, menacing grimace as
she studied the expression on my face. There was no emotion I
was capable of hiding from her right now. As far as my training
went, I was far from military, further from mercenary.

My panther screamed for release, roused by the scent of
blood and the need to defend. She snarled, and I lost control as
my hands widened, my fingers thickened and furred, nails transformed into claws. I fought with my panther for control. I could
not give in to her now, not when she'd be vulnerable to the Rebel
leader.

It was all I could do to grab hold of Illyria's hand. I tried to
peel her fingers off, but she backhanded me so hard my neck
snapped backward and my teeth sank into my tongue. The taste
of copper flooded my mouth. Pain lanced through my tongue,
just like it streaked into my body as Illyria twisted the knife into
my side. I struggled for breath and stared at her, still confused,
still too slow to put it all together.

"Why?" I gasped the word out but didn't really care if she answered me. I was too busy struggling for control of my body as my panther kept fighting against my fragile hold.

Illyria brought her face close to me, ensuring she kept to my left, away from my microphone. In my ear, Logan was yelling for me to tell him what happened. But I suddenly cared why she'd done it. So I waited.

She took her time, her breath hissing in my ear. "You think you're so clever, Hunter. You have no idea who you are dealing with. I would never have known who you really were if you didn't tell my messenger the truth. Now we don't need your mother. And now we have you." Her gray skin gleamed in the fluorescent light inside the metal-walled room. Her black demon eyes glared at me, and I wanted to laugh. Grams was going to be happy to say *I told you so*, and I wasn't planning to hold it against her.

I struggled for breath, managing to spit out my next few words. "But why betray us? What's in it for you? I thought you were helping us fight Widd'en's army?"

"That's where you're mistaken, my dear Hunter. Widd'en meant more to me than anything in the whole world. And you killed him. I had you in my sights from the moment I knew who you were."

"I don't understand. You've been killing Widd'en's men. Why kill the army that you follow?"

"Widd'en's men are weak, misguided. They refuse to answer to a woman, even though I am their rightful master."

"That's not possible. Widd'en would have had a second-in-command." I was speaking slowly, stalling for time, but she was lost in her thoughts.

"The army doesn't work like that. The reigning lord hands commandership down to his bloodline. Do you understand now?" she asked, spitting the words out against my cheek.

"You're Widd'en's daughter." I gasped, slowly losing

consciousness, my heartbeat barely a flutter. My fingers were slick with blood as she continued to twist the knife in my wound.

"Ah, the Hunter is smart too."

"You're wasting your time. Logan will have the team here in minutes."

"Not if Wren'do has already eliminated them. And Wren'do is very efficient."

"So is Logan," said a rough voice from behind Illyria. She spun around, letting go of the handle of her knife.

Logan stood behind her. Everything moved in slow motion as I wondered how he'd gotten there. Was Logan a jumper? Then the air shifted beside me, orange embers swirling around and around to form the sexy Saleem. I smiled, but I was pretty sure it looked more like a grimace of pain.

He caught me as my legs finally gave out. "Hold on, Kai," he whispered as he jumped me out of the fridge and into my apartment.

~

WHEN KAI HAD SAID something was off, Logan had known it in his bones. He and Wren had been stationed on the rooftop on the next building, watching as best they could. The view to the driveway was clear, and he'd seen Lily and Anjelo take out the guards with a swift and silent ease that had impressed him. Perhaps Omega should be looking at those two as well as Kai.

From his vantage point, he could see the south and west ends of the building as well. He'd watched Kai and the Wraith Rebel leader enter the building without a hitch. But when Kai began to suspect things were a little too easy, Logan was forced to reassess their progress and had to admit she was right.

That could only mean that someone Kai had divulged information to was selling info to Widd'en's men. Logan stiffened, glancing over at the Wraith general beside him. Wren had barely said two words to him since they'd scrambled up the south fire escape and taken up position.

Right now, Logan could trust no one.

He shifted a little to ensure he had the Wraith in his full sights, ensuring the Wraith would be unable to get the drop on him. Then he fished his cell phone out of his pocket and sent a text to Saleem. *Sec yr loc meet me asap.* And he hoped the Djinn would know what he meant.

Minutes later, as Kai made progress toward the refrigerators, Saleem and Iain shimmered into solidity behind the Wraith and hunkered down beside an air-conditioning fan.

The wireless crackled with Kai's shocked voice. "Illyria? What the hell?"

The Wraith moved, sliding around to grab hold of Logan, but the general didn't get far. Saleem's first bullet hit him in the upper back, the second at the base of his skull. If the poison wasn't meant to kill, the second bullet would certainly have done the job.

Instead, Logan saw that Saleem had used the Wraith gun Illyria had given Kai. Kai had paid little attention to the weapon, and Saleem must have grabbed it at some point. *Good call, Djinn,* thought Logan. *We might need this dirt bag to squeeze him for info.*

Moments later, he heard Kai ask, "Why?" Her struggle to speak was clear, and Logan's gut twisted with fear. What had the Wraith done to her? The pain in Kai's voice was enough to confirm she'd been injured in some way.

Everyone on the wireless was privy to Kai's words, and one look at Saleem's and Iain's faces said they weren't wasting time either. Saleem motioned to Iain to wait for him, and Kai's brother gave him a curt nod. Then the Djinn held out a hand to Logan, jumping him to the yard outside the south entrance as Kai said, "I don't understand. You've been killing Widd'en's men. Why kill the army that you follow?"

Logan's heart raced. The flow of the conversation only

confirmed that Illyria wasn't intending to leave Kai behind. She had some plan to abduct Kai, and Logan wasn't going to let that happen. No fucking way.

They entered the building using the same door as Kai and the Wraith, headed right, and slipped through the double doors. Left then right then straight ahead.

"That's not possible. Widd'en would have had a second-in-command," said Kai in his ear. He knew she was stalling for time. Smart girl.

"You're Widd'en's daughter," Kai's voice echoed in his ear both from the wireless and echoing from inside the fridge, and Logan's muscles stiffened. This was getting worse by the second.

"Ah, the Hunter is smart too."

Logan and Saleem slipped inside the room

"You're wasting your time. Logan will have the team here in minutes." Kai was speaking, but she looked like she was about to pass out.

Illyria was standing close to her, her hand at Kai's side red with blood. The Wraith had her back to Logan, so confident that her plans wouldn't be thwarted. "Not if Wren'do has already eliminated them. And Wren'do is very efficient."

Sorry, bitch, this is not your day, he thought.

Then he spoke aloud. "So is Logan."

As Illyria turned, Logan moved toward her. She grabbed the gun at her waist and raised her hand, but he kept moving. Saleem appeared beside Kai and spirited her away.

The Wraith managed to get off one shot before Logan pulled the trigger.

The bullet hit Illyria's forehead dead center.

CHAPTER 37

*L*ogan watched as Kai tossed and turned. Her pain couldn't be relieved with normal drugs, and it would be a waste of time to procure the special pain relief she'd need as a Walker.

All they could do now was watch and wait until her fever broke. She'd been unconscious most of the day now. Ivy had confirmed that Illyria's knife had been laced with poison.

Logan sighed and rubbed his eyes. He was holding on to the faintest hope that Kai's run-in with the Wraith-sword poison would strengthen her body against this one.

The apartment reeked of tension. But the one person Logan had expected to lash out at him had merely thanked him and slapped him on the shoulder. His heart twisted at Iain's reaction, reminding Logan that he still had history with the Walker.

He left Iain with Kai and returned to the dining table. Cassie and Larsson had stuck around for a while before being called out on a mission for Sentinel, which left the rest of them waiting around for Kai to wake up.

Ivy touched his arm as he took a seat. "Don't worry too much, dear. She'll be well enough soon. She's a strong woman, your Kai."

Logan nodded at Ivy, giving her a small smile, but it was very disconcerting to have her call him dear when she was sizzling hot and looked not a day older than forty. The woman had to be at least sixty. Logan had to wonder if Walkers were part immortal. Something he needed to discuss with Kai.

He needed to think about something else or he would soon go crazy with the waiting. He cleared his throat. "Mel. Thanks for coming back. I was actually hoping you would."

Mel sat across from him and nodded. She looked tired and worried, and he knew Kai's injury had gotten to her. "What do you need?" she asked, getting straight to the point.

"We need you to track Celeste one more time. This time there is no Illyria to betray us. And I think it's best to move as fast as we can. They won't expect it—the last thing they'll expect is a full-scale rescue mission. Especially when they think Kai is injured and poisoned to boot."

"That's what they think. They obviously know nothing about Walker physiology or immunization practices," said Kai as she walked slowly out of her room.

Everyone stared at her in silence.

"What?" she asked, laughing softly as she slipped onto the one free stool at the kitchen counter.

"Are you freaking insane?" Lily asked as she got to her feet. Two bright spots on her cheeks revealed how livid she was.

"I'm fine, Lily. I promise. I wouldn't get out of bed if I wasn't."

A number of people in the room snorted, including Logan, and Kai's expression changed as she studied the faces watching her. Then she looked at Logan and asked, "So what's the plan?"

Logan got to his feet and walked to her. "The plan is for you to go back to bed and recover." She lifted her gaze slowly to his face, and Logan saw the warning in her eyes. He hid his smile and slowed his steps.

Kai pushed off the stool and reached for the hem of her T-shirt. She was wearing low-slung yoga pants and a fitted tee, and the sight of her bare hips sent sensations rippling through Logan that shouldn't really be there when staring at an invalid.

She bared her abdomen, then turned to the right so everyone could see her wound.

No, not a wound.

A scar.

Mel gasped, and Logan knew exactly how she felt. The only people that didn't look surprised were the Walkers in the room. And Logan, of course, having seen Kai's healing processes before.

"Kai? Are you sure you're fine for this?" Mel's face was still pale with shock as she met Kai's gaze.

Kai nodded. "Walkers just heal fast, and alphas heal faster." She shrugged and then sat back down. Logan retreated to his chair as Kai swiveled to face the Tracker. "You up for tracking Mom again?"

Mel nodded. "The key will be fine unless you have something else."

Kai glanced at Iain and then at Ivy, who both shook their heads and shrugged. "Okay then. The key it is. Do you want to do it in the room?" she asked the Tracker who smiled and followed Kai.

They didn't close the door, but the room provided a little privacy for Mel. Logan paced while they were busy. Right now, all he wanted to do was shake Kai for giving him such a scare. On the other hand, shaking wasn't the first thing that came to came to mind when he thought of what he wanted to do to her right now.

Logan shook his head and paced some more.

CHAPTER 38

As soon as I entered the room, I headed to the bedside table. Mel sank onto the mattress while I dug Mom's key out of my bedside drawer. Before I handed it to her, I asked, "Would you rather be alone? Do you need anything?"

She grinned and shook her head, sending her wavy black tresses bouncing all over her shoulders. Her hair looked unruly, as if she'd been running her fingers through it over and over again. My stomach tightened as I realized I must have been the cause of her worries. In fact, I'd worried everyone who sat in my apartment right now.

I handed the key to Mel and sank down beside her. The sun was streaming through the window. How long had I been in a recovery stupor? I listened to Mel's even breathing as she slipped into her astral projection, and my heart thudded with expectation. Where were they keeping her? Would we be able to get in and out easily?

I tried to distract myself by thinking about those last minutes when Illyria had tried to kill me. I had to admit that even now, even having heard her own admission, I still found it hard to believe. I wasn't sure if my death had been her goal or if she'd just wished to incapacitate me. The poison on the knife would have killed a human, but she knew very well I was a Walker.

What she didn't know was that I'd suffered the effects of Wraith obsidian poison before, and it seemed my body had built its own defenses against it. If in fact it was obsidian poison. I wondered if maybe she'd tried the Black Lake waters, but Wren'do would have informed her of my non-deadly swim. The fact that the Wraiths had actively used any poison against me was a concern. Would they advance to using it on humans? I shuddered to think how devastating that would be.

I'd woken briefly when Iain was sitting beside me, and he'd told me what Wren had revealed after the people at Omega had completed their interrogations. Illyria was the illegitimate daughter of Lord Widd'en, a rebellious member of the royal family. Illyria's mother had kept the secret for years and only revealed it to her husband Lord Wrathyan when the girl was being forced to marry. Apparently, her mother could not bear the thought of her daughter having to go through an arranged marriage the way she had.

Illyria found solace with her natural father, although Wrathyan hadn't formally denounced her. The marriage proposal still hung over her head, but Illyria had abandoned it all to follow in her father's footsteps as leader of the Rebels. She idolized her father and had been driven near insane when he'd been killed.

Everything she'd done since had been a means to finding her father's killer, who until I had revealed myself, had been assumed to be Celeste. I was thankful I'd taken the weight of that responsibility on my own shoulders, but I still feared for my mother's life. I recalled the Wraith's words, that my mother was no longer needed. The memory chilled me, brought my attention straight out of my thoughts and back to Mel.

My timing was excellent. Mel stirred, her face pale as she blinked and reconnected her mind with her body. "You all right?"

I asked, leaning toward her. Mel nodded, although she looked afraid. "What's wrong? Did you find her?"

"I'm fine." But her expression told me otherwise.

Fear spun through my mind, making me lightheaded. I forced myself to maintain some semblance of calm and waited for the tracker to speak. Then Mel sighed and leaned her elbows on her knees.

"We just have a bit of a problem."

"Which is?" I asked, trying to be patient.

"She's being held in a secure facility in the Nevada desert." Her words came out in one breath.

"Area 51?" I asked, my voice dying on an uncomfortably high note.

Mel shook her head, then stopped and met my gaze. "You know, I'm not sure exactly. I was inside, managed to get around the place a little. But it's not like I had coordinates or anything."

"Okay, so what do we have to go on?" I asked as I rose. "You want to tell everyone?"

Mel nodded and walked with me back into the dining room. I cleared my throat and said, "Right, let's do this."

Mel slid back into her seat beside Drake and took a breath. "So Celeste is being held in a facility out in the Nevada desert. She seems to be healthy and clean. She's still weak and is being held in a secure room. The facility looks a lot like a hospital or medical center."

"Guards?" asked Logan, his brows furrowed in concentration.

"Two at her door and two guarding a set of doors entering the wing she's in. Security is tight, key cards for doors and elevators, cameras everywhere. It's underground, so one way in one way out. We don't know what facility it is, so schematics are out of the question."

"I'm guessing you couldn't tell the specific location?" asked Logan.

"No. I couldn't see anything on the surface that would act as a significant landmark. Just desert and cacti."

"Guards on the surface?"

Mel nodded. "Two in a hut at the entrance to the facility about a mile away. And two in a small office attached to the entrance. You go to the security desk; they check you out and allow you to pass through. Inside is just a single elevator."

"Then that isn't the only way out," I said.

Logan nodded. "Yes. But there should be a maintenance entrance for larger equipment and maybe even supplies."

"If there is, they didn't bring her through that way. I tracked her through the top entrance."

"What if we got in and then tried to find the alternative exit, just in case we need it. If we're careful, we may not need it."

Logan pursed his lips and nodded. "I wish I could say it would likely be an easy in-and-out, but I can't. Not for a facility like this. And especially not for something underground."

Logan's words were certainly not designed to make me feel better. I rubbed my forehead. "Okay, so we know she's fine and not being tortured. She's alive. That's a bloody good sign."

"The problem is exactly who the hell are these guys and what are they doing with her? I didn't see a single Wraith anywhere I tracked." Mel sounded frustrated as a frown wrinkled her brow.

The silence in the room was tangible as so many minds considered so many possibilities.

I glanced at Grams. "An experimental facility?"

She frowned, but all the same, the color drained from her already pale features. Her blue eyes had darkened with worry so much that I could have sworn they were black. "You think Widd'en's men sold Celeste to an experimental lab?" Her voice shivered as she spoke and her gaze flitted to Iain who sat across from me, equally pale. At least he didn't look like it was so unbelievable.

I glanced back at Grams and nodded. "What else could it be?

It's not as if the Wraiths have the means to build such a thing anyway. A facility like Mel described is so Area 51 it's either governmental or heavily funded private."

"What would a governmental agency want with your mother?" asked Anjelo, shaking his head as if he couldn't believe we were even having this conversation. I'd almost forgotten he was there. He and Lily had been strangely silent, and I assumed my injury had taken its toll on them.

I cleared my throat before I said, "Mom is a Hunter. She's a Mage. She has powers similar to mine, including the glow when killing Wraiths. Any government agency investigating the paranormal would kill to study a paranormal like her." My voice and my words were harsh, partly to mask the emotion ripping up my insides. The thought of anyone experimenting on my mother made my panther snarl. But I refused to sugarcoat it. Everyone in the room deserved to be made aware of the risks. "It also means that going into a facility like this is more dangerous than anything you've ever done. We're all paranormals here. Each of us would be a scientist's delight. We have to be well organized. And we can't get caught."

"Okay." Logan got to his feet. "Let me do some digging. Maybe I can find information on similar structures. Perhaps that will give us a good idea of how something like that is built and where the likely emergency exits would be. If anything, at least it will give us a better idea of what to look for once we get inside."

I slid off the stool again and studied the table full of people who'd come to support me. For a moment, I was overwhelmed and had to swallow back my tears.

"Okay, everyone get some rest. Once Logan gets back with some schematics, we can plan a way inside. I'll message you all with the time to meet."

"We're going as soon as possible, right?" asked Anjelo. He was tossing his phone from one hand to another, and I knew it meant he was worried.

"Yeah. I'd go right now if I could, but yes, we aren't going to waste any time about this."

Anjelo sat back, looking satisfied. He'd kept his new look after he returned home, and although I liked it, I missed his super-short crew cut. He nodded and got to his feet. Chairs slid on wood and fabric rustled as everyone took that as their cue to move.

Soon, only Logan and Grams were left, and the apartment felt abandoned. Logan moved toward me, threw an arm around my waist, and gave me a hug. Despite my weakened state, my skin sizzled where he touched me.

"I have to go," he whispered in my ear. Pots clattered in the kitchen as Grams began dinner. Logan placed a heated kiss on my neck and said, "When I get back, I'm going to make sure you know exactly how you make me feel."

"And how exactly do I make you feel?" I whispered, our mouths inches from each other.

"Oh, you'll have to wait until I return. But if you want an idea, it's something along the lines that even when you're weak and broken, you still manage to get my blood burning."

"Mmm. Is that a good thing?"

"Definitely a good thing."

"I should get weak and broken more often, then."

He grabbed my ass and squeezed, simultaneously pressing me against his body, his arousal firm against my hip. "Don't you get any ideas. I quite like my women in one piece, thank you."

More clattering from the kitchen made me grin. Logan released my butt and kissed me firmly on the neck before hurrying to the door.

His woman indeed.

Logan returned within a few hours with plans he'd found in Omega's archives. "What are these plans for?" I asked as he set them at the far end of the table.

"If I tell you, I'd have to kill you," he said, his voice bland. Grams and I both rolled our eyes. We were occupied setting the table with deep plates and tableware. "What's for dinner?" he asked, staring at the pots on the stove. He looked like a man dying for a meal.

"Spaghetti Bolognese, and don't change the subject." I glared at him.

Logan grinned and headed to the kitchen, giving me a light shrug. "I actually have no idea. I didn't waste time trying to connect the coded number reference on the bottom."

He washed up, then waited beside the pot for Grams to hand him a deep serving bowl, which he proceeded to fill with the spaghetti sauce. Steam swirled around them as I watched Grams point him to a large colander in the sink. Logan seemed very domesticated as he dropped the pasta into the colander to drain, then tossed it in olive oil as Grams poured. The look on Grams' face said she approved.

So did I.

A wash of dizziness flowed over me, and I sank into the nearest chair, leaving the rest of the work to them. Soon, we settled in to eat, and the next few minutes were filled with "Pass the pasta" or "Sauce" or "Salad" as was required.

I was grating Parmesan very liberally over my plate when Logan said, "I have no idea how you can eat that stuff."

"Why not? It makes the pasta taste delicious," I said, breathing in the fragrant steam rising from my plate.

"Because it tastes like feet."

I almost splattered my food all over the table. "Feet? How the hell does Parmesan taste like feet?" I asked, laughing at him.

"Well, it smells like feet. Smelly feet," he insisted as he shoved a fork into his pasta and twirled it.

I shook my head. "Your loss, then. More for me," I said as I wrapped my mouth around a forkful of pasta goodness.

WITH THE TABLE CLEARED, we gathered around the plan drawings that Logan had brought over. Two-dimensional drawings of the building occupied the top left corner, while different floors were mapped out in finer detail on the rest of the map. Whatever this place was, it looked huge.

"Omega stores their maps by type of structure, so this one was filed as subterranean. Unfortunately, I would have wasted too much time trying to figure out the ID and location of the facility. I figured we didn't really need to know that."

"True," I said, placing a glass on one corner to prevent the map from rolling away.

We studied the different levels, air ducts, elevators, emergency routes, water purification, generator rooms. Everything about the way a subterranean building was built should have fascinated me, but all I could think of was Mom and if she was all right and still in one piece.

Once Logan finished studying the layout, he said, "Right. I think you can let everyone know. We can head out tonight. Facilities like this usually house the staff, so we can't guarantee the place will be abandoned at two in the morning, but it would certainly reduce the risk of being seen."

"At least we have the jumpers to case the place for us. Having them certainly makes things a lot easier," I said, nodding and thanking Ailuros that I knew a few paranormals.

THE DUNES SURROUNDING the facility sloped high enough to provide sufficient cover for us. Mel and Saleem had taken turns bringing Drake, Logan, and I to the location. I was still a little unsettled after Grams got a last-minute call from Sentinel. It didn't sit well, especially when I was unable to contact Cassandra or Larsson.

All Sentinel agents seemed to have been called off this mission at the last possible minute, and it made me suspicious. And worse, without the addition of Larsson, we were forced to leave Lily and Anjelo behind.

Logan had charged them with keeping all weapons primed and at the ready in case Mel or Saleem returned for additional supplies. Both were unhappy with having been left behind, but it made no sense to take them with us and give the two jumpers additional work during team extraction.

The one person who had joined us was the enigmatic Drake. Mel had hinted at a unique ability to thwart an opponent while fighting that could come in handy. And she'd insisted that between her and Saleem, two jumps each to get us to safety would be fine.

Now, Logan, Saleem, Drake, and I gathered in the sands and waited for Mel to scope out the area and find a place to transport us to. She held Mom's portal key in her hand, just to give her the extra juice to project. Then she pocketed the key and nodded.

Dressed head to toe in black, with our faces hidden behind black ski masks, the darkness hid our movements, but who knew if the owners of this facility had invested in thermal sensors, which would have already detected us by now?

"Let's get moving," I said as Logan also shifted restlessly and glanced at his watch.

Mel nodded. "Let me just show Saleem where to go." She glanced at the Djinn and held out her hand. He took it and they disappeared. Seconds later, they reappeared, seeming unaffected by the jump. I wasn't certain that I'd ever stop being amazed by their ability to teleport.

Mel and Saleem jumped the whole team directly to the floor Mom was being held on. To get to it, we would have had to pass the guards that watched the entrance. Thankfully, bypassing them was easy enough.

We slipped into a room immediately to our left, and Logan turned to face us. He patted his bag and said, "Saleem and I will look for the generator and set these detonators to time with the extraction. We'll do the same with the elevator. Make sure nobody can use it to get to this floor. Then we'll eliminate whatever guards there are around here. Keep an ear out on the comms at all times. Kai, Mel, and Drake, go for Celeste. Mel, first priority is Celeste. Extract her first, then come back for the rest."

Mel nodded, then looked at Saleem. "Saleem knows where we'll be."

Logan nodded.

With everyone set, Saleem held out his hand to me. He was ready to jump when Mel put a hand on his chest to stop him. "Wait. I just projected to check things out and there's someone in the observation room. We need them incapacitated. I think it's one of the scientists or technicians."

"Just incapacitated?" asked Saleem.

"Yes, Djinn. We didn't come here to go on a killing spree," she said, narrowing her eyes at him.

He just grinned at her with mischief in his eyes.

"Fine. Logan and I will go and see what we can do about *incapacitating* them," he said, his eyes still teasing Mel even as the both of them disappeared in an explosion of orange embers and ash.

Waiting for them seemed interminable. Pain lanced through my palms and I had to force myself to unclench my fingers. My panther had responded to my frustration again, finding her way through my defenses without my knowledge and lengthening her claws with such ease I hadn't registered the change.

At last they returned, both looking smug. Mel and I shared a narrow-eyed glance that didn't bode well for the men in our lives. Both took the hint and sobered up, which I ended up finding too funny.

"All clear," said Logan as Saleem came to stand with me.

Mel held out her hand to Drake, and then we all disappeared into thin air, arriving in the small viewing room attached to Mom's room. Saleem left us there, disappearing almost instantly. The viewing room was filled with equipment, monitors, and various machines keeping tabs on Mom's vitals.

Through the glass screen, the shadows hid most of Mom's face as she slept, but enough of her features were visible for me to heave a sigh of relief. She looked fine. I stepped toward the door, but Mel tapped my shoulder. I glanced back at her, and she whispered, "Wait. We need to make sure nobody is inside the room with her."

I nodded as Mel disappeared. She returned a moment later with a relieved smile. "All clear. Drake, you keep a watch on the door and alert us."

Drake nodded and we left him, entering Mom's room silently. We reached the bed and got a good look at her as she lay there, unconscious. Her black hair was held away from her face by a wide elastic band, her skin pasty and dry. At first it looked like she was being given a blood transfusion, and fear rippled through me like an earthquake. But when I looked closer, fury replaced that fear. They were bleeding her. When I glanced at Mel, her expression mirrored mine.

We scanned the rest of the equipment, and then I touched the microphone at my collar. "What time was the power hit set for?"

"Two forty-five," said Logan in my ear.

"We need to reschedule. We need to wait for the power pulse."

"Okay, we'll wait for your signal."

"What are we waiting for?" asked Mel as soon as I finished talking to Logan.

I pointed at the wires connected to Mom. "These look like they're monitoring her heartbeat. And the others seem to be measuring her vitals. If we detach her, then it would set off any number of alarms."

Mel was already nodding, "And if we wait for power shut-down, they might think that's the reason for the lack of measurements coming from your mom. It should buy us some time. Good thinking."

I merely looked back at my unconscious mother. I couldn't even take the chance of waking her up in case waking vitals would call someone out to check on her. I motioned to the outer room, and Mel and I tiptoed through the doorway.

To find a guard standing in the middle of the room, staring at the two empty chairs where he would have expected two medical staff to be. He flinched when we entered the room, his eyes going wide as he reached for both his walkie-talkie and his gun.

A finger tapped his shoulder, and as the guard spun around, he lifted his gun from its holster. As his hand came up to aim his weapon at Drake, both the guard and I gasped.

Drake slammed a fist onto the guard's hand and then lost all solidity, transforming into liquid smoke. Just in time. Having lost his gun, the guard, now infuriated, threw a left hook. And went right through where Drake had been standing, his hand drawing trails of smoke with it. As his hand passed through the black smoke, the guard made an odd sound, something somewhere between confusion and fear.

Drake took the opportunity to solidify and plant his fist into the man's throat. The blow was loud, and I winced. When the guard fell, both Mel and I caught him before he hit the ground.

"You didn't have to kill him," Mel snapped at Drake, who was fast becoming solid again. And then I knew what he was. A Gargoyle. And the only way I could tell was he'd lost his glamor as he solidified back into human form, revealing inky black swirling markings on gray skin. My jaw dropped, and Drake gave me a sweet smile before turning his attention back to Mel. "Broke a couple bones in his throat, yes. Killed him? No."

"Okay then. That's totally fine, isn't it?" asked Mel as if she were scolding a five-year-old.

Drake ignored her, and she just huffed. "How long 'til the power goes out?"

"Ten minutes," I said, glancing at my watch. I sighed and peered back into the room at Mom. "It's going to be a long ten minutes."

Time passed so slowly I felt like I would explode. Every time I looked at my watch, it seemed only thirty seconds had passed. I shook my head and wondered if I needed to learn a little more patience.

Might do me some good.

Something changed in the air, my panther picking up a jump in the frequency the generator set off. Then we were plunged into darkness. My panther sight kicked in immediately, and for the first time I didn't fight as my feline took over my senses.

"Let's go, Mel," I said as I ran into the room. I removed all the tubes and electric nodes from the body, moving as quickly as I could without hurting her. At last I reached the lure in her inner elbow.

As I began to remove it, Mel whispered, "How the hell are you seeing all of that? I can't see a thing in this pitch black."

I chuckled. "Sorry. It's my panther sight. Works well in the dark."

"Ah, that certainly explains it," said Mel as she waited beside me, unable to do much else.

As soon as I was done, I caught Mel's arms. "Here. She's ready. Take her home."

Mel nodded. "Okay, see you in a bit." She disappeared, and with panther sight, it was interesting what I saw. The air parted as if it were made up of beams of red-and-white light. Mel's body shifted, turned into shimmering particles, and melted into the streaks of red as if she were as much a part of it as it was of her.

Impressive.

I left the empty bed and hurried to Drake in the observation room just as the generators kicked in, the low-powered lighting a sickly yellow glow in the observation room.

"They gone?"

I nodded and spoke into the microphone. "Number one is home," I said, then felt ridiculous. But something made me wonder whether it was a good idea to use names or specifics even if we thought the wireless was untappable.

I sighed. The effects of my injury were slowly taking their toll on my body. All this jumping must be wreaking havoc with my wounds. I was about to sit on the counter behind me when a shadow closed in outside the door.

"Drake," I hissed softly, but he'd seen the potential visitor too.

There was no time to move and hide, so I remained where I was as the door opened with a soft whoosh. A man entered the room, his eyes on the clipboard he held in front of him. He'd walked within almost ten feet of me before he realized anything was wrong.

When he looked up, I stifled a gasp.

Our eyes met, mirroring in green.

The man staring at me was supposed to be dead.

"Uncle Niko?"

CHAPTER 40

He gave me a warm smile and was about to respond to me when Drake hit him hard at the back of his head. Niko crumpled into an untidy heap at my feet.

I stared at him, mouth hanging open, then slowly turned my gaze to Drake who was standing stock still, watching me with the oddest expression. "Uncle?"

"Yeah, long story," I said, my voice quivering, my heart hammering. How could he still be alive? There were a few new scars on his face and neck, but what did that really mean? Had someone saved him after he fell into the flaming pool? I'd been so sure he was dead when Widd'en kicked him in.

But Niko was most certainly not dead.

Drake bent and dragged him around the wider island desk, out of sight of the door and safe. "I'm assuming we need to extract him too?"

"Of course we have to," I said, feeling a little at odds with Niko's unexpected presence. Sure, we had to take him with us. I had to think of Grams, seeing as how I was looking at her son lying there unconscious.

"But he's working for these people," Drake protested, still looking thoroughly confused.

"We don't even know who he's working for," I retorted. And then it clicked.

Like a key turning into a lock, I recalled Illyria saying they had a capable scientist working on the ammo. Who better than Niko? No wonder she'd been reluctant to reveal his identity. And all the bloodletting they'd done to Mom in the warehouse? For all I knew, Niko was involved there too. "All I know is he needs to make reparation for what he's done. He's guilty of more than just experimenting on Mom. He has to pay for his crimes."

Drake grunted as he glared at the unconscious Walker.

"Oh, and just one more thing." Drake glanced up at me. "Don't let either Anjelo or Lily near him. If I know those two, they'll rip him to shreds."

"How do you know they'll do that?" Drake asked, clearly skeptical.

"Because that's exactly what I want to do to him right now."

I tamped down a grin as Drake threw me a startled look and lost his glamor just for a moment. As he regained his human looks, I leaned against the counter at last. My eyes fell on the file that lay open beside me. Someone must have been disturbed while filling in details in Mom's report. But it wasn't the report or the information on it that stopped me in my tracks.

It was the stationery the technician had used. I picked up the file and examined the paperwork to be sure. Then I sucked in a breath. "Drake?" I called without looking up from the file.

"What is it?" He came immediately, probably hearing the stark consternation in my voice.

I turned the file to face him. For a moment, he seemed confused, then annoyed, as if he thought I was playing games with him. He was about to look up at me when his gaze must have caught the letterhead and he stopped, mouth open and eyes wide. "You got to be fucking kidding me."

I had nothing to respond with, considering the Gargoyle had voiced my very thoughts with perfection.

"So? What are we going to do?" he asked, his voice as shocked as I felt.

And a voice behind us said, "Do about what?"

I spun around, the file still in my shaking hand. Saleem stood in front of me, looking endearingly confused. I forced myself to breathe. "We were getting worried. Mel's been gone a bit too long." I tried to keep my answer short. I had the tendency to ramble when I was lying.

Saleem shook his head sharply. "Don't worry. I'll take you home. Let's see what's keeping Mel." Then he turned to Drake, studying the Djinn, suspicion gleaming in his black eyes. "You mind waiting for me or Mel to come back?"

Drake glanced at me, and only when I gave him a quick nod did he say, "Sure."

Saleem gave him an odd look, clearly curious about the Gargoyle's strange behavior. Then he grinned at me and crooked his elbow. "Ready when you are, ma'am."

I forced a smiled onto my face, gripped the file in my hand, out of Saleem's sight, and took his elbow. Almost immediately, my stomach turned as if something were sucking the air out of me. Saleem's jumps were certainly more turbulent than Mel's.

We landed in my apartment just inside the front door. I didn't wait to speak to Saleem, just threw the file on the dining table and ran to my bedroom where my panther ears had picked up movement.

Mom lay in the bed, pale and still unconscious. Mel sat at the foot, silent and surly. Beside the door stood a man who I'd never seen before. He was burly and looked too strong for me to fight. My panther senses picked up Saleem's light tread through the floorboards. He was coming after me. I slipped one hand behind my back and waved it at the Djinn, hoping he'd see it and understand.

My spine remained stiff as I stared at the man by the door. "Who are you?" I asked coldly. And loudly. That should give Saleem enough warning.

"That is not important right now. At this time, our highest priority is to ensure you and the rest of your team are safe and not contaminated." There was a slight hesitation in his voice when he said the word *contaminated*.

"What?" I snapped at the man. "Are you going to give me some bullshit line about contamination? Who the hell are you?"

The man ignored me, then turned slowly to look into the dining area. I turned too, as if to see what he was looking at. When he met my eyes, I raised an eyebrow. "What?" I asked, determined not to make things easy.

"Where is the jumper?" His eyes never left mine.

"How should I know? He was here when I arrived. How else would I have gotten here?"

He didn't answer me, just tilted his head and spoke strangely, in much the same way I did when I spoke into my microphone. "The Hunter has returned. The jumper has left... No, no idea. I'd assume back to the facility to extract the rest of their team... Yes, sir. I'll let you know immediately." Then he fell silent, and I had the odd feeling he was restraining himself from saluting his absent superior.

I faced him and folded my arms. "So what is it you people want?"

"I'm sorry, ma'am. At the moment, I am not at liberty to say. Ms. Morgan here is also awaiting an answer. Which you will both get during debriefing."

I barely waited for him to finish speaking before I turned my back on him and headed to Mom's side. "How is she?" I asked as I brushed aside a lock of hair from her forehead.

I'd asked Mel, but the guard responded instead. "Her vitals are fine. She seems to be under the influence of some sort of drug."

My thoughts went straight to Niko, lying on the floor in the observation room. I stared at Mom, wondering if at any point she'd opened her eyes to see her brother-in-law experimenting on her. I had to force myself to concentrate on the guard's words as he continued to speak.

"We wanted to transfer her to our medical facility—"

Mel cut him off. "Ivy wouldn't let them," she said smugly.

She gave the guard a *take that* glare, and I had to laugh. "Grams told these jerks what to do and they listened?"

"They had to, or they would have gotten themselves into deep trouble," said Grams from the doorway. I twisted around and stared at her. It occurred to me that nothing that was happening was making the least bit of sense. "Come, girls. We need to talk."

We both got up and followed her out of the room. I was relieved to be out from under that guard's constant stare, but then I wasn't too sure about leaving Mom alone with him.

I hesitated in the doorway, then kept moving. Mel touched my arm as we headed to the lounge. "I think she'll be fine. They've taken good care of her until now."

"Yes," said Grams as she sat. "They will take good care of her."

"Who are *they* and what's going on?" I asked, not caring if she thought I was being rude.

"Mr. Ice over there is Jerry Winter. And 'they' are the security detail attached to the Supreme High Council."

My jaw dropped.

CHAPTER 41

"**W**hat are they doing here?" I asked, not bothering to hide my shock.

"They got wind that Celeste was in a bunker facility in Nevada."

"How did they get that information?" For the briefest moment, my eyes narrowed on her, and she laughed.

"It wasn't me, dear. Cassandra's phone was bugged. They saw your texts."

"That explains why she and Larsson never showed up," I said, sinking into the cushions at my back. I kept an eye on my open bedroom door, still unable to trust the stony guard. Suddenly, I stiffened. "Where's Lily and Anjelo?" The question came out edged with a hint of hysteria as I feared for their safety. We'd left them behind specifically to keep them out of harm's way.

"Don't worry, dear. The officials from the High Council spoke to the kids briefly, then sent them home. Even they don't think it's entirely necessary to arrest a couple of children."

"They're hardly children, Grams," I said wryly, trying to imagine Lily's and Anjelo's reaction to being referred to as children.

"You and I both know that. The High Council doesn't. Perhaps it's better they continue to believe that," Grams said a little sternly. "It seems you are responsible for those two now, Kai. I hope you make sure you keep them out of danger. One sojourn in the Wraith world should be enough for that young man."

I snorted. "If anything, it's juiced up his desire for adventure. I'm probably going to find it hard to get him to concentrate on school."

"Well, you do your best, Kai." Grams gave my open room door a quick glance.

I frowned, thinking of the remainder of my team. "Are they waiting here for Saleem and Logan?"

"Yes. They want to speak to both of them regarding the mission and what they saw."

"I don't think that would be a good idea," I said softly.

"Why not, dear? The High Council just wants to be sure Omega is still legitimate and that both those boys were involved only at your behest."

I heard Grams' words, but I got to my feet and went to the table. The file was still there, but it now lay open on the table. I was sure when I'd thrown it there if it had landed closed.

Saleem.

I decided at this point I didn't care. Let Logan and Saleem know what their organization was involved in, what their employers were doing to paranormals.

I picked up the file and turned on my heel, heading back to Grams. When I handed the file to her, I said, "Now, tell me what you make of that." Mel leaned over to peek into the file as well.

Her response was so similar to Drake's I had to laugh when she looked up at me with half-open mouth and wide eyes. "Tell me this isn't true."

"I'm afraid it is. It's right there for anyone to see. This facility certainly wasn't a secret from certain Omega employees," I said as concern rippled up and down my spine. Drake and Niko were still back there. Where would Saleem and Logan take them?

While Grams was studying the file, I caught Mel's gaze, then pretended to tuck my hair behind my ear. She gave me a sharp shake of her head. They'd taken her comms. But I still had mine, and I intended to use it.

I got to my feet. "Can I use your bathroom, Grams?" I asked, making a face in the direction of my room.

She waved me off, more interested in the file than my bathroom needs. I hurried over to Grams' room, closing her door. Once inside her bathroom, I turned on the tap and touched my microphone. "Logan," I said, my voice just a whisper.

"Kai, what's going on?" His voice held an edge of urgency that said he was borderline panicked. Good thing I'd thought to contact him, then.

I didn't answer. "Did you get Niko and Drake out?"

"Yes. They're at Drake's." From that, I assumed that would also be Mel's since she did say they lived in the same house.

"Good. The High Council is here. Just stay away until I tell you it's okay." My panther ears alerted me to the footstep as it hit the threshold of Gram's room. I tugged the microphone and earwig off and threw them in the toilet. Just as I reached to flush it, someone knocked so hard on the door that I jumped.

"What?" I asked angrily as I flushed. I waited only until I saw the comms disappear down the toilet, then flung the door open before turning my back and heading to the sink to wash my hands. "What the hell is your problem?" I flung over my shoulder. *Let Jerry think I'm pissed that he disturbed my pee.*

"Who were you talking to?" he asked, his eyes watchful.

"No one. You see anyone here?"

Jerry stared at me, his face implacable. I dried my hands and faced him. Then he leaned over to me, peered into both my ears, then checked my collar. He did all that without touching me.

That was a good thing.

Then he cast a suspicious glance at the toilet. He straightened, then said, "We would appreciate your full cooperation, Ms. Odel."

"Of course. You'll get it when you start telling me what the hell is going on."

Jerry blanched at the vicious edge to my voice. Neither my panther nor I had the patience for this.

Grams popped her head into the bathroom. "Are you two done here? This conversation can easily be held in the lounge," she said with a raised eyebrow.

Jerry exited meekly, and I grinned at her as I passed. When we entered the lounge, my heart stopped mid-beat. Logan, Saleem, Drake, and a still-unconscious Niko were gathered in the middle of the floor.

Grams, coming out of the room behind me, let out a sharp cry and ran to Niko's side. "Oh my, please tell me I'm not imagining this."

"No, Grams, you aren't imagining it," I said. Then I glared at Logan. "I thought I told you to stay the hell away from here?"

Behind me, I heard Jerry grunt something like, "I knew it."

Logan gave me a chilling glare. Uh-oh. That didn't bode well for me after all this nonsense was said and done. I'd pissed him off. And from the looks of it, Saleem was equally upset with me. "What? Not you too?" I asked. The glacial glares didn't warm even a degree. "I was just trying to protect you."

"Because of the file?" Logan asked.

"Yes," was all I was willing to say. I wasn't in any condition for a good fight. Maybe later, when I'd rested.

Logan's expression softened a little, and I took that as a good sign. Grams was fussing over Niko and beckoned Drake to help take her unconscious son to her bedroom. Once he was comfortable, they both returned, Grams with a worried look on her face.

I knew how she felt. There was no time to rejoice that her son was alive. The problem we faced right now was what was he doing for Omega and what did Omega want with Mom?

And what connection did Omega have with the Wraith rebellion?

"So what now?" asked Logan, his tone now unaffected and totally professional.

"High Council debrief," said Grams.

"Do they need Drake and me?" asked Mel, getting to her feet and giving her cell phone a glance. "I need to go. I have an ongoing case that I'm looking into, and something's just come up." She waved her phone in the air as if unsure what to do.

"Of course, you need to go, dear. I don't think the High Council will be too upset at your absence. You don't work for Omega."

Mel gave us all a weak smile and an equally weak wave before bustling out the door with her Gargoyle in tow. He gave me an odd look as they left, and my panther hearing picked up his words.

"Typical," he growled.

"What's typical?" Mel asked softly as their footsteps took them to the first flight of stairs down.

"Just when I find myself a nice, decent, hot woman, she happens to be taken."

Mel's tinkling laughter rang out as they descended the stairs, followed by a gruff, "Shut up," from the Gargoyle.

I was smiling to myself when I became aware they'd asked me a question. I glanced around the group. "What? What did I miss?"

"I was asking you if you prefer the High Council come here, or would you like to go to see them?"

"I'll go in. I don't want Mom disturbed."

Grams nodded. "Don't worry about her. They have a good doctor looking after her. And once that boy wakes up,"—she gave her room door a dark look that said Niko was in deep shit when he woke—" he's going to have some explaining to do. Especially regarding Celeste's treatment."

"He'll be awake soon. All he received was a blow to the back of the neck." My voice clearly was cold as I gave the door an even darker glare

Grams snorted. "That was less than what he deserved."

"Gee, please don't ever sit on a jury if I'm on trial for anything," said Logan, his eyes laughing.

Grams waved him off. "Will you two also go to HQ?"

They both nodded.

My stomach tightened. "But, Grams, what if they arrest them?" The thought had been bothering me ever since Grams had filled me in on the High Council's presence.

"What for? Just being employed by Omega? I think not."

"I suspect they're going use this opportunity to turn us into double agents," said Logan, his expression dark and worried.

"You know what my take on that is," said Saleem firmly. Something else was happening here and I had no clue what. *Mental note to ask Logan later.*

"So shall we get this over and done with?" Both nodded and Saleem offered each of us an arm.

CHAPTER 42

We arrived at the building and headed to the front door. The High Council had chosen a quiet residential area as their location, which I thought was a subtle touch. The house was located in one of the older parts of Chicago where the streets were still cobbled and the light posts were styled after old lanterns. Morning light gleamed on the stones of the street, teasing away the inky darkness of the night sky.

Up the concrete stairs, Logan raised the ancient lion's head knocker, tapping it a few times. A few seconds passed, and just as Logan raised his hand to knock again, the door opened. An older woman answered, blonde hair streaked gray, pulled back in a severe bun, black-rimmed glasses on her long nose as she studied us through the glass.

"How may I assist you?" she asked, her voice crackling like electricity lived in her throat.

"Kailin Odel to see the High Council as requested," I said.

The woman's eyes widened. Then she nodded and waved us inside, closing the door softly behind us. "Please wait a moment while I get someone to attend to you." I nodded, but she was already gliding out of the room.

We weren't made to wait too long.

Voices traveled to us down the passageway, and two men entered the room. The first, tall, slim, with auburn hair and a pair of glasses that distorted his eyes, gave us a nod. "Thank you for coming. We do appreciate your assistance in this matter."

I nodded and stared at him, waiting for this debrief to happen and be over. The second man cleared his throat. He was shorter and stubbier, with thinning black hair that he combed over his gleaming skull in a vain attempt to hide his baldness. "This is Michael Carter, and I'm David Horner. We are both members of the High Council. If you will follow me, we can talk in private. I hope you don't mind, but we do prefer to interview each of you separately."

He got nods all around. None of us minded. Then he gave us a thin smile that I assumed meant he was satisfied with our response. He turned and walked out and down the passageway. He reached a set of stairs with two flights, one going up and the other down. We followed Horner down the carpeted stairway and exited into an extremely clinical office area, so different from the warm wood and old furnishing of the upstairs.

Here, white walls and white-painted furniture gave an air of clinical indifference, but I refused to allow that to make me wonder what I'd gotten myself into.

I was shown into the first room while Carter led the guys farther down the row. Howard motioned for me to enter, and I took a seat in a room that looked identical to the one we'd transported into at Sentinel HQ. Horner seated himself on one of the chairs in front of me and glanced at the door. Seconds later, Carter appeared and took the spare seat.

He leaned forward and said, "Now, Ms. Odel, could you run through everything that happened to lead you to finding your mother at the facility in Nevada?"

I raised an eyebrow. "Everything?" I was annoyed now. I thought I was the one that was going to be filled in, but they were asking nicely and they were the High Council. Who was I to lie to them?

Both men nodded, and Horner said, "Take your time. And just so you are aware, this meeting is being recorded. It makes things so much easier. I'm sure you'll agree."

I merely nodded, registering the unsaid warning in his tone, and began my tale with the skinned Walker I'd discovered in the garden behind the rehab center. I followed the events from Niko's involvement to how the Wraiths featured in my investigation, the drug distribution ring, and Widd'en. When I described my visit to the Graylands, both men raised their eyebrows, but neither said a word. I covered Greer's death at Brand's hands and going to Wrythiin to look for Mom.

I finished the story with our extraction from the Nevada facility. Both men sat back for a moment, still processing everything I'd said. I'd deliberately left out key information that I wasn't prepared to discuss with them. Like Logan and his fire troubles, my whole Ni'amh issue, and the blood promise that hung over my head like the blade of a guillotine.

Horner cleared his throat and leaned forward. "Thank you for being so frank with us. I know you don't have any obligation to speak to us, so we appreciate it." I merely nodded. "The reason you and your associates have been brought in for debriefing is, of course, the organization to whom that facility belongs."

There was a moment of silence that I let pass. I wanted them to talk, so I said nothing.

Carter rested his elbows on the table. "Are you at all aware of who owns this facility?"

I shook my head and chose to lie. "I thought it belonged to the Wraiths." Then I frowned, remembering that both Saleem and Logan would be answering these questions too. "But while I was at the facility, I saw something that made me wonder."

"And what was that?" asked Carter.

"Stationery with the Omega letterhead." There, I'd said it. And from the looks on the two men's faces, I'd chosen the right option in the truth. They were both nodding.

"Thank you for your honesty. We have suspected the place belonged to Omega, and when we heard that Sentinel might send someone out there, we sent a directive for them to stay put." That explained Cassie and Larsson. "Obviously, we had no say in your Omega team members, so we just let it go, hoping things wouldn't blow up in your faces. But fortunately, it seems your team got out safely and you have Celeste safe and sound. In addition, you also brought us Niko Odel, who will be trialed for his crimes."

I nodded and sat back, hoping this was the end of it.

But Horner spoke. "We need to be honest about our intentions here too. We will be requesting the two Omega operatives to perform some investigations on our behalf. You don't work for them, but I just thought you should know what our request is."

"Can they say no?" I asked, suspecting these men were entirely capable of strong-arming both my friends.

But they both shook their heads. "We are aware of the way Omega operates. There may be reasons for either or both of these young men to decline to help us, and we see no reason to hold that against them."

I was relieved, but I suppressed my sigh and waited. I got the feeling these two were waiting to ask me something else. And when Carter met my gaze, I could almost guess what he was going to ask. "Will you consider working for the High Council?"

I opened my mouth, then closed it again, a little unsure if they wanted an immediate answer. "Do I have time to think about it?"

"Of course. You have a week before we will need your answer. I have to be honest, Ms. Odel. We do need your skills. So please, think seriously about it."

"I'll be working for Sentinel?" I asked, curious as what the whole process would be.

Carter shook his head. "No. You will belong to an elite task force that works directly for the High Council."

That was a surprise. I stared at them, a little confused but a little impressed too. "Okay, I'll think about."

When they both got to their feet, I was both relieved and at odds with myself. I remained silent as I walked with them to the waiting room. They took their leave quickly and politely and then left me to my own devices.

Logan appeared not too long after, and he took a seat beside me. He sat so close that his thigh pressed against mine. I looked up at him and laughed. "There's plenty of space on the sofa. Do you have to sit on top of me?" I shook my head at him.

All he did was stare at me and say, "Sitting on top of you wasn't exactly what I had in mind." The words sent a flash of heat rippling through me. The man didn't have a sense of place.

"We're in the High Council's headquarters. Have some respect," I scolded, my face hot.

"What?" he asked, looking around at the four corners of the room. "Do you think they have cameras?"

"How would I know? If I were them, I certainly would. And not the kind any layman would be able to find."

"Ah, secret cameras. Even more intriguing." He'd lowered his voice until it had a husky rumble to it.

"Will you just behave yourself?" I snapped, trying to keep a straight face.

"Can I at least hold your hand? That wouldn't get us in trouble, would it?" He sounded so innocent as he made his request, but I knew he couldn't be trusted.

I narrowed my eyes, watching his face, but his was pure innocence. "Fine. That's all you get."

He grinned and slipped his hand into mine. Then he threaded his fingers between mine and held tight. The action was intimate, bringing my fingers as closely to his as humanly possible. Then he let go and began to run his fingers through mine, in and out in a way that made me blush.

Just hold my hand my ass. The brute was dead set on embarrassing us in front of the High Council.

"Why, Kai, you look a little hot to me," he whispered into my ear, his warm breath blowing a tendril of hair loose from the tie at the back of my neck.

"I warned you to behave."

"Or what?" he whispered. "Will you spank me?" He spread his fingers and ran them down mine, heat sparking all the way from the tips of my fingers to my thighs.

I laughed as I tried to glare at him. "What's gotten into you? Did they give you funny water to drink while interrogating you?" Then my eyes widened as he drew his fingers back along mine and pulled them tight. "I know. You're a ShapeChanger pretending to be Logan. That's it."

"I'm not pretending to be anyone, as you well know. What I am pretending is to be in control. In fact, I'm not so sure how much longer I can control myself." His hand went out then in again, the heat in my core rising to melting point.

Someone cleared his throat at the door. "Not that it's not entertaining, but are you two done?" asked Saleem, a huge grin on his face as he stood in the doorway.

I glared at Logan and got to my feet, but when I tried to tug my hand from his, he held on tight. The look he gave me was hot and filled with sizzling promise.

Then he let go.

SALEEM JUMPED us back to my apartment, bustling with activity.

"Seems we should have called ahead," said Logan with a wry smile.

From where I stood, I could see my father sitting beside Mom on my bed. "Why do you say that?" I asked, a little distracted.

"Probably a good idea not to give people the shock of their lives at Saleem's arrival. Or better yet, to avoid arriving on top of some poor guy." Saleem laughed at that.

I snorted at the image he drew.

Lily and Anjelo waved from the kitchen where a kettle was boiling and cups and plates were set out. I left them to their task and kept walking, while Logan and Saleem headed toward the counter.

Both room doors were open. Niko sat up in bed. There was a guard at the window and one beside the door, making sure my uncle didn't make a run for it. He met my eyes as I walked toward his door, then lowered his gaze. I wasn't surprised that he felt guilty. He deserved to be, considering everything he'd done.

"How do you feel?" I asked, standing a foot away from his bed. Not that I was particularly concerned. I just wanted to ensure he'd survive to be held accountable for all his crimes.

He lifted his gaze to mine. "A sore throat, but mostly I'm fine. They've taken good care of me." He left the rest unsaid, but I knew what he was thinking. They were taking care of him despite what he'd done.

I couldn't wait for the right time to ask. As far as I was concerned, there was never a right time for anything. You made the time to do the things that mattered. "I take it you weren't dead when Widd'en kicked you into the pond?" He shook his head. "Was it Illyria who fished you out?" A nod.

I waited a moment, my patience running thin.

"What were you doing to Mom?"

"What I was doing to her was nothing. I pretended to take blood for research, keep her sedated so she wouldn't inadvertently give anything away, and I made sure she wasn't experimented on in any direct or harmful way. I made them wait, buying time and hoping someone would come for her."

There was something in his voice that said that wasn't all. "What were you supposed to be doing to her?"

"Testing the obsidian poison, how her body reacted to it, and the Synthe effect using her blood. They wanted to go to the next level, testing her ability to kill Wraiths with her golden hands, but Celeste was too weak for that and they knew it, so they scheduled that particular testing for last."

I took a moment to absorb his words, but it was just too much. "What would you have done if we hadn't come?"

Niko shrugged. "I hadn't thought that far ahead, to be honest."

"Why did you protect her?" I asked, keeping my tone even.

"Because I'd already done enough to hurt my family. I'd seen what the Synthe did to Greer, and I blamed myself. It seemed to have sucked the soul out of her. She became vicious, and I never liked to see that in her. But the Synthe, it took control... Its strength is terrifying."

"You know she's dead?" I asked, feeling nothing. I watched his face and was satisfied to see the sadness in his eyes, the droop of his shoulders.

He nodded. "Yes. Mother told me. It's my fault, I know. While she was with me, she was my responsibility and I didn't look after her the way I should have." He nodded to himself almost as if he'd forgotten I was still standing there. "My fault."

I didn't say anything to make him feel better. Mainly because I didn't feel he deserved to feel better. He deserved to be punished. I wrapped my arms around my body and took a deep breath. "I need to know something." When he met my gaze, a question in his eyes, I asked, "Clancy. Why?"

At first, he didn't react, as if the name meant nothing to him.

"The girl you killed with the metal claws," I snapped, my voice edged with hurt that I hoped he didn't notice.

"That wasn't me. Brand. He thought it would be a good way to teach you a lesson. Abduct your friend as a message to make you stay away. Unfortunately, I never had control over Brand. I couldn't stop him. And the Synthe… By that time, it was having a terrible effect on me. My memory, concentration, emotional control. Everything."

I shook my head, not wanting to hear about his distress. Frankly, I didn't care if he suffered. "And what about Lily? What reason do you have for what you did to her?"

He shook his head again. "Lily? I don't know a Lily."

I sighed, already having had enough of him. I moved away from the bed, expecting him to try to stop me. But when I paused at the door and looked back at him, he gave me a sad smile. I couldn't rouse even a hint of good cheer toward him. Not yet. And he seemed to understand, giving me a resigned look.

I hesitated at my door.

Grams, Dad, and Iain surrounded Mom, who looked very much awake and well. They all turned to look at me, and Mom beckoned for me to sit beside her. Iain shifted, and I slid onto the mattress and moved closer to her. I stared at her face for a moment as if I needed to be reassured that she was truly there. But she was.

I'd saved her. I'd brought her home safe and sound.

I sighed and a sob caught in my throat as I looked at my little family that was missing one person. I lay my head on Mom's chest and listened to her heartbeat. Then I whispered, "I'm so sorry."

I felt her hand trail across my forehead. Butterfly kisses is what she used to call them. The barest touch of her fingers on my skin that had always soothed me, that had once brought a little girl peace. "Sorry for what, honey?" she asked, her voice just as soft.

"For Greer."

I heard her heart stutter, then settle back into its regular pace. "Greer is not your fault, Kai. You can't carry her death on your shoulders. You did everything you could to save her, but maybe this was her fate. Perhaps she wasn't meant to be saved.

You need to accept that, honey. Accept it and put it behind you."

Her words enveloped me with so much love. She didn't blame me.

I nodded, and Iain held out his hand. I placed mine in it, and he squeezed. "You did good, Kai," he said, and his deep-green eyes agreed. Dad watched his family from Mom's feet, and for once I saw happiness shine in his eyes.

And though there were still things I needed to face, a job to decide on, a blood promise to fulfill, a lover to help heal, I felt something new deep within my heart.

A sense of peace.

~ TO BE CONTINUED ~
The SkinWalker Series continues with Blood Promise.

ACKNOWLEDGMENTS

To Mel, Cassie & Kate – three ladies who fill my heart with happiness. Not sure what I would do without them.
The amazing Ella James who is always ready to help even when she herself needs like ten hours more per day.
To my editor Cassie and my proofreader Karen, –you always manage to help make things fall into place so I'm saved from having a nervous breakdown.
To Doris Orman who had been fabulous taking over my PA work. Woman, you are amazing.
To hubby and the girls for nagging me to eat on time and for reminding me that all humans need sleep.
And to my readers. Keep on turning them pages...

FREE STARTER LIBRARY - JOIN MY NEWSLETTER

Get the following titles FREE when you subscribe to my newsletter.

Tee's Newsletter

http://smarturl.it/TeesMailingList

ABOUT THE AUTHOR

I have been a writer from the time I was old enough to recognize that reading was a doorway into my imagination. Poetry was my first foray into the art of the written word. Books were my best friends, my escape, my haven. I am essentially a recluse but this part of my personality is impossible to practice given I have two teenage daughters, who are actually my friends, my tea-makers, my confidantes… I am blessed with a husband who has left me for golf. It's a fair trade as I have left him for writing. We are both passionate supporters of each other's loves – it works wonderfully…

My heart is currently broken in two. One half resides in South Africa where my old roots still remain, and my heart still longs for the endless beaches and the smell of moist soil after a summer downpour. My love for Ma Afrika will never fade. The other half of me has been transplanted to the Land of the Long White Cloud. The land of the Taniwha, beautiful Maraes, and volcanoes. The land of green, pure beauty that truly inspires. And because I am so torn between these two lands – I shall forever remain cross-eyed.

Stalk Tee here:
www.tgayer.com
tee@tgayer.com

facebook.com/TGAyerAuthor

twitter.com/TGAyerAuthor

bookbub.com/profile/t-g-ayer

www.ingramcontent.com/pod-product-compliance
Lightning Source LLC
Chambersburg PA
CBHW021232060726
47590CB00005B/1734